OOzooland Adventures

CANDLE AND THE MAGIC BOAT

Created and Written by Robert E. Wood

Illustrations by Gina Femrite

A *Life's Footprints* Children's Book
OOzooland Series — Story One

Watch for these other fun and exciting Life's Footprints books coming soon.

 The Mouse Who Wanted to Stay in the Trap is a magical story about a little girl and a mouse. By caring for the mouse, the little girl learns a valuable lesson about herself. This storybook will become one of your very favorites. In fact, many teachers read used this book to their classes and report that children love it. You might want to share this with your class friends as well.
Suggested reading from "read to them age four" up to readers age ten.

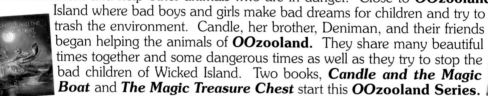 ***The Father of All Trees*** is a classic story about one tree that spans time and cultures. It reminds us of the nature of Mother Earth and how this one tree affected the environment, animals and birds and different cultures of people over many years. It will delight children of many ages and adults as well.
Suggested reading from age seven to age fourteen.

OOzooland Series are stories about a magic place where Candle first visits. In *OOzooland* the citizens are animals saved from their homes in many places around the earth that people have destroyed. The citizen animals manufacture beautiful dreams for children and many other wonderful things. These good animals use their magic boats to deliver these beautiful dreams to children. They have probably delivered some of these dreams to you. The animals also care for the environment and help other animals who are in danger. Close to ***OOzooland*** is Wicked Island where bad boys and girls make bad dreams for children and try to trash the environment. Candle, her brother, Deniman, and their friends began helping the animals of ***OOzooland.*** They share many beautiful times together and some dangerous times as well as they try to stop the bad children of Wicked Island. Two books, ***Candle and the Magic Boat*** and ***The Magic Treasure Chest*** start this ***OOzooland Series.***
Many other stories will follow as Candle, Deniman and their friends continue visits to ***OOzooland.*** You will love their stories and the citizen animals of ***OOzooland.***
Suggested reading from "read to children age four" to readers age ten.

You can register with Life's Footprints to receive information about when these additional exciting books will be available. We guarantee that your name and personal information will not be sold or released to any other person, company or entity.
Name _____
Address _____
City _____ State _____ Zip _____
My age is _____ I am a girl reader _____ I am a boy reader _____
I purchased this book from _____
(Name of store or other source)

Published in the United States by:
Life's Footprints.
905 Long Road
Centralia, WA 98531
lfbooks@yahoo.com

Printed in Korea

Typography by:
The Kraze! Inc.
12798 NW 98 Place
Hialeah Gardens, Florida 33018
ghalligan@thekraze.com

Table of Contents

THIS BOOK BELONGS TO: _____

Reading books and things is so much fun.
My "Reading Reminders" will be done.

I will ask my parents and grandparents to help me improve my reading and writing by:

🐨 Reading to me 30 minutes a day.

🐨 Helping me read signs when we travel.

🐨 Letting me help them write the grocery lists.

🐨 Writing notes to them and asking them to write responses.

🐨 Discussing my books with them and asking them to tell me about the books they have read.

🐨 Setting aside a special shelf or a special "Treasure Chest" for my books, pencils, crayons and paper.

🐨 Having them take me to the Library to get a Library Card.

🐨 Asking them to help me write stories about my experiences at school, our vacations and other things I do.

🐨 Asking them if I can share my books and reading with my sisters, brothers and friends.

🐨 Asking them to help me keep a diary so I can enjoy reading about my important experiences and feelings as I grow up.

Here is a list of other things that I will do to improve my reading and writing.

I will _____

_____

_____

A note to my parents about my own diary!

Assure me please, I'd like to know
You'll help record me as I grow.

The toys you buy for my delight
To play by day and hug at night.

The things I do to make you glow
My problems too — of course you know.

Let's add some pictures here and there
of times I smile — of things I care.

Someday I'll read my book with glee
Including things you did to comfort me.

The treasure is — because I'll see
The love you gave — my life to be.

By Robert E. Wood

v

This story is one in a series of Candle's adventures in *OO*zooland. Before reading the story, you can review the glossary of the many different terms and places in the back of this book. Also, the human and *OO*zooland characters are introducd below so that you will know and enjoy them as you read Candle's story. Candle also invites you to look for other *OO*zooland adventure stories at your bookstore or inquire by mail only at: Life's Footprints, 7905 NW 54 Street, Miami, FL 33166.

Characters
Story One

HUMANS

CANDLE: Young girl from Oregon
DENIMAN: Candle's older brother
GRANDFATHER: Candle's grandfather
CANDLE'S PARENTS

THE GANG FROM WICKED ISLAND

DANTA: Dirty young girl
PENDAM: Evil leader of the Gang

COOZOO: (COO-ZOO) is the first *OO*zooland citizen that speaks to Candle the evening of her birthday party. He asks her to return his magic boat. When Candle arrives in Wisdom Square, Coozoo tours *OO*zooland with her and introduces her to the many magic places and citizen animals.

LENZTELLI: (LENZ-TELL-E) is the elder citizen of *OO*zooland and he is very wise. He conducts the Oath of Unfractured Love to Candle. Also, LENZTELLI helps plan a dangerous mission when Candle and her brother return to *OO*zooland.

FOOFOOTH: (FOO-FOOTH) manages the Magic Mirror Factory in *OO*zooland. He makes a magic mirror for Candle and teaches her something all children should know.

CANULIT: (CAN-U-LIT) manages the Magic Furniture Factory in *OO*zooland. He builds a Magic Boat for Candle to return home in. Candle uses her Magic Boat for many future adventures with her special animals friends in *OO*zooland.

SNIFFNU: (SNIFF-NEW) is another *OO*zooland citizen that greets Candle in Wisdom Square. He helps Candle and his citizen friends solve many problems when Candle returns for many more adventures in *OO*zooland.

GRABBER: (GRAB-BER) is also among the citizen animals who greet Candle. He takes care of the Golden Sand in *OO*zooland. When Candle and Deniman return, GRABBER is very important in helping to rescue the Magic Treasure Chest.

PUSSOLPUTS: (PUSS-OL-PUTS) manages the Dream Factory in *OO*zooland. He and the other citizen animals design beautiful dreams to deliver to children all over the world. PUSSOLPUTS makes a special dream for Candle to take home with her.

SAVALLA: (SA-VAL-LA) joins in greeting Candle in Wisdom Square. SAVALLA is the one that first finds the Magic Treasure Chest at the bottom of Golden Bay and helps recover it during a dangerous mission when Candle brings Deniman back to *OO*zooland.

HOPPHI: (HOP-HI) joins in greeting Candle and tells her that he will show her more of the special places in *OO*zooland when she returns. HOPPHI has special ways to get around in the wonderful places in *OO*zooland that Candle and her friends enjoy on future visits.

ZIPPER: (ZIP-PER) is a fun-loving citizen of *OO*zooland. He helps in many adventures and he is always willing to help in the Dream Factory. Later he hlps Candle to pick out a place in *OO*zooland for her own Magic House.

LOVEFOO: (LOVE-FOO) is always among the citizens of *OO*zooland to help with many adventures to solve problems. She can fly high to spot the things that help the other citizens of *OO*zooland solve many problems.

You will meet many more citizen animals as Candle, Deniman and their friends travel to *OO*zooland.

Introduction to
OOZOOLAND ADVENTURE SERIES

CANDLE AND THE MAGIC BOAT

It all started when Candle's Grandfather gave her a rocking boat for her birthday. He did not realize that it was really a Magic Boat. The Boat takes her sailing through the moonlit sky and through a big window that has bright rainbow patterns and finally to OOzooland. There she visits the Dream Factory and FOOFOOTH makes her a Magic Mirror. Then Candle takes the OATH OF UNFRACTURED LOVE, and becomes a citizen. She worries

about her parents concern that she is away from home, but she had to go to help the citizens of *OO*zooland and she knows she'll be home soon.

On her second trip to *OO*zooland, two of her new friends, GRABBER, the turtle, and SAVALLA, the dolphin, help her find the Super Magic Treasure Chest which had been stolen and buried at the bottom of the ocean. The Treasure Chest can make time stand still and contains the Golden Rings of Knowledge.

Candle, Deniman and many of Candle's friends make many more trips to *OO*zooland. You can continue read-

Candle leaves for OOzooland.

ing about them in many more books that tell of these exciting adventures. Perhaps you, too, can travel to *OO*zooland with Candle.

But wait! Candle's story is so important that if you have not yet traveled to *OO*zooland with Candle, you should share her adventure from the beginning.

Candle in OOzooland.

CHAPTER ONE

Candle's Birthday Gift Of A Magic Boat

In Oregon there is a beautiful river named the McKenzie River. Along the river is a quaint little town with friendly people. Close to the town is a white covered bridge. Across the bridge and down the road along the river, there is a lovely house where Candle lives with her parents and her brother, Deniman, who's two years older than Candle. It is near a little lake that the river runs into. The house is surrounded by many fir and oak trees.

There are also some dogwood trees that bloom with many beautiful white and pink blossoms. Wild flowers and beautiful bushes grow all around the house.

Friendly animals such as rabbits, squirrels, deer and raccoons live in the woods near Candle's house.

Candle and Deniman live in a beautiful house surrounded by beautiful trees, flowers and animals.

Beautiful owls, bluebirds, robins and other birds nest in the many trees. In front of the house there is a little path that leads down to the lake where there is a wooden dock for boats. A small boat is tied to the dock. Here, ducks, geese and fish live and play, in the emerald-green waters.

Candle's real name is Mary, but her grandfather started calling her Candle because he says that she brings a beautiful glow into his life. Soon her parents, her brother Deniman and all her friends started calling her Candle as well. Candle loves her grandfather very much. He has told her many things about nature. They often go on walks and talk about the flowers, plants and animals. Sometimes they watch puffy white clouds that swirl across the sky the quickly change shapes — one moment they look like a castle, the next moment a turtle or some other familiar object. Grandfather has also taught Candle and Deniman how to play leapfrog and other fun games.

Candle's grandfather is very special and wise.

Candle enjoys her house, especially her own room. It has many bright colors and her favorite pictures hanging on the walls. Her mother allowed her to pick out her own bedspread and pillows. They have many colorful designs on them. She has many stuffed animals and dolls. Her favorite doll is named Anna. Her room also has a big window that allows her to look out at the flowers, trees and the lake.

In the wintertime she loves to watch the big snowflakes drift gently down. The flakes turn the trees and ground white or they disappear into the water in the lake. Springtime is her favorite season. She can listen to the birds sing and watch the many animals scurry around gathering food. Her mother gives her bread crumbs and birdseed so she can feed her wild-life friends. The birds and animals sing and chirp at Candle as if to thank her, and she talks to them, too.

Among Candle's favorite things to do is to have Deniman take her out in the small wooden boat, which he paddles. Their father has taught them to be very careful. They always wear life vests and they never go out when the wind is blowing. Both Deniman and Candle love to feed the baby ducks and geese that hatch in the spring. They give them all names and watch them swim behind their mothers until they are big enough to fly. They also like to watch the multi-colored fish that dart here and there in the clear water between the boat and the rocks at the bottom of the lake.

This particular spring, Candle is almost finished with school. She loves

Candle's brothers, Deniman, often takes her for a boat ride on the lovely lake near their home.

Candle loves the wildlife around her home.

school, and she has learned to read books and to add and subtract numbers. Candle is proud that she can add numbers and she often practices with her wildlife friends. For example, she may see one mother duck that has four baby ducks and another mother duck that has five baby ducks. She quickly adds them and knows that there are nine baby ducks in all. She also loves learning to play at school with her many friends. After school, Candle does her homework assignments. If there is time, she sometimes helps her mother make dinner. Before bed, she plays with her dolls and reads them stories.

A few days ago, there was a special excitement for her, because it was her birthday. Her mother had helped her write invitations to all of her friends and decorate the house for her party. She had planned to play many games and have prizes for everyone. Then she would share her lovely birthday cake along with her favorite ice cream.

Candle's mother and father had bought her some nice presents, including a new dress, a new bicycle and other games and toys. However, she was also to receive one very special gift—a rocking boat. It had caught her grandfather's eye in a pawnshop window. The boat is made of beautiful wood and has paintings of beautiful animals on its sides. On the bow is a monkey, then an alligator, a tiger and other animals along the sides. The

Many friends came to celebrate Candle's birthday.

animals all appear friendly and are dressed in stripes, polkadots and other designs of different colors. After Candle's grandfather bought the rocking boat, he found it was too big to wrap with birthday paper, so he put a big, colorful pink bow around it.

At one o'clock, all of her friends had arrived. Each of them brought her a birthday gift and a card. She opened the cards first, and her friends passed them around and admired them. Most of the cards were happy cards that the children had colored themselves; they were very pretty. Next she opened the gifts from her parents and Deniman's gift of several colored jump ropes.

Then her Grandfather brought out the rocking boat. Candle's eyes were so bright; she could hardly believe how beautiful it was. The animals on it almost looked real. "Oh," she said breathlessly as she hugged him, "it is my favorite present of all. Now I can rock my dolls in it and share it with

Candle is ready for bed wearing her new fluffy nightgown.

my friends." Because there were so many children at the party, her father carried it to her room so she could enjoy it later.

When the party was over, Candle went to her room and put on her new fluffy nightgown that she had received from her Aunt Crystal. It was white and had many colorful strips on it, like the animals on the boat. After she hugged all her dolls, her mother came in to tell her goodnight and tuck her into bed. Her mother smiled down at her and said, "Candle, you are such a wonderful daughter. All of us are so lucky to have you."

"You are so wonderful, Mother," replied Candle, "and I am so happy with my family and all my friends. I had a great birthday party. Oh! I almost forgot. I wanted to rock Anna in my new boat for a little while before I go to sleep. May I?" Candle's mother told her that she could, "for a short time," and then she should get to sleep, as she had to get up early for school the next day.

"Okay," answered Candle, "I will rock only for a few minutes. Good night, Mother. Thank you again."

COOZOO explains to Candle that his picture is on the bow of his magic boat.

CHAPTER TWO

Candle Returns Coozoo's Magic Boat

Candle pulled Anna, her favorite doll, into her arms and stepped into the boat. Soon she was rocking and singing to Anna. Suddenly a very sweet voice said, "Please bring my boat back to me." "Who said that?" Candle asked. "Oh, it is me, COOZOO," the voice answered. The voice sounded so friendly that it did not frighten Candle, but she was very puzzled.

Candle's favorite doll, Anna.

"COOZOO is a strange name," she replied, "and this is my rocking boat. Today is my birthday and it is a special present from my grandfather, but you can rock in it with me."

COOZOO talking to Candle from OOzooland.

"Oh, you don't understand," COOZOO continued. "I will explain why your grandfather found the boat in the pawnshop, but first let me show you who I am. Look on the bow of the boat and you will see my picture. I am dressed in colored polkadots, and I am able to talk to you through my picture from my Magic House."

7

Candle looked at the pictures of all the animals on the boat and saw one with polkadots on it. "Oh, you are a pretty monkey," she said excitedly. "But please tell me about the boat, and where your Magic House is?" "I am one of the citizens of *OO*zooland," COOZOO replied. "I live here with many of my friends. But let me explain about the boat and why I need it back. Then I can tell you more about *OO*zooland when you arrive. It will not take you very long to get here."

COOZOO continued his explanation. He told of how the many different animals had found their way to *OO*zooland over the years. He said LENZTELLI, the owl, was the first and he is very wise. All of the citizen animals came because their homes had been destroyed by pollution or greed. As a result, their families had become ill from the unclean air and other poi-

The bad children of Wicked Island do not keep it clean and they make ugly dreams.

sons around them. Candle understood this, as she knew that children sometimes become ill from unclean air and other pollution.

The animals that came had to have very loving hearts, or the Magic Atmosphere around OOzooland would not have allowed them to enter. COOZOO told Candle that most of the animal citizens now worked in one of OOzooland's many factories and she would understand more when she arrived. One of the most special places was called the Dream Factory. This is where some of the citizens of OOzooland design and produce beautiful dreams for good children all over the world.

The dreams are made using GOODOOS, which are all kinds of pleasant thoughts, praise, encouragement and other kind ingredients that cause children to feel secure and feel very loved. Then the children grow up sharing and doing good things to help others. They also will do things to keep the environment clean so that all fish, birds and other animals can live in healthful and safe homes.

COOZOO explained, "The Magic Boats are what the citizens of OOzooland use to deliver these good dreams. Each citizen has one. However, a short time ago a boy named Pendam and a girl named Danta suddenly appeared in OOzooland. We citizens thought that they were good or they could not have gotten here through our Magic Atmosphere Screen. They even took the OATH OF UNFRACTURED LOVE; they were very clever at lying." At that point, Candle asked what the Oath meant. COOZOO replied that she could understand only by visiting OOzooland in person.

"As for Pendam and Danta, we finally discovered they were from Wicked Island, not too far from OOzooland, where ugly dreams are made. Their citizens are nasty and even fight among themselves. They do not clean up after themselves and allow trash and pollution on their island. They also make their dreams from MUDOOS which are bad thoughts, like insults, that cause arguing and fighting.

9

"These dreams cause children to feel hurt, guilt and loneliness. Then the children start living their lives the same way. They treat other children poorly, and they even throw trash and poisonous things into the water. These can kill fish, birds and other animals. If children are treated with MUDOOS by their parents and friends, then they will be far more likely to allow dreams from Wicked Island to replace the dreams that we produce out of GOODOOS, here at *OO*zooland."

COOZOO continued: "Pendam and Danta soon started doing bad and even painful things to the *OO*zooland citizens. They would not help, except to try to make some ugly dreams when no one was looking and Pendam was caught throwing trash into Goldfish River.

The citizen animals of OOzooland tell Pendam and Danta to leave.

"Within a few days, the citizens asked them to leave, but they would not go. LENZTELLI finally discovered how they got in. He flew around until he found a hole in the Magic Atmosphere. Then he repaired it after

Pendam and Danta left to deliver a bad dream. The mean children were not aware that their secret entrance had been sealed. So, when they returned, they were surprised to discover that they could not get back into OOzooland.

"However, they managed to do two very cruel things before they left. The first thing they did was to steal the Magic Treasure Chest and hide it. Then they stole my Magic Wooden Boat. But the Boat would not work for

Before Pendam and Danta left OOzooland, they stole the Magic Treasure Chest and hid it at the bottom of Golden bay.

them, because they did not have happy hearts. They probably sold it to the pawnshop on their way back to Wicked Island. Since then, I have not been able to deliver my share of good dreams. So many children have had to do without their GOODOOS or, worse yet, they have been tricked into dreaming MUDOOS from Wicked Island."

Candle clearly understood the importance of the dreams. And as she thought about it, she realized that not one of her good friends had talked about beautiful dreams lately. They always shared such things. At this point, she started to ask COOZOO the many questions she had about the Treasure Chest . . . the Dream Factory . . . about the citizens, and many, many more things about OOzooland. However, COOZOO assured her that she would understand more when she arrived, and that it would be beautiful and fun to see.

"Why can't the boat come home by itself?" she finally asked. "Oh, it needs to have someone guiding it that has a happy heart," replied COOZOO "That is why we couldn't find it until now, and if you hurry and open your window, you will be here very soon."

CHAPTER THREE

Candle's Exciting Trip to OOzooland

Candle thought about her mother telling her to go to sleep soon. But she had been rocking Anna for only a little while when COOZOO started talking to her. Surely the short time to deliver the boat would be okay. She dreaded the thought of not having the boat any longer, and what might her parents say? But more important, no child should go even one more night without beautiful dreams. She knew that her mother and father would understand and would want her to help in any way she could.

Candle stepped out of the Boat and over to her big window. The moon was shining so brightly, the night was al-

Candle stepped out of the Magic Boat to look out the window.

13

most as light as the day. The lake and tree leaves glistened, and Candle saw two little fawns playing in the grass. As she opened the window, a light breeze picked at her long, soft hair. Without further hesitation, she stepped back into the boat, picked up Anna and said:

"Oh beautiful boat, from my happy heart,
it is time for us now to depart.
I'll sit right here and hold Anna's hand.
Please take us now to OOzooland."

The boat then lifted from the floor and gently slipped through the window. Candle heard an owl hoot as the Magic Boat rode the warm breeze, up through the tree-tops. She looked back at her house and the shining lake. She noticed that she had left her light on, but she was comfortable with the thought that she would be back home soon.

The boat sailed higher and higher toward the west. Soon she could see the lights of a large city below. The stars looked brighter than she had ever seen

Candle leaves to deliver the Magic Boat to COOZOO.

Candle looks down at her favorite picnic beach and the Pacific Ocean.

them. She thought she could almost touch them. Then the city was out of sight and more mountains appeared and, in another instant, she recognized the Pacific Ocean. She was absolutely sure of this fact, because she saw the tall white lighthouse near the beach where her family had picnicked on many Sundays. It was a favorite outing to look for shells and interesting rocks. Moments later all she could see was the endless ocean bathed in every direction by moonlight. Soon the wind changed and the boat turned south. There were a few dark forms on the ocean with some twinkling white lights which Candle guessed were ships.

Suddenly, she saw a large window ahead. Through the window appeared the most beautiful colors she had ever seen, even more spectacular than a rainbow. All she could say was, "Oh, Anna, that has to be *OOzooland!*"

Candle arrives in OOzooland in Wisdom Square.

The boat slipped through the window and started to descend. Candle could soon see things taking shape among the colors. Within seconds, the boat settled on gold-colored sand in what seemed to be a lovely courtyard.

"Hello," said a now familiar voice. "I am very pleased you came." Candle looked around and saw COOZOO, polkadots and all, hanging by his tail from a tree. He had a big welcoming smile. The tree had a blue trunk with big pink leaves. There appeared to be odd-shaped fruit on the tree, of many different colors.

"Hi," responded Candle as she stepped out of the boat with Anna. "I am very happy to meet you and to return your boat. Is this all there is to OOzooland? Where are the other citizens you told me about?"

"Oh, there are many more areas in OOzooland than this," COOZOO replied. "You have landed in Wisdom Square. This is where we have all of our meetings. They are conducted by LENZTELLI, the owl, and he will be

COOZOO meets Candle at an OOluciouss Tree in OOzooland.

here soon. The other citizens are doing their duties at our factories. If you want, you may visit any of our many areas and visit with the citizens for as long as you wish. But because you do not have much time, if you will take the *Oath of Unfractured Love*, you can come back here again anytime you want. You may even want to have your own house here to stay in when you visit. There are many fun things to do."

"But I have so many questions, I don't know where to start," Candle said. "Like what is the *Oath of Unfractured Love?*" "Oh," COOZOO replied, "You will understand as soon as we go on a brief tour. Then everything will be explained. I will tell you about the *Oath* after we go to the Magic Mirror Factory. But first let me tell you about Wisdom Square and how you travel to the many different areas from here. I also noticed you looking at the OOluciouss trees. While we are talking, you are welcome to try an OOloopop or a SWilizie or something else. Just pick one off any tree." Candle did feel a little hungry, so she picked an OOloopop and found it delicious, while COOZOO continued to inform her about *OOzooland*.

"The Golden Sand you see here in Wisdom Square is brought in from Golden Beach each month by the citizens. The sand comes from mountain tops where it erodes little by little from the rain, snow, wind and heat. It is carried by streams and rivers to the many oceans. The ocean currents then carry and deposit each grain on beaches all over the world. The Golden Sand is special, as it gathers all the knowledge and events from *everywhere*. Special ocean currents bring most of it to *OOzooland*. The reason some of

Wisdom Square has many different lands around it and lots of different things to do.

the sand is brought to this Square is to sift the knowledge from it with the Magic Scanner.

"The knowledge chips are then sent to the *OOzooland Print Factory* and published in the *OOzooland News*. At the monthly meetings, the citizens gather in the Square to discuss and share the things we read about. Then we decide on how it will benefit our country or help build better dreams. Sometimes we even send some grains of sand with our dreams to help people sleep. You may have noticed some in the corner of your eyes when you awaken in the morning."

"You're right," said Candle, "I always have to wash my face in the morning to get the sand out. By the way, could I attend your meetings sometime? I do like to read, and I know I could help design good dreams."

"Of course you may," said COOZOO. "Perhaps you would like to design and build a dream in the Dream Factory. PUSSELPUTS, the elephant, runs that factory. He could help you choose a child who really needs a good dream and show you how to run the equipment. Some children are poor, some don't have nice parents and some don't have enough food, but really, all children need a good supply of beautiful dreams."

Then they walked to the Silver Fountain in the center of the

Candle selects one of the many delcious drinks at Silver Fountain.

Square. There were lots of liquids spouting into the air and returning into many little basins. There was also a list that had many strange names on it with little silver cups beside each. "Try any you would like," said COOZOO. "All the drinks are made from the special fruits and berries we grow here. I think you will find them all delicious."

Candle accepted his invitation and sampled several. "Oh, these are so tasty!" she agreed. "I shall try to learn all the names of your drinks so I can select my favorites. But please hurry and show me the other areas of OOzooland because I must soon return home."

CHAPTER FOUR

Candle Meets Many New Animal Friends

andle had noticed all the doors in the decorative walls around the Square. Each door was a different color and had a strange name on it. The first door was white and named, Snowy Forest Road. COOZOO opened it. The cool air and beauty took Candle's breath away. "This path leads to White Mountain Slide and Glassy Ice Lake," COOZOO motioned. "You can go there anytime and play with your friends. If you are playing here and say 'please snow,' you can have gentle snowflakes when you are sledding, ice-skating or playing 'Fox and Geese.' You may also make things out of the snow, like a snowman. They will last until you wish them away." Candle could hardly believe how white and clean the landscape looked. She could see the shiny ice lake

Candle opens one of the many doors from Wisdom Square and looks out at White Mountain Slide and Glassy Ice Lake.

21

Another door leads out to Lily Brook Way.

and the beautiful mountain in the distance, with snow-covered trees and bushes. She could hardly wait to visit there soon.

The next door was blue and the sign said Lily Brook Way. Upon opening it, Candle could see the little brook and hear it gurgle. It sounded happy. Small fish jumped and splashed as if they were playing. She also saw a path leading away between white lilies and other beautiful bushes and flowers. She could see where the brook ran into a river, and beyond, the river flowed into the lake. COOZOO said, "They are named Goldfish River and Greatfun Lake." Even from a distance Candle could see the reflection of the trees in the clear water. It reminded her of the lake in front of her own house. "I will spend a day here soon and I'll bring some food to feed the friendly fish," Candle said.

The next door was decorated in many colors and designs. Nutritious Road was its name. This led to all the factories where the foods, cookies, desserts, ice creams and refreshment drinks were prepared. They were all made from the many pure fruits, vegetables, berries and other things that grow in OOzooland.

"All the citizens develop recipes from time to time," COOZOO said. If some of the citizens like a recipe, it is manufactured or grown on special magic trees. Then it is available for everyone to eat." Candle thought about the super delicious Swilizie and juice drinks she had minutes ago and she was looking forward to tasting all the rest.

Because time was slipping by, Candle and COOZOO agreed that they would explore Moonbeam Lane, Candy Cane Drive, Star Blinking Path and Sunbeam Loop at another time. "However," he said, "there are two more very important areas for you to tour before you leave." Candle felt disap-

pointed because she was not able to see all of *OOzooland*. But she also knew that this would add more special excitement for her when she returned.

They walked by several other doors to one that was covered by a mirror and a sign that said, *Land of Life's Footprints*. This time, they entered and started to walk down a street that was just like glass. The street sign read Magic Mirror Street. There were mirrors of every shape and size. Some made Candle's reflection look tall, some short and some fat. She laughed at all her funny shapes and those of COOZOO. They passed by

Candle and COOZOO walk down the street in the land of Life's Footprints.

the Magic House Factory and the Magic Dreams Factory. They then entered the Magic Mirror Factory, where they were greeted by FOOFOOTH, the tiger.

"Hello Candle," he said as he gave her a hug. "We all heard you were coming to bring COOZOO's boat back. We all are so lucky and thankful that it ended up with

FOOFOOTH greets Candle and COOZOO at the Magic Mirror Factory.

someone with a happy heart. Many selfish or mean children would not have returned it." Candle liked FOOFOOTH immediately and said "You're welcome, sir." He then told her that he was almost finished with a Magic Mirror for her very own. He would then program it, to help her record her heart's feelings.

Candle still did not understand, but she knew that LENZTELLI, the owl, was supposed to explain it later. Then she would take her *Oath of Unfractured Love* and become a citizen of *OO*zooland. She was excited to think about having the official status that would allow her to come often and play or help the other citizens with all their good deeds. Suddenly her thoughts were interrupted as a big screen lighted up and she could see a big fluffy rabbit. "Hello, Candle," said the rabbit. "My name is CANULIT and I manage the Magic Furniture Factory where we also build the Magic Boats. I have just completed a new boat for you. I will take it to Wisdom Square and

CANULIT talks to Candle from the Magic Furniture Factory.

meet you there in a few minutes. But remember, the Factory can make only one boat for each citizen. So you must take care of it and never lose it."

Candle realized then why it was so important for COOZOO to have his boat back. "What a special gift," she thought. She had been so busy that she hadn't even asked how she was going to get home. "Thank you," Candle said, smiling. "You all are making me feel so happy. I look forward to meeting you in person and riding home in my new boat."

By now, FOOFOOTH had finished Candle's Magic Mirror. "Please step into the wishing booth," he said to her. "You are to hold the mirror close to your heart and make the following wish: 'Mirror, I wish for you to record all the GOODOOS and MUDOOS that enter my heart each day.' This will tune the Mirror to your heart." These were more of the new words that COOZOO had mentioned, but she still did not clearly understand all of them yet. After she stepped into the booth and repeated the words, COOZOO then suggested that they hurry back to Wisdom Square for her *Oath* ceremony.

FOOFOOTH tells Candle he will tune her Magic Mirror to her heart.

CHAPTER FIVE

Candle Takes the Oath Of Unfractured Love

As Candle entered Wisdom Square with COOZOO and FOOFOOTH, she was amazed to see so many animal citizens there to greet her. They were dressed in all their specially colored designs. Some were wearing funny ties and hats . . . and even glasses. LENZTELLI, the owl, graciously invited her to sit in a big, fluffy chair at the front of the meeting. Everyone then shouted "Welcome!" to her and even sang Happy Birthday.

When they finished the song, they introduced themselves one by one. There was ZIPPER, the alligator, who had a giant grin on his face. Next,

The OOzooland citizens gather around Candle to greet her in Wisdom Square.

PUSSOLPUTS, the elephant, brought her a cup of one of the delicious juice drinks from the fountain. Then SNIFFNU, the bear, GRABBER, the turtle, LOVEFOO, the dove, CANULIT, the rabbit and all the rest said hello as well. Candle knew that she wouldn't remember all of their names now. But she would when she returned and got to know them better.

The last one to introduce himself was CANULIT, the rabbit, who had already talked to Candle through the Magic Vision Screen. He also brought her new Magic Boat up to the front and presented it to her. It was shinier than the one she had returned to COOZOO. Besides all the animals' pictures on it, her picture had been added on the bow, in order to identify the Boat, as hers. "Oh, Anna!" she exclaimed. "Isn't it beautiful?" Then she continued by thanking all the citizens for their kindness, and she gave a special big hug to CANULIT for making the beautiful Boat for her.

CANULIT brings Candle's new Magic Boat to her in Wisdom Square.

It was now time for her *Oath of Unfractured Love* which would make her a citizen. LENZTELLI opened his own Treasure Chest and took out a big sheet of paper with a golden border. At the top, it said, "OOzooland's *Citizen Oath of Unfractured Love.*" Holding her Mirror and Anna tight to her heart, she repeated the oath that LENZTELLI read to her:

"I, Candle, do hereby promise to do my best to be a very good girl. I will help others and be kind. I will play fair and be honest. I will try to eat and drink only healthy foods and drinks. I will think only good things so that I can truly love myself. This will mean I will have more love to give others. I will accept and give GOODOOS. I will not

LENZTELLI presides as Candle takes the Oath of Unfractured Love.

accept or ever use MUDOOS. I promise to look at my *Magic Mirror* each night to see the record of what I have done each day. And I promise to write the *Mirror*'s record in my *Life's Footprints Diary* and keep it in my ownspecial *Treasure Chest*. I promise these things to all the citizens of *OOzooland* from my loving heart."

LENZTELLI then asked whether any citizen objected to citizenship for Candle. The response was a friendly, loud "No" from everyone. Then LENZTELLI pronounced her an official citizen, and everyone shouted "Welcome!" once again. Candle was starting to understand, but she still did not know the real meaning of *Unfractured*, or GOODOOS, or MUDOOS. LENZTELLI told

her to look in her Magic Mirror and tell him what she saw. Candle looked and saw her reflection. In front of it was a white line across the center of the Mirror. Above the line there were many red hearts of different sizes. She noticed that the bigger each heart was, the higher it was placed to the top of the Mirror. There was writing on each heart. Three of the big ones had *Birthday,   Boat   and OO*zooland on them. One smaller words close to the white line read, "Sally thanked me."

The OOzooland citizens explain GOODOOS and MUDOOS to Candle as reflected in her Magic Mirror.

LENZTELLI explained that the white line reflected her feelings, when everything was normal in her day; like making her bed, or walking to the school bus on time. The red hearts represented special things that happened. For example, the big ones surely include her birthday party, coming to *OO*zooland and receiving the boat. Smaller hearts probably represent little things, like one of her friends telling her that her dress looked nice, or thanking her for the party.

LENZTELLI then pointed out that the hearts had no lines or "cracks" in them. Therefore, they were called *Unfractured Hearts*. Candle then asked why there were no hearts below the line. "Oh, that is to record bad things you do each day or bad feelings caused by someone saying something nasty to you." LENZTELLI continued. "Then the red hearts would have lines or cracks in them. That is *Fractured Love*. If it was something you did bad, the cracks (fractures) would break the heart into pieces. If it is something someone *else* did or said to you that might hurt your feelings, the cracks or fractures would appear white. But it is still a *Fractured Heart*. So that you will clearly understand, let's pretend to use some MUDOOS while you look in your Mirror."

LENZTELLI asks Candle to pretend.

Candle agreed, so LENZTELLI said to her, "Your hair is very ugly!" A heart suddenly appeared below the line. Between the white cracks she saw the word "insult." Candle felt bad for just a moment. Then she quickly remembered they were pretending, so the heart faded away.

To demonstrate a heart with a MUDOO, LENZTELLI then asked her to pretend that she did not like FOOFOOTH, and say something nasty to him. She had a difficult time pretending, but she was finally able to blurt out, "FOOFOOTH I don't like the mirror you made for me . . . it's ugly."

Another heart appeared below the line, and it was shattered. She could hardly tell it was a heart. Again it faded quickly, as she knew that what she had said was not what she really felt.

"I don't like pretending to use MUDOOS," Candle said, "It makes me feel very uncomfortable." "Oh, I understand," said LENZTELLI, "but do you now know what the *Oath of Unfractured Love* means?" "Yes," replied Candle. "I will think of the hearts as footprints of my mind. I am going to practice living by my OATH when I return home. I will explain it to Deniman and my friends, even though they don't have a Magic Mirror."

"Well, if you know them to be good children, you can invite them here to visit," said FOOFOOTH. "Then I will make them a mirror in the Magic Mirror Factory."

"Oh, I know many good children who would be most happy to do that," said Candle.

CHAPTER SIX

Candle Helps Plan A Dangerous Mission

At the thought of home, Candle suddenly realized that she was getting very tired, but she wanted to know about one more thing before she departed. "Please tell me about the Magic Treasure Chest that Pendam and Danta stole," she asked LENZTELLI. "Oh!," responded LENZTELLI "as far as we know, the Magic Treasure Chest has been here forever. We designed our own Treasure Chests like it so we could keep our own *Life's Footprints'* Diaries, other special books and our color sticks in them.

"But what makes it even more special is its magic power. It contains a Time Spell to make time stand still for up to one hour at a time, except for us. We push the Magic Button when we know that the Gang from Wicked Island are delivering bad dreams. By doing this, we can sometimes deliver a beautiful dream before the bad ones get to a child. That's why they wanted to steal the Chest so badly.

"The Chest also contains Golden Rings, made out of the Golden Sand, that we process here in Wisdom Square. Because the Rings con-

The Magic Rings of OOzooland.

OOzooland is beautiful and not very far away.

tain all knowledge from the beginning of time, the Rings allow us to talk and listen to children, fish, animals and birds anywhere.

"We were planning to start excursions to go and visit with children and animals in different areas of the world. This would allow us to find out where the pollution is coming from. We could show the children how to color pictures of these once beautiful places being destroyed by pollution. They could then color beautiful pictures of the same landscape. This would show how these places would look if they were cleaned up. In this way, the children could educate their parents. This would help explain why cleaning up pollution is so important for the health of all life. Then the parents could help make laws and take actions to stop polluting and to help clean-up our world.

"We believe that Pendam and Danta somehow found out about our plans and hid the Chest. Our friend, SAVALLA, the dolphin, thinks she saw Pendam and Danta sink it out in Golden Bay near the border of our Magic Screen over OOzooland. They probably plan to see if they can get through our Magic Ocean Current and take it to Wicked Island. It is sad to think that they would be able to deliver bad dreams faster than we could deliver beautiful ones. And, I'm sure they would use the Magic Rings to say MUDOOS to make fun of the animals that are sick from pollution."

"Then we must find it and bring it back before they take it," said Candle. "Surely SAVALLA would be willing to help GRABBER search the bottom of the sea for it. And then GRABBER could tie several ropes to it and we could all pull on

GRABBER offers to help search for the Magic Treasure Chest.

the ropes from our boats. I will bring Deniman back with me soon. I know he would want to help and he is very strong and brave."

All the citizens agreed that it was a good plan and that they must do whatever it would take to find the Chest first.

"However," LENZTELLI cautioned, "we must plan carefully. I suspect that Pendam and Danta poured poison on a small section of our Magic Atmosphere to get through the first time. They might be planning to do the same thing. It will take a long time and much poison to weaken it, but they might get through again. So we must hurry, before they succeed. They might also try to poison the Magic Ocean Current. So we might all have to wear protective clothes when we go."

Candle said she would ask her grandfather what kind of material they should use for the clothing. She felt sure he would know. Then everyone agreed to help with the plan. All the animal citizens agreed to make the protective clothes as soon as Candle found out what material to make them with.

LENZTELLI did not say any more about his deep concern for this dangerous mission. He knew the Gang from Wicked Island would do anything to re-capture the Chest. But he also knew that somehow they must get the *Chest* back first. His hope was that Deniman was a very strong and wise boy.

Candle offers to return and bring Deniman to join in the dangerous mission to get the Magic Treasure Chest Back.

CHAPTER SEVEN

Candle Says Goodbye To Her New Friends

Candle stepped into her new Magic Boat and sat Anna beside her. She noticed a book on the seat entitled "How to Design Your Magic House." She realized that CANULIT had left it for her, so she could give him building instructions when she returned, if time permitted. Then Candle looked up and faced all the citizens. She thanked them by saying:

"I'm so happy I visited your OOzooland.
Where beautiful colors touch golden sand.

Candle steps into her new Magic Boat and says goodbye to her new OOzooland friends.

37

All of you citizens are so happy and free.
And you really have been very nice to me.
Your sky and water are brilliantly blue.
Your happy flowers all sparkle with dew.
My family will miss me, so I'm on my way.
But I surely will think of you most every day.
I will tell my friends of moonbeams on trees.
And how I arrived, in a boat on a breeze.
GOODOOS and MUDOOS I'll remember so clear.
The *Oath* that I took, I will always hold dear.
FOOFOOTH's gift of a dream I'll sleep on tonight.
So hugging my Anna, I'll sleep peacefully and tight."

Everyone waved as she gave her "Happy Heart" command to her Boat to return home. It rose slowly from Wisdom Square and circled all of *OO*zooland to gave her a spectacular view of the beauty below. Then it turned toward the big Magic Window.

"Candle, sweetheart, you are usually awake and up by now," she heard her mother say. "And who gave you the book that is in your boat? I did not see it at your birthday party." Opening her eyes, Candle was greeted by her mother's smile, followed by a big hug. "Please don't forget to wash your face this morning," her mother continued. "Your eyes look like the sandman visited you with a nice dream."

Candle had an excited urge to tell her mother all about *OO*zooland and her new friends and the beautiful dream she brought home with her. But she knew that her story would have to wait because she was never late for school. "Oh, mother, I'll tell you all about the new book later," Candle replied. Candle smiled when she realized that her mother had not noticed her picture on the bow of her new Boat.

Candle's mother wakes her to get ready for school. Candle must wait until later to tell her mother about OOzooland and plan her next exciting trip to help her new friends.

For more books about Candle's travels to OOzooland
and to meet more of her OOzooland friends,
please write to Life's Footprints.

39

GLOSSARY

OOzooland: The place where good dreams and GOODOOS are made by many wonderful and colorful citizen animals.

Magic Mirror: They are made in *OO*zooland's Magic Mirror Factory. These are mirrors tuned children's hearts and they display the fractured and unfractured feelings every day.

Fractured Hearts: These are hearts that have cracks in them. The cracks represent bad thoughts or deeds or any other unloving or unkind actions.

Unfractured Hearts: These are beautiful hearts with no cracks in them. These represent good thoughts and deeds, kind actions by children and others and special, happy moments.

GOODOOS: Means good thoughts, dreams and wishes.

MUDOOS: Means bad thoughts, dreams and wishes.

Magical Wooden Boats: These are colorful little rocking boats that are made in the Magic Furniture Factory. OOzooland citizens use these to fly anywhere they desire. The boats are also used to deliver beautiful dreams to children.

Wicked Island: This is a dirty and polluted place where the "Gang" of evil and naughty children live. They make MUDOOS and bad dreams for little children.

Wisdom Square: This is the meeting place for the citizens of *OO*zooland. It is where the Golden Sand from Golden Beach is brought to sift the knowledge from it. It is also where all the doors open to the many Magical areas of *OO*zooland.

OOluciouss Trees: One of the trees in the *OO*zooland forest where OOloopops, SWilizies, Fruitacrisps and other delicious foods are grown.

Super Magic Treasure Chest: A wonderful and very old chest that contains the Magic Time Spell Button that can make time stand still for one hour for everyone except the citizens of *OO*zooland. It also contains the Golden Rings of Knowledge that have been made from the Golden Sand of Wisdom Square. The rings give the citizen animals the power to speak to all people and animals.

Protective
   Atmosphere
     Screen: A magical barrier around *OO*zooland that prevents anyone with an unloving heart from flying in and polluting the atmosphere.

Protective
   Ocean
     Current: A magical and very strong ocean current that prevents anyone with an unloving heart from sailing into *OO*zooland by boat.

The OATH OF
   UNFRACTURED
     LOVE: The oath and promises one makes when becoming a citizen of *OO*zooland.

Dream Factory: Where good dreams are designed for children and then delivered to them by animal citizens in their Magic Boats.

MAXIMUM EXPOSURE

X Rated titles from *X Libris*:

Other titles in the *X Libris* series:

MAXIMUM EXPOSURE

Roxanne Morgan

X
RATED

www.xratedbooks.co.uk

An *X Libris* Book

First published in Great Britain as a paperback original in 2004
by X Libris

A CIP catalogue record for this book
is available from the British Library.

ISBN 0 7515 3400 5

Typeset in Palatino by
Derek Doyle & Associates, Liverpool
Printed and bound in Great Britain by
Clays Ltd, St Ives plc

X Libris
An imprint of
Time Warner Book Group UK
Brettenham House
Lancaster Place
London WC2E 7EN

CHAPTER

1

Fern Barrie switched her cellphone to her other hand, and, with her free hand, flicked the button on her vibrator. 'Come on, Danila! You've *got* to be kidding me! You want us to film an "erotic art classic" at a *farm*? What are you expecting – sex in green welly boots?'

The jelly-vibrator's soft buzz was not loud enough to be heard over the phone connection. Sprawling back on her bed in the shared university lodgings, naked in the summer sun that fell hot through the open window, Fern began to run the tip of the vibrator over the sides of her small breasts. She felt her nipples harden instantly.

The mirror on the wardrobe doors at the foot of Fern's bed reflected her back to herself: pink limbs sprawling on a rose-and-gold Indian bedspread; curling ash-brown hair long enough to trail in tendrils over her bare shoulders.

'Look . . .' Dragging her attention away from the image, Fern protested, 'Dani. I want to make a *good* movie.'

'A porn movie!' Danila's voice had a smile in it.

'A *good* porn movie. For women.' Fern grinned to herself. 'Women like us . . .'

Trailing the jelly-vibrator down over her tummy, shivering, she played with the soft brown fuzz at her crotch, teasing the nub of her clit.

Oh, man, it's *such* a pain. With Danila and the others, I've got talent, enthusiasm, a cast . . . everything we need . . . just, no money! We can't even afford to hire a studio to shoot the action.

Fern had the mobile phone pressed up against her ear with her free hand. The voice of the newly graduated student, Danila Martinez – Danila Esperanza Martinez Kapiasynska, in full – came clearly to her.

'But this place's *perfect*, Fernie! They'll let us do all the shooting there! It's way out in the country – nearly in Wales. No one's going to see us. We can film all the sex scenes we like there; it'll be great!'

Fern smiled to herself at Danila's enthusiasm. *That girl wants to be behind the camera more than anything . . .*

The touch of the vibrator sent a shiver rippling across her skin.

She brought her attention back to what the young woman said. 'Yeah, but . . . We're supposed to be making a serious entry for this competition. And you want to shoot it on a farm? OK, we're amateurs, but we don't want to look *that* amateur! Not if we're aiming to go pro afterwards, and make a career out of this.'

'It won't be amateur, Fernie! And it's not a farm, it's an estate!'

Fern caught her image in the mirror again. She found herself picturing Danila's pale latte skin against her own . . . and automatically framing it as a film-shot: white and brown against the soft rose of the bedspread . . .

Damn, I need to make this movie!

2

Dani's going to be a real good director, I've written a great script – I *know* I have – I just know we can win the competition. And that'll give us the funds to go pro, and then ... watch out, world!

Fern shook her head. The rest of her bedroom, where it wasn't piled with clothes that needed a visit to the laundrette, was lost under a drift of papers, ring-binders and books that ought to have been back at the university library a week ago. Not exactly sensual.

She mentally shut out that evidence of the last term of the course, and the thought that she would soon need to vacate the shared house, and draped herself over the bed, stroking the vibrator across her crotch.

The voice in her ear said, 'Fernie? You still there?'

'Sure.' Fern teased the very tip of the vibrator over her clit's hood, feeling the straining urge to fill herself. 'Been thinking. OK, an estate, a farm – what's the difference? You're right, Dani. It's somewhere to do the filming, and that's what matters. You know what? You're *cool*.' She grinned. 'So, tell me about this place.'

'Like I say ...' Danila's voice came treacle-thick and sensuous over the cellphone. Fern thought she sounded pleased. 'It's a big old country estate. There's a fancy manor house, but I don't think we'll get to see much of that. That's where the owner lives. Jonathan Parnell. My cousin Eugenie put me on to him, and he sounded fine over the phone when I talked to him.'

' "Talked"? When you persuaded this guy into doing something he never would have considered otherwise!' Fern said it with a grin, having grown familiar over the last twelve months with Danila's ability to persuade.

Then she frowned, picking up on something Danila had not said.

'You haven't been down there?'

3

'No. But my cousin has, last summer. There's farm buildings and gardens, Eugenie says. Main thing is, there's *woods*, Fern – woods where we can go out and strip off, and film, and no one will see!'

'Woods.' Fern spread her legs more widely. The mirror reflected the soles of her feet, and the inside of her thighs, and the pink lips of her sex between the soft curls of her hair. 'Sex outdoors. Sex in the open. That could work . . . That really *could* work . . .'

The brightly coloured vibrator's tip rested on her clit. She squirmed. Danila's excited voice continued in her ear:

'The guy who owns the place, this Jonathan Parnell, he wouldn't charge us anything *like* what we'd need to rent a studio. He says we could use one of the barns, too, as well as the woods! I mean, think about it, Fern! We'd have an outdoor *and* an indoor set—'

Fern stopped stroking herself, and frowned. 'That'd mean a lot of lighting. We're not going to be able to afford expensive equipment. This is your basic video-cam stuff and you edit it on the laptop—'

'But we'll need somewhere indoors.' Danila suddenly sounded plaintive. 'Do you have any idea how wet it is on the Welsh borders?'

Fern spluttered; choked back a laugh. 'I know how wet it's *gonna* get!'

'Oh, funny, girl, funny!'

Or, Fern reflected, arching her back, how wet it already is . . .

Danila's squawked protest went unnoticed for a moment. Fern wriggled her bum-cheeks on the soft cotton bedcover, and oh-so-gently stroked up and down the lips of her labia with the vibrator. The ache of desire made her tease herself, pushing the rounded thick tip of the jelly-prick inside – just an inch—

Smiling, and keeping her tone level with an effort,

4

she said, 'Have you talked to the others about this? Hope? Lindsey? Tessa?'

'Yeah, they're all cool with it. I mean, it's the only way we can afford to do this, and I can't see any other way we can get a competition entry ready. Besides, they just like the idea of *doing* it, after all the talking about it. What do you think, Fern? Are we good to go?'

Fern closed her legs together, trapping the vibrator against her wet lips, and reached over for her diary on the bedside table. Final exams over and done with, and now . . .

Fern trapped the mobile phone between her ear and shoulder, and flicked through the pages. 'I'm clear from the start of July through to the end of August.'

Danila sounded cautiously satisfied. 'Allow a couple of weeks at the finish for final editing, and we could get it into the competition well before the start of September . . .'

Fern leaned back against her pillows. The vibrator slid off to lie on the bedspread, buzzing on the soft cotton. She reached down, grabbed it and lifted her knee to give herself better access to her outer lips.

Teasing herself again, she said, 'Yeah. You know, we could really do with another guy, as well as Lindsey.'

She heard Danila sigh.

'I asked around, but I couldn't find another guy who didn't just think it was all a big laugh and free shagging.' Danila's voice had an edge to it now. 'Bloody students! OK, so I know we've only just graduated, but . . . This is *serious.*'

'But it has to be fun, too.' Watching herself in the mirror as she rolled over, exposing the neat curve of her bottom, Fern said, 'You should have been here a couple of years back, when Professor Mayhew was on the staff – you know, Vivienne Mayhew; she does research into female sexual fantasies?'

Danila sounded diverted. 'Don't tell me *you* got into that? I've got her books. They're . . .'

'Serious works of research?'

'I was about to say "really hot".'

'That too.' Fern rolled over on to her back again, stroking herself between her legs, strong strokes along her outer lips. Her thigh muscles fluttered. 'Prof. Vivienne's last book, on women who live out their sexual fantasies in real life? She did the research for that one right here at our university.'

Danila snapped, 'Maybe *she* could have talked some sense into the Media Department!'

For a long moment, sprawled in the sunlight, Fern remembered her second year at the university.

Vivienne and Alix and Sandro and Professor Axley – I could have made one hell of a film about what *we* did! And I've been working too hard, because it's been way too long since I've done anything like that . . .

Danila broke into her memories: 'I want us to make a film so cool it just knocks people on their arse – so cool we get independent funding to make another one. We've got to be able to make a career out of this! There's got to be more women-directed erotica. You with me?'

'Sure I am.' Fern was used to the anger just under the surface of Danila's voice. Not her fault, though – making good porn is difficult enough. Convincing the Media Studies staff here that a woman can direct it . . . Huh. They won't believe it till they see it.

Till it gets them hard. Or wet.

But if we can win the Arts Foundation competition, then *everybody* has to take us seriously . . .

Danila Martinez's voice faded as Fern's attention wandered. Her wardrobe mirror reflected back a skinny girl in her early twenties. Fern stroked a hand over her hip, feeling her skin quiver, and sucked at the piercing in her lower lip, shivering at the sensation of the hard steel.

She spread her legs, pushing the vibrator down until it softly buzzed against the tiny bud of her anus. Fern watched as a thin film of sweat covered her pale skin, her long thighs and tight abdominal muscles.

Dani's a good mate. And the only girl I know who doesn't hate me for being thin!

Her attention was snagged by the end of Danila's last sentence:

'. . . *still* not have enough people to film what we've written, Fern! What are we going to do about that?'

A little breathlessly, Fern managed, 'I guess . . . that means you and I are both going to . . . you know . . . join in? As well as be behind the camera?'

Danila chuckled. Fern could visualise her smile perfectly even without seeing it; the Polish-Hispanic woman's wide, curving mouth. '*You* can star! Just because it's a videocam, that doesn't mean any moron can use it. But you'd be good, especially if we want to do an all-girls scene with you and Tess and Hope . . .'

'Oh, I think we should, don't you?' Fern said, mock-innocently. She rolled half on to her side, reaching out for another toy lying on the bedspread. A thick, curved black dildo, made of latex, too wide for her to close her hand around. As she spoke, she rubbed her hand against her own wetness, and stroked that up and down the dildo's thickness. 'I just wish we had – better equipment.'

'I don't know about you, girl, but my equipment's just fine!'

'I meant the *videocam* – oof!' Fern shut her eyes, re-positioned the dildo, and thrust again. The hard rounded head pushed at her wet labia, and with a shiver she felt herself open to it. Slowly, steadily, she pushed it up herself, spreading her legs wider and leaning forward. The sensation of fullness verged on the unbearable, and she felt her inner flesh clench involuntarily, and almost bring her to climax on the instant.

'You OK, Fernie?'

'I'm just fine, yeah ... OK, right, now we've got somewhere to shoot. Have you done the *final* final version of the script edits? Or have I got to rewrite that last scene again?'

Danila's voice filled with enthusiasm. 'I guess we can make adjustments as we shoot. But I did edit your last new scene, just to put some more stuff in. I think it's pretty hot!'

'What—' Fern swallowed. 'What else does he do to her?'

The thick latex dildo slid home to its wide base, filling her vagina completely. It took her breath away momentarily. She looked at the mirror, seeing her wide-spread thighs, and the enormous girth of the dildo penetrating her pussy. Wetness slicked the sides of it as she slid it out a fraction, and then back in. In the mirror, her slightly freckled face shone with sweat.

'Well—' Over the cellphone, Danila could be heard flicking pages. 'He ties her legs apart . . .'

Fern spread her feet until her heels touched the sides of the bed, holding the dildo in with one hand. *For now, I'll have to imagine my ankles are tied.* Her back arched, involuntarily, and she almost fumbled the cellphone. 'Then what?'

'Then he holds her hands over her head, so she can't move, and he stuffs her arse full with a super-big butt plug . . .'

Damn, I need my hands, Fern thought. She took a firmer grip on the dildo and pushed it suddenly up her cleft, feeling the slick, hot wetness there easing her way.

'. . . and then he fucks her,' the voice from the cell-phone continued, brutally frank.

A hot, red flush rose up from Fern's breasts; she could see it clearly in the mirror. Her face shone, pink and sweating. She yanked the latex dildo down, and slammed it back up her vaginal canal, every muscle of her thighs straining at how widely she spread herself.

'. . . and he grabs her tits – I don't know, maybe he bites them; what do you think?'

Fern caught the phone between ear and shoulder again, and closed her other hand hard over her breast, digging in her fingertips, squeezing hard. 'Yeah, I th-think—'

'Or clothes-pegs.' Danila's voice sounded full of wicked amusement. 'Maybe he puts clothes-pegs on her nipples.'

'Dani!'

'*I* know what you're doing. Go on: I dare you!'

With one hand cramming the thick bulk of the dildo up inside her, Fern reached into her toybox, scrabbled for a moment, and found a wooden clothes-peg.

Her nipples were hard, erect enough that she didn't need to roll or rub them. Slowly she opened the clothes-peg – and let the wooden jaws close down on her nipple.

'Shit!' A white jagged line of pleasure-pain shot from her nipple to her crotch, and her inner walls clamped down hard on the rubbery texture that filled her.

Danila giggled. 'Now you leave it there a minute.'

'You just wait till *I'm* directing *you*!' Fern almost lost the phone. The burning constriction on her erect nipple shot pleasure through her.

Danila's voice came with a gasp. 'Now, when I say, you're gonna pull that peg right off – no opening it; just pull. Just one, two, three . . .'

Fern positioned her fingers to grip the side of the clothes-peg, clamping her eyes shut, feeling the sweat running down her face. With her other hand, she stuffed the dildo as far up herself as she could, the heel of her hand pressing against her clit.

'One, two, three – *go!*'

Fern's yelp and gasp of pleasure echoed in the room. The blazing pain of circulation returning made her feel as if her breast had swollen to twice its size. She clamped her palm down over it, grabbed a handful of her breast hard, slid the dildo rapidly and solidly in and out of her cunt, and brushed the heel of her hand across her swollen clit.

Orgasm pierced her from her toes to the crown of her head.

As she let go of the dildo, circling her middle finger furiously on her clit, she came again, and then for a gasping, sweating, third time before she flopped back, the dildo sliding out of her on to the cotton bedspread; after-shocks still convulsing through her flesh.

It took a minute or two to find the cellphone, lost in the Indian bedcover as it was.

With as much self-possession as she could manage, Fern said, 'So – when can you get the van?'

'This week. We're really going to do this? *Cool!*'

Danila sounded as if she were bouncing. Fern, having known her a year now, thought she had never seen the woman's enthusiasm for anything flag.

Fern shook her head ruefully. 'Of course we're going to do it, Dani! I haven't looked at anything but exams for *months*. If we can only win the competition – at least get placed ... You know yourself that could make all the difference to our careers. So – when *can* we borrow the van?'

'Thursday.' Danila's tone became a purr. 'I'll have

10

all the equipment at my place by then. And my cousin's lending me her laptop, so we can edit what we film as we go. The sound equipment's crap, but we can dub over it later. Hey, Fernie! If everybody gets their act together, we could be doing the first shoot by this weekend!'

CHAPTER

2

You wouldn't think, Nadia Kay ruminated, that you could be rich and bored at the same time, now would you?

Or at least, I would never have imagined it of myself.

She swung the wheel of her bright red MG hard over, avoiding a tractor pulling out of a farm gate with inches to spare, and simultaneously put her foot down on the accelerator and her hand on the horn. Her rear-view mirror showed the tractor's driver gesturing in a traditional manner.

Well, not rich, exactly. Pleasantly well-off, after selling up the antiques business. But bored . . . oh yes. Bored to tears. It's time I did something new.

But driving too fast through country lanes on the Welsh borders probably isn't it . . .

She slowed down, cresting a hill.

Green slopes went up on one side of her, swimming under the July heat; in front of her, the hill fell away. Nadia Kay swung the sports car off the road and into a lay-by, cut the engine, and sat for a long moment looking out across the valley at the rising hills. The leather upholstery of the car had a wonderful odour, she thought, although she appreciated rather less how it felt now, hot and sticky against her bare thighs.

Oak and beech woods hid the valley below her. Further off in the west, past these near, lower hills, a darker blue against the milk-blue of the sky argued the presence of the Brecon Beacons. She pondered driving on into Wales.

After all, it doesn't matter exactly where I go; I'm bound to find a hotel with vacancies somewhere. People do take spur-of-the-moment holidays . . . While they're trying to work out what to do with their lives.

The hot metal of the car ticked, the engine cooling down. Nadia reached across and wound down the passenger-side window. Little air stirred. She sweated. She caught a glimpse of herself in her cotton sundress as she sat back – diminutive, long-legged, her face scattered with a tiny gold dusting of freckles across the nose and cheeks. Her copper-red hair was cut in a neat bob. One or two silver hairs glinted among the red at her temples, but the lines at the corners of her eyes were laughter-lines. She knew, without vanity, that she could pass for younger than early forties.

If I wanted to. She smiled to herself, opening the car door to allow air in, but not getting out yet. There's something to be said for experience, after all.

The silence and isolation of the road appealed to her. She swung her legs carefully around, the upholstery peeling sweatily away from her skin, and stood up, gravel under her sandals. A brief breeze caught the hem of her ivory cotton dress. She walked a yard or two to the edge of the parking place, and the welcome shade of an ash tree in full leaf.

I didn't expect to come home to a heatwave . . .

She smiled. Two months in Venezuela had left her

13

habitually rising early, and staying up late in the warm dusk, with the middle of the day a desert of siesta, lying in her room with windows and doors open, trying to coax the humid air through, and sleep. Flesh beside her own flesh had proved hot and sticky; male sweat pungent, male muscles heavy and hot where an arm lay carelessly across her hips ... Her memory had made of England a green, damp, cool place.

Distantly, she could hear intermittent traffic: a main road a few miles off. The sound of a skylark went up into inaudibility. She smelled the sun-hot gravel, and the exhaust of the car. Abruptly, she peered forward, down the slope in front of her.

She saw rough grass, and more trees at the bottom of the hill, not far away, their long narrow leaves hanging motionless in the air. Willows? And, between the thick ancient tree-trunks, the glint of a stream?

That would be cooler, she thought.

On impulse, Nadia strode back to the car, wound up the windows and locked it, tucking her clutch-bag under her arm. I'm hardly dressed for country walking ... but it's only a few hundred yards ...

She was not wearing tights or stockings; it was the work of a moment to pull off her sandals and carry them with the straps hooked over her finger. Despite the heat of the day, the depths of the grass were cool and slightly moist. She trod with caution, but not slowly, and a minute or so brought her to the foot of the hill, where willows shaded the sun. She breathed a sigh of relief.

A pool the colour of whisky had a clear-water stream flowing into and out of it. A long spear-shaped leaf circled in the slow current.

Without the least care for her dress and the marks the willow bark might leave on it, Nadia seated herself on the nearest tree root. She stretched out one slender tanned leg, and dipped her bare foot into the water.

That's cold! She smiled to herself. That's what I wanted . . .

She shifted herself about on the willow's root, and put both her feet into the chill water. It felt like silk and ice, caressing her ankles and calf muscles. Looking down, she saw how the pool turned her feet pale.

She dipped her fingers in, sprinkled a few drops of cold water over her forehead and the V-front of her dress, and leaned back against the willow tree's trunk, closing her eyes.

Without opening them, she reached up with damp fingers to undo the top button of her cotton dress.

Nobody's going to see me, Nadia thought. *Perhaps that's a shame . . .*

I've been spending too much time with young Corey, out in Venezuela – Corey Black can get away with *any*thing . . .

Nadia smiled.

But it's not just that. I've stopped caring about what 'people might think' of a woman my age doing this. Because there, 'a woman of a certain age' is interesting, exciting, glamorous.

And now I'm home, and I feel restless – yes, I've had my adventurous moments in the past, but coming back to England, that all feels rather distant now . . .

'You,' a deep voice cut abruptly into her thoughts, 'are trespassing.'

Nadia Kay slowly opened her eyes.

Two months out of England haven't changed me that much, she reflected calmly. Except to relax me; make me feel like myself again. If this had happened when I was going through all the stress of selling the business, I dare say I should have jumped up like a startled rabbit. As it is . . .

The voice was male; she automatically glanced in

15

that direction, expecting – since she was in the country – that the first thing to meet her gaze would be green wellington boots, standing foursquare in the rough grass that lined the stream's edge.

Like all of Oscar's country friends, who used to bore me rigid, and no wonder he and I divorced if he could never understand why.

She saw a pair of dark, expensive brogues.

On a country path? Well, it's hardly a day for mud, in this heat, but still . . .

Curiously, she raised her head and looked up, her gaze travelling up incongruously smart and expensive suit trousers. No flat cap. No tweed. No shotgun carried broken over the man's arm.

Cradled against the willow-trunk, Nadia found herself gazing up at a man who might have been her own age or a little younger, and who was wearing an elegant, dark Armani suit.

'Trespassing on my land,' his voice repeated, with a touch of irony.

Nadia smiled. 'I'm terribly sorry. I'm afraid I didn't realise.'

The man continued to look down at her. She had a brief impression of authority in the way he carried himself. Might he be ex-military? she wondered. His dark brown hair fell over his forehead in the kind of casual cut that only comes at great expense. His shoulders were broad, she noted. What made him stand out, in the dappled shadow of the willow trees – and gave her a surprising, familiar jolt in her lower belly – was his face.

His eyes were a brown as rich as the pool in which her feet were now chilled to numbness. His features were strong. A very masculine face, she thought. And his mouth had a combination of strength, and lips that looked as if they would be both soft and hot if she touched them with her own . . .

A slight colour touched the man's cheekbones as his gaze swept her from her water-immersed bare feet to the red-gold of her hair. It doesn't look like embarrassment, Nadia thought. He doesn't look like a man who's easily put off his stride.

'Sorry.' He was frowning slightly now. 'I thought you were one of the girls from the village. They bring their boyfriends up here . . . Did you have an accident? Your car break down?'

He raised his head and looked about, as if he expected to see a car somewhere along the stream's bank, or out in the field among the wildflowers.

Nadia prickled, slightly, at 'girl'.

I'm hardly a girl; does that mean I can't sit down in bare feet? She sighed to herself. I'm back in England now; perhaps it *does* mean that.

The man looked tall, she thought, but any man is tall when seen from so low down. Nadia let her gaze fall to her own level, momentarily appreciating the length of his legs and his well-cut suit.

She found her eyes were almost exactly on a level with the flies of his trousers. She looked away.

'My car's up there.' Nadia lifted one bare foot from the pool, and shook off drops of shining water. She gestured towards the grassy slope. 'I didn't have a breakdown; I was just passing. I didn't see a NO TRESPASSING sign.'

Irritation briefly coloured his tone. 'You wouldn't, no. The little sods take it down.'

Nadia removed her other foot from the water's chill. Putting it on the cool earth, she felt the pattern of the grass and roots under her bare skin. She had tugged her hem down to cover her knees before she remembered that she had undone the top button of her dress.

17

She made no move to close the V of material, to hide the shadowed cleft inside the bodice. Still without rising from where she sat, she raised her eyes.

He really does look attractive – and if he took that suit jacket off, I'm sure he'd look even better.

'Nadia Kay,' she said, looking into his amazing clear-brown eyes.

The skin at the corners of his eyes creased very slightly. 'Jonathan Parnell. May I give you a hand?'

She found herself reaching up automatically. His hand was large and powerful; she had a moment to notice that he was well manicured, if not overly so, before his grasp closed about her own hand.

She was effortlessly lifted up on to her feet. As effortlessly as if she weighed nothing: a moment of weightlessness. It dizzied her to the point where she stumbled slightly as her bare feet took her weight again.

Nadia thought, *Oh!*

The briefest sensation went through her mind and her body – what would it be like to have those powerful hands close about her waist and lift her up, and put her down on a bed? How small she would feel; how fragile.

Nadia felt her cheeks heat in the shifting shadows of the willow leaves. *I wonder if this is obvious to him . . .*

Jonathan Parnell was not, in fact, so very tall, now that she stood in front of him. A little under six foot, she thought. Still tall enough for her to have to gaze up, but she was long used to that. His skin was just touched with sun, rather than tanned; his Armani suit looked out of place by this streamlet, in these green fields. He wore an expensive silk shirt open at the throat, and no tie.

She smiled to herself. Farming obviously pays better than I thought.

18

He said nothing. She expected his grip on her hand to loosen and let her go. But the warmth of his flesh continued to enclose her fingers.

Nadia did not loosen her own grip. She looked up from under her eyelashes. 'Jonathan – may I call you "Jonathan"?'

The shifting light and shade of the willows made it difficult to judge how dark his hair might be. A very dark brown, at the least. He stood with a self-possessed elegance that sat oddly with his definite, stark features. Now she was on her feet, she could see the sharp lines of his jaw and brow; see how his mouth was turning up very slightly at the corner.

'Perhaps,' Nadia said, 'I should be going.'

Jonathan Parnell held on to her hand. 'Nadia . . .'

She could feel a thin film of sweat between his skin and hers. Her mouth was suddenly dry with arousal. She smelled his scent, standing so close to him; a masculine odour of soap and expensive cloth and the heat of the day.

'It's hot out there.' His gaze went over her head, to where the sun shimmered over the rough grasses, and then abruptly dropped to lock with her own. 'It would be a shame to rush off.'

She smiled, holding his gaze. 'But I'm trespassing.'

'No. You're not.' His smile became crookedly encouraging. 'The owner's given you permission to stay here.'

'Has he, indeed?' Nadia very deliberately looked down at her hand, her fingers now interlaced with his. Her skin, a little sun-touched, was not as flawless as a twenty-year-old's, but her hands were slender, and from long experience she knew that men envisaged them doing things that seemed pleasingly incongruous in comparison with their well-kept elegance.

She still expected him to let go of her hand, she

found; probably to apologise for forgetting that he held it.

He turned her hand over, bent his head and kissed each of her fingertips in turn, his lips soft and hot and smooth.

' "Nadia" . . .' He looked up at her, under lashes that were black as ink and astonishingly long for a man. His eyes seemed almost elongated, and his brows very slightly tilted; without the civilised suit and shirt, she found herself thinking, he would be an aristocratic satyr. A man of contrasts. 'You don't have to stay, of course. But if you'd like to rest here longer . . .'

The thin cotton dress she wore had been chosen to give her relief from the sun's heat. Now she was conscious that her hardening nipples must show where the slightly sweat-dampened material clung to her breasts. She glanced away, down at the pool, where it reflected the shivering willow leaves that overhung the water.

On the periphery of her vision she saw that a slight bulge now spoiled the well-cut line of his suit trousers.

She had a natural poise and balance, which she knew worked to her advantage. I can look self-possessed, Nadia reflected. But sometimes, that doesn't quite get me what I want . . .

Without protest she slid her hand out of his grip and leaned over to pick up her sandals from the grass at the foot of the willow tree.

The movement was not blatant. If it happened to raise the hem of her skirt, so that the material showed her enviably slim calves, that might be construed as an accident. That she presented him with the fabric clinging to the smooth curve of her bottom was less excusable. She smiled to herself, and turned very slightly, so that the cloth just whispered across the front of his trousers as she reached for her shoes. The deep V of her dress was within his line of vision.

Straightening, she let her weight rest back on one hip and heel, sandals dangling casually from her left hand, and swept him with her gaze from head to heels.

The blunt head of his penis became outlined against the thin material of his suit. As she watched, it filled out still more. She lifted her eyes and gazed at him.

There was no trace of embarrassment on his face.

'I wonder,' he said thoughtfully, 'if I might offer you somewhere more comfortable to sit?'

The corners of his mouth just slightly curved up. As if he could be ironic about his own arousal, and hers.

Heat played up and down her spine, and flushed the insides of her thighs. Nadia smiled back at him. 'I suppose you might do . . .'

With the decisive movements of an athlete or sportsman, the man shrugged his jacket back off his shoulders, let it fall, and swung himself down to sit between the spreading roots of the tree.

Under his ivory shirt, Jonathan's shoulders and arms were more muscular than Nadia had imagined. He had a build somewhere between a rugby player's and a runner's. She watched him swipe his dark hair back out of his face with an unexpectedly boyish gesture, look up at her, and put his hands to the crotch of his trousers.

Nadia nodded silently.

His fingers were steady, she thought, as he undid his belt. The cylinder of flesh under the material of his suit thickened and grew. She wanted to reach down and touch it herself – wanted to grab and squeeze, enticing it to grow harder. Instead, she stood as if spellbound, watching him lower the zip of his flies, and reach inside.

Her labia both itched and ached with arousal. She

found herself squeezing her thighs together. To stop her hands shaking, she put her palms against her breasts, feeling her flesh swell, and dug her fingers into her bodice. Her nipples were two hard nubs against her palms; she chafed at them, and watched him staring up at her.

He unzipped his flies and parted the opening of his boxer shorts. As he took hold of it, his cock jutted out of his fist, a cool ivory against his sun-gold hand. She saw the shaft was thick enough to make him a solid fistful. The head was cut, purple; weeping a clear liquid already.

'Would you –' his voice didn't falter '– care to sit down?'

Nadia, barefoot, stepped delicately on her toes and straddled his legs.

She looked down at his open trousers, and the flies of his boxer shorts just visible underneath; something about the vulnerability of his exposure sending a hot shiver through her cleft. She dropped one hand to her crotch, fingering herself through the thin material of her dress.

Lowering her other hand, she began very slowly to raise the summer dress's hem.

Who am I teasing, him or myself?

Arousal throbbed through her, her mouth dry, her cunt aching. She could anticipate thrusting herself down on his rigid cock, foresee the bulk of it piercing her, pushing aside her hot flesh . . .

Jonathan Parnell looked up into her face. As she pulled her dress high up to her waist, exposing her legs and her soft tummy, he reached up to the ice-green lacy panties that she wore.

Taking a pinch of fabric at each side, he began to ease them down.

The cool air from the stream glided over her skin,

and she felt her bottom exposed, naked.

With her knickers down to her calves, she reached down, grabbed his wrists, and lowered herself to kneel astride his thighs.

The cloth of his trousers rubbed against her inner thighs. The contrast of him clothed and herself bare made her muscles flutter delicately. As she straightened up on her knees and reached down for his cock, he raised both his hands to the buttons of her dress and began to undo them all down her front.

She took hold of him. His prick was iron velvet, hot in her hands.

Nadia wiped the pre-come down his shaft, lubricating him, gripping his flesh, teasing with her fingertips. Her own flesh loosened. She needed nothing, she knew; she could feel herself sopping wet between her legs, knew her red curls there must be pearled with liquid already.

'Jonathan . . .' she said, her voice thin with desire.

He peeled aside her dress, and reached up with large hands to cup and then squeeze her breasts hard. She jerked her head in a nod, robbed of words. Her breasts had never been large, but they were still firm, even past her fortieth birthday, and they were exquisitely sensitive. Stabs of pleasure jolted from her nipples direct to her clitoris. She felt her pussy aching to be filled.

His voice remarkably steady, he said, 'Come to me, Nadia . . .'

Supporting herself with one hand on Jonathan's hard-muscled shoulder, she gripped his cock and guided the head to the lips of her pussy.

Not to thrust herself down on him was an unbearable tease of her own flesh. She felt her clothing against her skin in disarray; somehow welcomed the fact that she was half naked while he merely sat there with his flies unzipped. He dipped his head forward, nipping at her breasts. Her eyes shut automatically. She gripped his shaft and spread her knees, easing herself down, slowly, slowly, as his thick pillar of flesh entered her.

His hands left her breasts; his arms clamped about her waist.

Before she could do more than squeak, he held her body still, locked hard against his chest and belly; braced the solid muscles of his thighs, and thrust his hot cock up into her dripping body.

The surprise of it, and the sheer sensation as his bulk filled her, almost made her come on the instant.

Her knees gave way. She felt as if no muscle in her body had strength. Suspended by his embrace, she found herself helpless to move; his hands were now flat against her buttocks, pushing her against his hard chest, where he was sweating under his shirt. All she could do was attempt to spread her legs a fraction wider, to admit him to the deepest part of her.

Slowly, his tight embrace lifted her, while his hips dropped, and the thickness of his cock slid down.

She whimpered at the loss of it.

Squirming her hips against him, her bottom rising and falling, she whispered, 'Please . . .'

'Since you ask so nicely.' His voice rumbled in her ear, sending a shiver down her neck and spine.

Without warning, he thrust up again, plunging himself home inside her. She felt herself open and hot, squirming against him, trying to pump with her hips but held helpless in his grasp. She felt too much fabric, too much of his shirt and trousers, and not enough of his wonderfully smelling skin against hers. All the skin-to-skin contact she could feel was his cock, thrust up home into her pussy, pulsing against her vaginal walls. She shivered, squirming, on the brink.

'Again!' she whispered. The heat outside the trees, the shifting shadows, the cool of the stream; all of these vanished beside the desire to have his cock inside her. 'More. Please!'

His voice sounded roughly breathless, but still in remarkable control. 'Please what?'

'Please . . . come inside me.' She could feel her face flame as hot as the rest of her skin, all over her body. *Here I am, begging . . .*

His voice was rough, teasing. 'You want me to cream you?'

'Yes. I want . . . I want.' She swallowed, licking dry lips. 'More. Fill me! Please! More.'

One of his arms clamped around her, pinning both of her arms to her sides.

His other arm went around her waist, his muscles flexing as he gripped her. The sweat soaked her dress where it clung to her skin between them. She was held, suspended, moving restlessly on her knees, trying to push herself lower.

'Beg me,' his voice rumbled, breath hot at her ear.

'Please . . .' All thought of self-composure or pride vanished. She dipped her head, kissing at his throat, feeling the faintest abrasion of stubble under his chin. 'Please, do it; do me . . . Fuck me . . .'

The blunt head of his cock nudged at her opening.

She was wet enough that he slid in instantly again, thrust up, and settled to a driving rhythm that lifted her up on her knees as he bucked under her, her legs gone limp, her head falling back, eyes shut.

As if from a distance she heard herself pleading: 'Now!'

He panted out, 'My pleasure!' with a sound like a ragged laugh in his voice. Then he was breathing harshly against her bare neck, her body gripped tightly against him. His powerful thighs thrust up under her, and her body filled with his cock as it heated and swelled.

'Now!' Nadia cried out. 'Oh, now, oh please, please, do it—'

His body gathered under her into one great thrust upwards that impaled her; her belly filled, her pussy clamping about his cock even as it jerked and spasmed, so that as his red-hot seed spurted into her, making her head swim and her vision fade, she lost every last ounce of control, coming fiercely with an unashamed yell at the same moment that he came inside her.

CHAPTER

3

'We're lost,' Fern remarked, on the woodland path, just as Dani's mobile phone gave out her ringtone.

Danila Martinez, swearing, put down four cases – including a camera bag and the padded case for the laptop computer – with a delicate care that was entirely at odds with her vocabulary. Fern grinned, and put the tripod and prop bags down on the winding earth trail.

'*What?*' Danila barked into the cellphone.

It was just possible to make out Lindsey Carter's voice, tinged with his usual sarcasm. Fern thought she heard him asking, 'How is it possible to get lost on a hundred metres of straight *path*?', but the young woman's angry splutter was too loud for Fern to make him out clearly.

The path through the woods here faded away to thinner trees, and impassable brambles and bracken and other undergrowth. Insects bobbed in the sunlight that glimmered in Fern's eyes. She stretched her arms out, making fists of her hands, easing the kinks out of her back. She felt her muscles begin to relax. The *thrum* of the van's tyres on the motorways, and the back roads that wound into the countryside, had got into her bones. Now she drank in the sun and the silence, the lack of traffic or other people . . .

Not all other people, she thought. We got here, we're set up to sleep in the barn, and the others can't be that far off – I think I can hear voices.

'Naturally they're in front of us,' she murmured to herself, listening to Dani argue on the phone. '*They're* not carrying half a vanload of equipment . . . Bloody drama students!'

'Back *that* way,' Danila announced, hitting the end-call button and stuffing her phone back in the pocket of her cut-off red combat pants that she wore as shorts.

'How far?'

'I don't know. I don't care! If we had decent lighting equipment, we could have done this back in the barn!'

' "Let's do the show right here" . . .' Fern murmured, with a grin.

Danila glared. 'And you can stop being so cheerful!'

'It's a gift.' She toned down her grin – *So Dani won't be too pissed off!* – but couldn't hide the sparkle of excitement that began to burn inside her. The slightly sour odour of woodland vegetation, mixed with her own sweat, was at the same time disturbing and provocative. She inhaled deeply.

'We're going to *do* it,' she said softly. 'Not just shooting tests in classrooms. We're going to make an erotic movie – *for* women, *by* women.'

After a second, the tension went out of Danila's spine. She nodded. An uncharacteristic hesitancy sounded in her voice. 'You think this'll work? People won't . . . laugh?'

Fern shrugged, suppressing what she felt must be a whole flock of butterflies in her stomach, and concentrated on the excitement beyond them. 'Maybe.

Sex is funny sometimes! But the film . . . You just got to have the confidence, Dans – that, if we like what we're doing, there'll be enough women out there like us who'll like it too.'

Slowly, the other woman nodded. 'Yeah. I guess. OK, let's go. They can't be *that* far away.'

With care, Fern lifted the prop bags, settling the straps over one shoulder. She rested the camera tripod across her other shoulder. Her short pink T-shirt rode up far enough that she caught the flash of her navel-piercing, silver in the sunlight. 'Think they've got their kit off yet?'

Reluctantly, Dani smiled. 'Linds probably has. That boy drops his shorts at every opportunity.'

'Yeah, like you don't enjoy the view . . .'

Danila snorted, shouldered her camera cases and turned about, padding back down the path. Dust kicked up behind her battered trainers. Following her, Fern thought Dani, with her mixed Polish and Hispanic family, looked exotic in the extreme here, down in the Welsh borders, several hundred miles from London and the university. The sunlight through the oak trees dappled her soft coffee shoulders and breasts in her skimpy white T-shirt, and shone back from her short black hair.

'You know,' Fern said, picking her way down the trodden-earth path behind the other woman's swaying hips, 'you really ought to get in front of the camera, Dani.'

'I *direct*,' the dark woman said, without looking around. 'It's what I do, girl. I'll leave the acting to you and Linds and the others.'

'I *script*,' Fern remarked, in as close an imitation of Dani's tone as she could manage. She couldn't stop herself laughing. 'OK, so I happen to have written myself a large part . . .'

The woman in front of her grunted.

Oh, we *are* pissed off, Fern thought. In another mood, Dani would pick up any comment about 'large parts' and run with it, naff as the humour might be. But she does take things seriously . . . Too seriously, maybe.

Maybe it's because we're finally here. About to start. This is it: we make it work now, or it's all for nothing. We win – or we lose.

The path opened back out to the edge of a field that Fern didn't recognise. She followed Danila down under the outstretched branches of the oak trees, grateful for their cool shadow. After two or three minutes of walking, she made out the sound of voices ahead – and a glitter of water, where a shallow stream ran between willows.

Lindsey Carter sat on a fallen tree-trunk, not far from the water, his white polo shirt catching the sun through the leaves. Two twenty-two-year-old women – Fern recognised them as Hope Frost and Tessa Garza from the uni's drama course – stood on either side of Lindsey, both apparently talking flirtatiously at him.

'That boy's jam,' Dani murmured under her breath. Sweat gave a soft shine to her brow. 'Look at the honey bees!'

'Hope's more of a wasp, if coming down in the van is anything to go by! She's nearly as vain as Linds is. And *she* hasn't got his sense of humour . . .' Fern lifted her shoulder so that she could wipe her cheek against it, sweating flesh against more sweating flesh. 'And Tessa, good grief! Does that girl ever speak above a whisper?'

Fern paused, watching the three of them engrossed in conversation. The blonde, Hope, put her hand on Lindsey's thigh. Seeing that, a thought lifted her mood. 'Still – I guess we won't be needing a fluffer . . .'

'*Fern*ie! How many times have I got to tell you? This is a *class* act!'

Fern raised her eyebrows, deliberately mock-practical. 'If Linds doesn't get it up, there won't be much to film.'

'Somebody taking my name in vain?' Lindsey Carter stood up, coming forward across the leaf-mould and trodden earth to greet them.

He wore blue jeans below the polo shirt, and his feet were bare. Brown-blond hair flopped over his fore-head. Fern saw, again with surprise, that he stood perhaps two or three inches shorter than both the female drama students.

I always forget that. He makes me *think* he's taller.

'Hey, Linds.' Fern let the prop bags and tripod slide to the ground. She leaned forward and gave him an air-kiss that allowed her lips to skim his warm, perfectly shaved cheek. His scent seemed compounded of the earth of the woods, and some masculine tang that would be an expensive aftershave – Lindsay Carter's family had not had to scrimp to send him to university, Fern knew.

'Hey, Fern . . .' Lindsey's blue eyes were on a level with hers, and the long dark lashes lowered over them as he gave a grin of welcome. He nodded at her navel-ring. 'Is that a new thing for you? Looks good.'

'Yeah.' Fern nodded. 'Thanks.'

He may be vain, but he likes everybody around him to feel good too. Maybe that's why I'm not going to strangle him for letting *us* carry the bags up here . . .

Her gaze slipped from her silver navel-ring to his body, not a yard away from hers. The soft blue denim jeans Lindsey wore clung to his slim, muscular body; worn almost white at the seams and the flies. She appreciated the shape of his thighs, and the flatness of his abdomen. The short sleeves of his polo shirt meant that his cut biceps were visible. His skin was pale from indoor studying; it gave him what Fern thought of as a coolly intellectual air.

Attempting to sound more offhand than she felt, Fern said, 'You read the script for this scene?'

Hope Frost came across the clearing with her model's walk, putting the blond hair back out of her face. 'Does this need a script? What does it say? "Take out your dick and fuck"?'

'If you'd read it, you'd know,' Fern managed to stop herself saying. She caught Danila's eye. The dark woman lifted her brows slightly; enough to remind Fern that drama students were, as Dani had said at the start of the project, the closest to actual actors that they could get.

Unless we pay them. And it cost more than we really had to hire some of this equipment . . .

Danila exclaimed briskly, 'OK!', and clapped her hands together. Fern stopped herself from jumping, annoyed at being momentarily startled.

'Now, what I need from you guys—'

As Dani began a directorial pep-talk, Fern settled the bags and moved away. She paced around the woodland clearing, looking at the rocks and lichen, tree-boles and stream, with an eye to framing shots.

I've heard her talk before. Although . . . now we're actually going to do *it . . .*

For a minute, she stood bemused, not looking at the green leaves or the water.

Indoors or out – this means filming people fucking*. I hadn't thought what that was going to be like, not up until now. And it's . . . strange. Even though I like doing it, like watching it, making a movie out of real people having sex is . . .*

Kind of a turn-on, actually, Fern found herself

32

thinking. Wow. The benefits on this job may be better than I thought . . .

In the background, she heard Dani's voice continuing.

'. . . Just a warm-up scene, first, so that we can get used to what we're doing here, and test the equipment. The filming equipment. Shut *up*, Linds!'

Fern laughed under her breath.

The second of the drama students, the long-haired and long-limbed girl Dani had introduced as Tessa Garza, shot a similarly amused glance at Fern, catching her eye. Fern nodded. The dark girl hadn't said much on the drive down from London.

Now she walked up to Fern, and stood gazing upstream beside her. Her blue sundress showed her golden, sallow skin and the contours of her full breasts. She did at least move with that kind of confident self-possession that Fern particularly associated with drama students.

Which is good, because if she's as shy as she looks, we're finished here! But *looking* that shy – now that's good, that's a plus . . .

Tessa lowered her eyes, and fiddled with the end of her long black-brown braid where it hung over her shoulder. When she spoke, her voice was soft but amused.

'Listen to Danila. It's not possible to talk about this, is it? Everything turns into innuendo!'

Fern grinned. *Maybe she can speak, after all.* 'Oh, you get used to that. It's like writing the script. Everything turns into *Carry On Bonking*. But it's not the words that are important.'

Crouching, Fern trailed her fingertips in the water. It was surprisingly cold. And welcome, too. She dabbed chill liquid over her temples and forehead, and straightened up. 'You done anything like this before?'

The woman shook her head. She looked at Fern from under long dark lashes. She might have been Italian or Spanish by birth, Fern guessed, realising that English wasn't her first language.

One of the foreign students. That's cool. She'll make things look 'exotic'. Fern grinned to herself. Because I'm all for ideology – but I'm also all for playing with it behind the bedroom door . . .

Tessa said, 'What about you?'

'Sure. Sort of. Not on film.' Fern glanced back at Danila. 'And I guess this is going to be a lot more like hard work.'

'Linds said we'd have fun.'

Looking up at the tall girl, Fern was hard put to it to suppress a grin.

Dani had Linds recruiting for her? No wonder we didn't have any trouble getting female volunteers!

And no wonder there aren't any more men. Perish the thought that Mr Carter would let any other guy share his spotlight . . .

'Fernie!'

She came out of her thoughts at Dani's summons, and for the next three-quarters of an hour lost herself in technicalities. Here is too bright, there is too dark; those trees don't make a contrast; Hope looks washed-out in sunlight, Tessa vanishes into shadow. A clearing thirty yards on was perfect, but the power cables run up from the farm sheds wouldn't go that far . . .

'And I'm bored,' Lindsey Carter interrupted, in the middle of a heated argument between Fern, Tessa and Dani. 'Maybe we should go get some lunch?'

Three voices snapped, *'No!'*

Mouth still open, Fern looked approvingly at the two women who had spoken in chorus with her.

'Let's move back, if we can't move upstream,' Fern said, filling the gap that Dani left. 'Linds, if you're

34

bored, we'll do tests so we can see how your skin shows up under these lighting conditions.'

Before she could say more, the lithe young man reached over his shoulders, grabbed his polo shirt and stripped it off over his head.

After a startled moment, Fern said, 'Yeah, well, that wasn't *absolutely* necessary.'

She heard the blonde drama student behind her mutter, 'Oh, I don't know . . .'

Lindsey heard Hope too, she thought, by the glint in his eye.

He must go to the gym, she reflected, taking notice of the swell of his pectoral muscles. A thin line of dark hair grew down from his navel and vanished under his jeans waistband; she found herself feeling hot at the thought of running her hand down it, following it . . .

'We should just get on with this!' he said forcefully.

Danila picked up the hand-held videocam. 'Most of movie-making is sitting around waiting, Linds, didn't you know? But, OK, we'll do some rough shots, just to get a feel for it – shut *up*, Linds! Let's move down there a way.'

The cool shadows of the wood enclosed them, branches arching together over the stream, long thin leaves spindling in the breeze. Fern, following the others with the carry-bags, didn't hurry.

Dani's probably right . . . Have a day messing about with more screen tests, to get them into this. They haven't done this before. As soon as they're used to getting their clothes off and getting down and dirty . . .

'This'll do,' Dani's voice called, ahead.

By the time Fern had sat down, broken a Coke out of the coolbox and downed half of it, she found the place set up. Soft green grass grew between the path and the edge of the stream, and Danila was kneeling

35

on a fallen tree-trunk, pointing her lens down at the sunlit greenery, playing with the focus of the video-cam. Tessa Garza stood watching her, leaning against a willow, one palm flat against the bark. Hope Frost had put on sunglasses, despite the shadows, and her face could not be read.

Maybe they're nervous, Fern thought. It wouldn't be a surprise, after all. What I did with Professor Mayhew ... well, these guys didn't. They don't have much practice in living out their fantasies. So I guess Dani and I will have to go easy to start off with.

'Hey, should I get naked?' Lindsey bawled across the clearing.

With the perfect self-possession that rarely deserted him, he began unbuttoning the flies of his faded jeans. Fern blew him a kiss, sat down on a fallen log, and didn't bother to pretend she wasn't watching. She lifted the can to send the cool drink down her throat.

As she lowered it, Lindsey slid his hands under the sides of his unfastened jeans and eased them down to his shins. His legs shone pale in the shadow as he stepped out of the garments. Letting her gaze travel up his smooth, muscled calves and thighs, she realised that she was staring at white, uncovered buttocks.

'You went commando?'

'Thought it would save time ...'

She almost choked on the soft drink.

Naked and grinning cheekily, Lindsey Carter put his fists on his hips and gazed around the clearing. Those hips were narrow, Fern saw, and as he turned she stared at his flat belly. The thin line of dark hair growing down it spread out into a dark cluster of curls, in which his genitals nestled, white and flaccid.

Mock-plaintively, gazing down, he said, 'I need encouragement here.'

Hope took off her sunglasses. Fern saw the rather

blurred look on her face. 'I could—'

Danila interrupted her. 'You could, but I want you over *there*.'

With a pout, the blonde girl slouched across the clearing, to where Danila busied herself framing her with a shot. Fern saw Lindsey grin. He sauntered across the grass, appearing indifferent to both his bare feet on the earth and his bare dick on display. He murmured, 'Yes, oh mistress of pain,' just loudly enough for Fern to hear him. She couldn't hold back a snigger.

A mutter from Dani made her stifle it.

Looking from Hope, now sitting on the grass with an expressionless face that told its own story, and Tessa with her back to the tree-trunk, her hands behind her, Fern found herself speaking up without forethought:

'I'll go first, if you like.'

Break the ice. Those two may be used to going on stage – but they're not used to going on stage and fucking . . .

Hope's pale shoulders slumped a little in relaxation. Relief, even. Tessa nodded.

Dani's black curls bobbed as she lifted her head from the viewfinder, and Fern saw her glancing about quickly. 'Good idea, girl. OK, Linds, you and Fernie take the first dance . . . We won't worry about the script right now; just – improvise.'

Fern got to her feet. Sweat was making her T-shirt cling to her torso in any case, she realised, and her shorts were not as cool as she'd hoped. Not in this hottest part of the day.

'It's no big deal,' she added, looking over at Hope and Tessa. 'I mean, you'll be using stage names and all . . . I'm going to be Julie Blue . . .'

'I'm going to be "Lindsey Carter",' Lindsey said,

grinning. 'My ego can take it!'

'You'll be "Victor Steele", like we agreed, and like it . . .'

Fern unzipped the denim cut-offs and stepped out of them, pulled off her T-shirt and, wearing only her panties and a white crop-top bra, padded across the cool earth towards the young man.

He reached out a hand – and she walked past him, to the edge of the stream, and stepped down into the cool water. It slid over her bare toes and the arches of her feet, up to her ankles.

'That's *good*.' She gave a sensual sigh. Looking across the sunny clearing, she saw Dani peering at the videocam, and Hope sitting with Tessa on a fallen tree, as if the two other young women had constituted themselves an audience to the act. She glanced at Lindsey.

The long strands of hair falling over his forehead cast a shadow, so that she couldn't see an expression in his eyes. His full lips were slightly parted. At the base of his belly, his cock began to fill and stand up.

Leaving the water, Fern walked the couple of yards across the cool green grass. A gap in the branches above evidently let enough sunlight penetrate down to allow it to grow. Further towards the edge of the clearing, the fresh grass grew lush and thick, and high as her knees. Here, she could kneel down and be in full view of the camera.

Fern dropped down lightly on her knees, and rested her hands on Lindsey's hips.

His skin was white and soft, and she shivered, thinking of it covered by his clothes and protected, day after day. The solidity of bone and muscle under it gave him surprising bulk for a slim-looking man. She trailed her fingers down the bare skin of his hips to his thighs, where a fine covering of brown hairs felt

38

rougher under her palms.

Above her, Lindsey took a sharp breath.

She lowered her head, nuzzling into the soft, man-smelling skin at the side of his inner thigh; licking up the crease of his groin. Beside her cheek, his cock leaped and swelled, growing quickly, jutting up almost flat against his belly.

Fern turned her head sideways and, pulling her lips back, began to nibble with the lightest possible bites up and down the side of his cock. His smell of arousal increased. She felt his fingers winding in her hair, then pulling it as his hands clenched into fists.

The furred skin of his balls shrank, tightening, as she kissed her way across them. She took one hand from his hard, sweating hip and trailed her fingertips over his scrotum. The softness of the texture, and the way it reacted under her touch, made her realise that her groin felt hot.

Oh, he *is* cool . . .

In one smooth movement she knelt up, wrapped her hand around the base of his penis, and put her mouth over the top of it.

For a small, short man, she thought, Lindsey was oversized in at least one respect. Just the head of his thick, long cock stuffed her mouth full. She lay her tongue flat, curving it about his shaft as she licked; then opened her mouth wide enough that her jaws ached, and pushed him into the back of her throat. She swallowed, hearing him make a stifled cry above her, and abruptly lifted her mouth away from him.

He moaned, half in pleasure, half in pique.

Fern looked over her shoulder at the two students, and grinned.

She must make a good shot for Dani, that much she could guess – a tiny girl with ruffled brown hair, kneeling in skimpy cotton pants and bra. Holly Frost's face still showed no emotion, but her gaze was riveted on the two of them. Tessa had the fingers of one hand over her mouth.

Fern spoke just loud enough to be heard. 'Maybe I could use some help over here . . .'

Lindsey's thigh quivered under her palm. She didn't look up at his face. The thick, heavy cylinder of flesh jutting out from his crotch spoke for him. *I don't think he even remembers Dani's got a camera . . .*

Swiftly and decisively, Tessa Garza stood up. She pulled her hair-tie loose, grabbed the hem of her blue sundress and stripped it off over her head. Her black hair fell down about her face in a ruffled mane.

I was right about her boobs, Fern thought.

In the dress – which hadn't suited her – the girl had looked heavy, and her dark colouring rather intense. Now, naked in the woodland clearing, she stood with her head up and her shoulders back, her eyes glimmering darkly, the expanse of her golden skin setting off the long curls of her black-brown hair perfectly.

Her shoulders and hips were wide, her stomach had a gentle curve to it, and her nipples were large and brown against her large breasts. She carried herself with her head poised. As she looked at Fern, what had looked like thick brows and a too-wide mouth now seemed perfect sensuality.

Tessa held out her hand to the woman beside her. As if hypnotised, Hope put her fingers into it, and let herself be raised up on to her feet.

After a second, Tessa began to lead her across the clearing towards them. Fern, sitting with her cheek resting against Lindsey's warm thigh, felt her mouth go dry. Tessa's expression spoke of control; the other girl followed her, her head down and her gaze on the earth.

'Here.' The Spanish girl took hold of Hope's shoulders, and held her in front of Lindsey.

Fern got to her feet, bending to hurriedly brush bits of twig and dead leaf off her skin. Lindsey Carter had his lips parted, looking at the blonde girl as if he was imagining everything he might do with her . . .

Fern slowly reached out her fingers to Hope's dress. With her hands at Hope's bodice, she stopped. The slightest lift of the blond head let her see the woman's expression. Awe, excitement, shock, arousal . . .

Giving her time to move away if she wanted to, Fern began to unbutton the dress. She stopped when it was undone to the waist, and pushed the sides of it so that they fell down, trapping Hope's wrists beside her in the sleeves.

Hope had not worn a bra. Her small pink-brown nipples hardened in the air off the stream. Milk-pale skin gleamed under the trees. Fern reached out and cupped the deep curve of her breasts, feeling the other woman's flesh hot and swelling in her hands.

Behind Hope, Tessa reached around her waist and put her hands into the unbuttoned dress, pushing it further down. Fern watched Tessa slide her fingertips under the waistband of the blonde woman's panties.

'Hey!' a plaintive male voice said at her ear.

The warmth of Lindsey's breath sent a shiver down her skin, and an ache blossomed at her crotch. Fern gave him a challenging look. 'Feeling left out?'

'I'm neglected!'

'I guess you can work for it, then . . .'

Fern took a step back and to the side, making sure she stayed within the range of the shot. The brown-blond boy reached for her. She gave him a grin and darted back, the longer grass tugging and brushing at her shins and calf muscles. Lindsey took two swift strides towards her: she backed up and turned around

41

to run, or pretend to run—

'*Shit!*' A white bar of pain hit her across her shins.

She felt herself overbalance and fall, sideways and forwards; she reached out for Lindsey's hand and missed it.

She twisted as she fell. The ground came up and hit her solidly under her bare arse.

'Shit, I'm going to have a *bruise!*' Sprawling, she sat up, rubbing at herself, swiping at the grass as Lindsey, Tessa and Hope broke off and ran towards her. She glimpsed Dani taking her eye off the videocam and standing up.

Her hand knocked against something hidden by the long grass.

'What is it?' Lindsey Carter squatted down, peering.

Within a few seconds, Fern yanked the covering grasses away.

A wooden plank stood upright. Supported by two small vertical stakes, it could not fall over. Fern stared at it in blank surprise.

On the far side of it, Tessa knelt down, frowning. 'Look at this.'

'Let me see . . .' Fern ignored Lindsey's hand and got to her feet, rubbing at her bruised buttocks. Awkward for a moment, she walked around the standing board and looked.

Tessa was staring at lettering.

A noise echoed through the wood – not a loud one, and Fern would not have noticed it if she hadn't thought she ought to recognise it.

The lettering, partly obscured by lichen and not well-maintained, read WILDLIFE WALK. A small red number 6 occupied the bottom part of the plank.

'Fern . . .' Lindsey's voice held a warning note. He straightened and looked onwards, down the path.

*That small sound, that whirr, is the noise of a 35 mm
camera loading a film.*

A very clear, very loud voice said, 'The map shows
us purple loosestrife through *this* way.'

Colour glimmered through the trees, all of it in
pastels.

Around the bend in the path that Fern had not
noticed, a crowd of fifteen or twenty people appeared.

She had a split second to recognise the familiarity of
bubble perms, pale cardigans and men in short-
sleeved summer shirts, and think, Coach party – a
pensioners' coach party—

The elderly woman at the front of the group
stopped, her jaw slackening. The voice cut off as if
someone had clapped a hand over her mouth. She
stared.

In the sudden silence, Fern stared back. Her faded
blue eyes and yellowing whites fixed themselves with
appalling clarity in Fern's mind. She saw the woman
gaping at her almost-naked body. Fern's pulse
drowned out every impulse she had to think. She
could only stare as more and more of the grey-haired
men and women strolled around the corner of the path
into the clearing, stopped, and gawked at her.

The silence vanished, replaced by voices rising
rapid and shrill.

A white-haired, plumpish man at the back of the
growing crowd lifted his camera and quickly pressed
the button.

'I . . .' Tessa backed up, arms dangling loose at her
sides, evidently too shocked even to think of covering
herself with her hands.

'Oh, f . . .' Fern began to whisper.

Hope squealed, turned and ran, all in one move.

Panic had frozen thought. Now, with the blonde
girl's bare arse flashing in her vision, Fern found

herself triggered into action.

Only just aware of Lindsey beside her hesitating a moment to scoop up his clothes, Fern swung around, grabbed her T-shirt, realised she couldn't see her shorts anywhere on the ground – and ran.

CHAPTER

4

The sudden shrill beeping of a mobile phone sent Nadia's heart into her mouth. She simultaneously jumped and bit back an exclamation of '*Bloody* things!'

'Sorry.' Jonathan Parnell lifted his arm from around her shoulders, leaned over and reached into the inside pocket of his discarded jacket. 'Parnell here: go.'

Talk about spoiling the moment! Nadia thought.

The warm and sensual glow of their fucking had left her sprawled on the grass, cuddled up beside the tall man, with her dress unbuttoned and the imprint of grass-stems on her naked flesh. Now, sitting up, she felt suddenly less relaxed than dishevelled.

Did you *have* to answer the phone? she thought, as the call continued.

Now that he was leaning away from her, his dark tilted brows lowering as someone on the phone obviously told him something he didn't like to hear, Nadia felt slightly put out.

It isn't that he's deliberately turning his back on me . . . except that it is.

As a younger woman, she might have leaned

forward and nibbled at that point on the nape of his neck where the softest curls grew at his hairline. Licked at the soft skin, and buried her nose in it to smell him.

But I know enough to estimate my chances of him being irritated at the interruption – him or any other man. And so . . .

Swiftly, Nadia set about retrieving her appearance of poise. It took a few moments to button up her sundress; there were grass stains on it for which the only cure, right at the moment, was a dignified refusal to acknowledge their existence. The green lacy knickers she rolled up swiftly and tucked into her clutch-bag. She put her sandals on, and the heel-strap of one slipped down; she reached with a quick hand to pull it back into place.

There. She sat with her legs curled under her, skirt demurely just hiding her knees. *The picture of a picnic in the English countryside.*

And when he's finished with that abominable phone, we can get back to what we were doing . . .

'Who?' The black brows lowered, giving his expression even more of a severe cast. 'They saw *what*?' he demanded.

Nadia saw his eyes go vague with listening as he sat up. His gaze passed across her without the slightest reaction to her presence.

'That's out of my hands,' he added curtly. 'Yes, keep them with you. I'll come and talk to them. *No.* Not on any account. I want repeat business from that firm.'

Nadia raised a brow. While the man's gaze fell full on her, she realised that in the last sixty seconds he had gone from seeing a sexual woman beside him to seeing nothing whatsoever outside his own head. His frown contained anger, and something else, she thought. Concern? Worry?

46

'I'll be ten minutes.' Without a goodbye, Jonathan Parnell ended the call, and slipped the mobile phone into his trouser pocket. He scowled.

'Nothing too bad has happened, I hope?' Nadia said, still sitting delicately on the grass.

His attention came back as if a door had opened: she saw him take in the sight of her. She felt sensitive now, able to catch any slightest hesitation that would signal he had forgotten she was there.

'I'm very sorry.' He nodded his head, and if he had been of an older generation, Nadia would have thought he intended a bow. 'I really do have to go. If you're sure your car isn't broken down – no? Then, again: I'm sorry.'

His muscular bulk shifted effortlessly up from her side. In almost the one movement he had got to his feet and swung his jacket on. Nadia tilted her head back, almost made an undignified scuffle to get up, but found herself left sitting by his speed.

'It's been a pleasure.' He flashed a momentary smile down at her. 'Goodbye, Nadia Kay. Excuse me.'

'But—!'

The willow leaves and the turn in the path swallowed him up within seconds. For a few more moments, she heard his tread on the path. Then, nothing.

'But,' Nadia repeated, with a frown of her own.

What was all that about?

Slowly she got to her feet. The slide of the cotton dress on her naked belly and bottom reminded her that she was not completely dressed. She gazed after him, for all she could see or hear nothing of him now.

'Damn,' she said softly to herself. ' "Can I have your phone number?" ' wouldn't have hurt. Or ' "Here's my number." '

But then ... the phone call did sound potentially serious ...

I hope he'll be all right.

After a long moment, she lifted her hand to shade her eyes and walked out into the sunlight.

The climb up the hill was not as easy as walking down it, and before she reached the top, she felt the underarms of her dress hot and soaking. Sweat made a dark patch between her breasts. The relaxed sexual glow in her body was fading.

The red MG's metalwork stung her fingers, too hot to touch. Nadia unlocked the driver's door and the passenger door and left them wide open, along with the windows. The upholstery will be too hot for me to sit on, she thought.

Waiting for the interior of the sports car to cool, she walked slowly back to the edge of the lay-by and peered down at the land beyond.

Maybe, she thought. Just maybe I *will* find a hotel close at hand . . .

If this is his land, then Mr Parnell shouldn't be difficult to find.

And don't they say that too much of a good thing is wonderful? I rather think that I want to resume our – interrupted conversation . . .

'I never promised you exclusive use,' Jonathan Parnell said curtly.

Danila spluttered.

Fern got her words out a split second before Danila: '*Coach* parties! You have *coach parties* of people here?'

With a complete lack of humour, the tall, dark-haired man who was apparently the estate's owner remarked, 'Our nature trail is very popular.'

Behind Fern, Lindsey Carter muttered something about it being even more popular now. Fern ignored him.

Danila had one hand clenched into a fist at her side,

hiding the pale gold of her palm. 'But *I* thought— I understood we— How can we shoot a movie if there are people all over the place? I thought we'd have the place to ourselves!'

'I have no idea why you should think that, Miss Martinez.' The man's brows lifted. 'I assure you, exclusive use of the estate would cost far more than you and your friends here could afford.'

Oh *would* it? Fern seethed, finding herself for once wordless. Well – yes. But I thought he— And Dani said—

Conscious of Danila trying to recover herself enough to make conciliating remarks, Fern could only stare at the tall man in the Armani suit.

Jonathan Parnell stood with his hands clenched into fists, resting his knuckles on the desktop. She thought him in his late thirties, maybe a little older – and either a man who worked out, or one who was into sports. The lines of his expensive, well-made suit accentuated his body: elegant but strong. His eyes, under dark brows, glared down at her.

It made Fern recall being fifteen, caught smoking behind the school sheds. A flare of rage energised her. She looked up into his face, hands on her hips. 'Why didn't you *tell* us?'

Coldly, he said, 'I assumed you had been told.'

Her shorts still missing, Fern had thrown on her battered leather biker jacket over her T-shirt and panties. She thought grimly that it was not an outfit that gave one much advantage in an argument. Well, not if you're as cold as ice, and this guy *is*. Because I look hot. I know I do. But as far as he's concerned, I could be something he scraped off his shoe. He thinks I'm .. tacky. He thinks this whole thing is tacky. Beneath him.

Conflicted, she thought, this would be less

embarrassing – and less irritating – if he wasn't so good-looking . . .

And now he's going to tell us to get lost, Fern realised.

She glanced about the old-fashioned office with its white-painted sash windows and green leather-topped desk, purely so that she wouldn't give free rein to her temper. As she did, Dani caught her eye.

I know, Fern thought. I know. We're here now. We haven't got the money to go anywhere else. Or the time. And . . .

And I didn't know how much I wanted to do this! Not until now, when it looks like we're screwed.

Danila muttered apologetic promises in the background. The man turned his head, and after a moment walked to stare out of the window at the farm buildings that clustered here at the back of the manor house. Fern could not help her gaze going to the firm body hinted at under the well-cut suit and crisp white shirt.

It's not just the body, she thought, her eyes on his face. Warmth stirred in her groin, despite herself. *It's that face. And his attitude.* I'd like to have him at my feet. I'd like to be at his—

She cut off her wandering thoughts, feeling her cheeks heat.

He's an arsehole, that's all. A pretty arsehole. Plus, he keeps us waiting two hours just to tell us we're going to be kicked off the place? Face it, this guy is a prick—

Danila's voice ran down and stopped.

'Look.' Biting back an instinctively rude remark, Fern kept her gaze on Jonathan Parnell's profile. Making herself speak quietly, she said, 'We can – fit in. Without scaring off other people who come to the farm, I mean. We can do that. Dani, can't we?'

It was not really a question. Jonathan Parnell looked back, coldly, over his shoulder. For a moment, it seemed as if he would say nothing.

He finally sighed, turning to face them. 'We have a number of activities involving the general public here at the estate. I should be very reluctant to allow you to continue your – disruptive actions—'

'We won't!' Dani blurted out. 'I mean, we won't be disruptive. Will we, Fernie? Mr Parnell, you'll hardly know we're here!'

Fern bit at the lip-stud she had chosen to wear this morning, holding back derision with difficulty.

Look at him! she thought. Posh suits, manor house, all this land – he doesn't *need* our piddling few hundred pounds. He just *wants* it. And it looks like Dani just assumed we'd be on our own here – and he never thought he needed to tell her different. Just pocketed the cheque . . .

And now watch us get escorted out of this place fast enough to leave skidmarks!

Fern lifted her chin, gazing up at Jonathan Parnell. It was too hot in her biker jacket, even with it only draped about her shoulders. She was conscious of the scent of leather. Attempting to catch the man's eye, she succeeded – and caught herself unawares.

A stab of shock and arousal went from her throat to her pussy the second she encountered his direct gaze.

His lip curved, very slightly, in what might equally well have been an ironic smile or a sneer. His eyes shone dark and brilliant under his heavy brows. She saw his gaze shift: felt as if he were stripping the biker jacket off her and surveying her in her bra-top and panties – without being moved by it in the slightest.

Wouldn't I like to take that smile off his face!

If I could do to him what I was doing to Linds just

51

now ... Make him moan, Fern thought. Rumple that jacket and tie ...

Jonathan Parnell's brows lifted. 'You do realise that I'm doing you a favour in permitting you to use the estate for filming?'

Patronising bastard! Fern frowned.

His expression seemed bland – businesslike – with only that puzzling touch of irony or mockery that she couldn't place.

Does he want something else? More than rent money for the barn and the land? Does he think that, just because we're filming porn, we have to be sluts? OK, he hasn't *said* that, but . . .

A sizzle of annoyance grew in her, until she found herself gritting her teeth to suppress it.

What's annoying? she wondered. That he might be thinking that – or that he might not? That he's *not* playing lord of the manor, and asking one of us to be 'nice' to him before he agrees we can stay here?

She had a momentary fantasy, so strong that it made her flush from her breasts to her hairline. This man, behind his desk, unruffled, standing with as much self-possession as he was showing now – and herself bent forward over the desk, face-down, as he put one hand in the small of her back to keep her there, and with his other hand pulled down her panties . . .

What am I *thinking*!

Fern blinked. She glanced around, embarrassed. The others seemed too involved in watching the man to hear his decision to have any attention to spare for her. And as for the man himself . . .

His gaze went across her as if he saw nothing there.

Jonathan Parnell moved to sit down, seating himself with authority in the chair behind the desk, and steepled his fingers for a moment. The pause seemed to stretch out for ever.

'Talk to my estate manager.' He reached for a manila file, and spoke without looking up from it. 'He'll have a schedule of what parts of the farm are open to the public, and when. You will avoid them. I do *not* want a repetition of this, do you understand me?'

'Yes!' Danila yelped.

Fern exchanged a wordless glance with her. The other woman was grinning, and she had surreptitiously reached behind her and grabbed Lindsey's hand in her own. She looked at Fern with something approaching triumph.

They were not even back to the van and the barn in which she had parked it before Hope Frost and Tessa Garza put their heads together, talking intensely as they walked down the path, and then stopped, looking anxiously from Fern to Danila.

Fern shot a glance at Dani. Dani's abstracted look had not vanished since they left the office at the back of the manor house. Mentally shaking her head, Fern turned back to the two women.

'What's up?' She caught a glance from Lindsey as she said it. He rubbed a hand through his hair, with the air of a man not wanting to take part in any discussion.

'We've been talking,' Hope said sharply. At her shoulder, Tessa nodded energetically, but didn't speak. The blonde woman said, 'We've made up our minds.'

Oh *shit*! Fern thought.

In the moment it took her to fail to think of a conciliatory remark, Danila came out of her abstracted mood.

'What?' Danila demanded. 'Made up your minds about *what*?'

Fern groaned under her breath. Not the right tone to

ask that question in. And it would have been better not to ask at all . . .

'Hey,' Fern broke in deliberately. 'I've got some cans still in the cooler; why don't we go sit up behind the barn and chill out for a—'

'We've made up our minds.' Hope repeated it firmly, her pale eyes shifting from Fern's face to Dani. 'Tess and me. This was a crazy idea from the start! You can get someone else. We don't want to do this any more.'

CHAPTER

5

'You *will*?' Nadia smiled as she looked happily at her barely unpacked suitcase, feeling her mood rise at the realisation that she need not unpack it any further. 'Vince, you're such a sweetie. You're a doll!'

It was possible, she thought, to feel Vince Russell's blush over the telephone without the benefit of actually seeing the man.

'You can have the cottage.' His London-accented voice came gruffly over the connection. She pictured the broad shoulders, shaven head, and heavy features that went with that voice – a thuggish look that served him well in the surprisingly up-market security firm that he now ran.

'Great. But – the keys?' Nadia could feel her smile fade. 'If you have to post them, that means I'll have to stay at this abominable hotel for at least a day.'

She glanced around the room as she spoke, needing both hands to hold the mock-1930s telephone stand and mouthpiece. A mixture of aubergine and grass-green chintz patterned the too-soft sofa, the curtains, the bedspread and the drapes that hung from the frame of the four-poster bed. Numerous ornaments made the hotel room almost as cluttered as her antique shop before she had sold it, but considerably less welcoming.

Worst of all in this heatwave, it had taken her barely five minutes to discover that not only did this hotel not have air-conditioning, the sash windows had been painted over and wouldn't open.

Add that to the lack of a mini-bar, and the two television channels the set seemed to receive . . .

My fault for going for an 'olde-worlde' and wilfully old-fashioned 'English country' hotel, Nadia thought, her lips pushed firmly together as she suppressed her irritation with the room.

Although, as I have reason to know from Oscar's family home, these people have one thing right – the English aristocracy's country houses *are* bloody uncomfortable . . . I hope the tourists appreciate that aspect of it.

No, somehow I don't think I want to put my money into the hotel business.

Vince's voice came back on the phone. 'No prob, darling. Had a word with Steve – he can courier 'em down to you, if he diverts on his way to Brum. You have dinner and then take a drive out to the cottage, love, and he'll be waiting there with the keys in his hot little hand.'

'Really? And you're sure your lady-friend won't mind?'

'She's not back till October. She asked me to keep an eye on the place. You'll be helping me out if you're staying there, so it's a good thing you phoned me.'

Nadia knew her smile must be audible in her voice. 'It's a good thing I phoned up to have a bitch about things, you mean.'

'Always is,' he said simply. His tone deepened. 'You

gonna come and see me when you come back to the Smoke? You've been missed, you know that? You've been gone too long.'

'I might pay you a visit . . .' Knowing it would bring a hotter touch of colour to his face, even if she couldn't see it, Nadia purred, 'Has Vincent been a naughty boy?'

The pause at the other end of the line spoke volumes.

She added, in a leisurely way, 'Does Vince need a spanking. . . ?'

'Aw, shit, girl!' Vince Russell groaned. 'And now you're going to leave me to deal with what you just gave me?'

Nadia couldn't suppress her laughter. 'You're so *easy*, Vince!'

'Yeah, that's what all the girls tell me . . .'

She could tell he wasn't displeased. After a further brief interchange of sentences so that she could be sure to find the country cottage, she rang off, repacked the few items she had removed from her case, and went down to the gloomy restaurant.

The quality of the food was not such that she desired to linger over it. Settling her bills and stepping out into the still-light evening, she felt her spirits lift as she slid in behind the wheel of the MG.

Vivid memories of encounters with Vince Russell went through her mind as she began the drive.

He's a good man, Vince, and a good friend – and nowhere near as much of a thug as he likes to make out. But thinking about him isn't the safest thing to do when I'm behind the wheel . . .

Forcing her concentration back to the road, she followed narrow country lanes west and north, manoeuvring with skill and verve.

A spanking pace, in fact. She smiled to herself, her

mind going into automatic as she drove.

Yes, that's Vince. He's as kinky as they come – which is another thing I like about him. Not to mention that he's also full of surprises . . .

It had been Vince's idea, a month or so before she had travelled out to South America, that they should switch, and she try a day of pure submission to *him*.

The ongoing stress of selling up her antiques and ephemera business had undoubtedly contributed to her agreement. Just for once, Nadia had thought, let someone *else* make all the effort! Give me the illusion that I can't do a thing about it, it's all out of my hands . . .

She had serious doubts about Vince's ability to carry it off, though. It would be difficult, she had mused, as she finally drove back to her flat over the London shop at lunchtime, after another session of viewing impossible properties for sale. When you've seen a man submissive on his knees, begging for mercy – and enjoyed seeing him that way – is it possible for him to be dominant?

Well, I suppose we might try . . .

The phone rang as she sat down with a glass of wine, before she had managed to have more than a sip of it. Vince's voice said curtly, 'Five minutes!' and the line went dead.

My. That *was* convincing.

His no-nonsense tone put a little shiver through her. Nadia found herself making rapid preparations, visiting the bathroom, dressing in a plain and elegant ivory-coloured linen skirt and blouse. When she came back into the living room, she stood there uncertainly for a moment. *My stomach feels as if this is the top of a roller-coaster . . .*

The doorbell rang. Nadia swallowed. It's only Vince. And I've seen Vince bound, whipped and begging . . .

She glanced in the mirror by the door as she went to let him in. Her hair was neatly combed; small pearls shone at the lobes of her ears; she wore no make-up. She might have been a businesswoman, an academic, perhaps even a junior politician – certainly a woman grown to maturity and confidence.

She opened the door.

Vince Russell grinned.

He was wearing dark slacks and a bomber jacket, both of which might have been bought at a market stall. His head had been shaved recently, and the brown fuzz growing back added to his thuggish look. It was not merely his height or his broad shoulders that made other men step out of his way on pavements, Nadia thought. His work in security gave him an instinctive and almost tangible confidence.

'Vince—'

He reached out and knotted his fist in the front of her shirt, squashing her breasts together as the material pulled tight.

With his arm stiff, he shoved Nadia back into the flat and kicked the door shut behind him.

Stumbling awkwardly as she was forced to walk backwards in front of him, Nadia realised she was being pushed towards the door of her bedroom.

'I've got something for you to wear,' Vince said. He pushed the door open with his free hand, not letting go of his grasp on her blouse.

Pushed into her own bedroom, Nadia opened her mouth to object, and found herself making only an undignified squeak. She realised that her knees were already loosening from the helplessness she felt in his grasp. Vince Russell stood six feet tall, and weighed nearly sixteen stone.

Dry-mouthed, she thought, Yes, we've got a stop word, but unless I use it, there's nothing I can do to prevent him doing anything he likes to me . . .

An undignified, squishy feeling of arousal started between her legs.

Still holding her by the front of her blouse, he popped the buttons of her skirt with his other hand and yanked it down. Nadia felt her panties come down with it, dragged over the curve of her bottom, leaving her buttocks and belly bare. Shock and startlement, as well as arousal, made her tentatively squeak and thrash her legs.

Vince took a folded carrier bag out from under his jacket and upended it. A collection of rubber and straps and objects fell out on to her bed.

'What—?' Nadia began.

'Nadia, darling, you just got to learn to stop yapping!'

She felt his big hand close around her jaw and squeeze. Nadia opened her mouth – more to protest than because she was being forced.

Immediately, a thick black latex-rubber gag, shaped like a fat cock, was shoved into her mouth.

She choked, losing co-ordination. While she strained her lips to accommodate it, feeling it press down on her tongue and almost trigger her gag-reflex, Vince buckled the straps tightly around the back of her head.

For the first time, Nadia thought, *How am I going to use my safeword?*

Fear went through her. Her leg muscles loosened. She didn't want to play, now – still less so now that she couldn't tell him what was beyond her. *What I can't take.*

She flailed at Vince, and he caught her hands.

Her legs were hobbled by her pulled-down skirt and panties. As she struggled, he wrestled padded cuffs on to her wrists.

No – Vince – I want to *talk* about this—!

Nadia shook her head, feeling her jaw strained by the thickness of the rubber gag. When he held her wrists, it was as if he held a doll.

And yet I could pull my hands free, she realised, as the catch on one cuff snicked shut. He's holding me tight, but I'm not bruised. And – this *is* Vince.

She didn't relax into his grip, but some part of her ceased to feel fear or tension. With that gone, what remained was a feeling of indignity – of delicious indignity, Nadia thought, and realised that her face was hot; she must have gone red. And what a picture she must present to Vince.

I wish I could ask him, she thought, squirming as he put both her cuffed wrists into the grip of his left hand, and held her effortlessly. Is this what he wanted to see? Do I look undignified? Humiliated? Helpless?

Her hair had swung into her face; she could not reach to push it back. Sweat glued it to her forehead and cheek. Her face must be pink. The buttons of her blouse had pulled undone where he had grabbed her, and now she stood with her bare bottom on display, her ankles hobbled by her clothing. One pearl earring lay on the carpet beside her bare feet.

Vince held her bound wrists up over her head, and bent down. She felt him pulling her skirt and panties completely off. He reached behind him for what looked like a belt.

Nadia stared. It looked two inches wide, and made of quarter-inch rubber, with a hefty buckle. Deftly, still using one hand, he whipped the belt around her waist, pressed it into her belly and buckled it up.

The constriction of her body made her shiver. Heat spread between her legs, and she couldn't look Vince in the face. He chuckled under his breath, and she felt her face flame.

Very carefully, he pulled the tail of her blouse out from under the belt, and then tightened it another notch. It felt like being gripped irrevocably: a grip she couldn't shift. With her hands now held above her head, there was nothing she could do.

She yanked at his grip – which didn't move. Irritation stirring in her, she tried to kick at him.

Vince shoved his knee between her legs.

He pressed her back against the cool plaster of her bedroom wall, holding her with one hand, and shifting the cuffs quickly so that her wrists were cuffed in the small of her back. His knee forced her legs humiliatingly wide apart and lifted her up on tiptoe. She squirmed furiously, finding herself hot between the legs at this enforced vulnerability.

He reached around her, the movements of his hand puzzling until the hair fell away from her eyes and she could see that he had clipped a strap to the back of the belt. Her thighs quivered as he brought it up between her legs. She had time to glimpse it, to see that it had a couple of holes in it. And a small – pouch?

Vince grinned and jerked the strap taut between her legs.

Nadia felt herself blushing. The 'pouch' fitted into place over her clit. She could guess where the two other holes were. As she looked away, she felt Vince snap-fasten the end of the strap to her belt at her navel.

'That's better.' Vince grinned at her. 'Now, you remember: I'll stop just as soon as you tell me to. Nadia?' He paused. 'OK, I guess I don't stop.'

Nadia found herself half coughing and half swearing, the thick rubber cock filling her mouth, making it impossible for her to form words no matter how she pushed at it with her tongue. It stuffed her cheeks wide. She narrowed her eyes, glaring hatred at her captor.

'Kick if you like,' Vince Russell said amiably. 'Helps, sometimes. At least you can't bite me . . .'

His smile snapped her temper.

Nadia thrashed, trying to wrench her wrists apart, pinned helplessly to the wall by the hand that he planted firmly between her breasts. She could feel the heat of his palm through the sweaty wreck of her blouse. She kicked up, not able even to make contact with his shins, and the rubber strap between her legs slid up between her labia, making her grunt out a noise between yelp and squeak.

He laughed.

Oh, you wait! It was a growing relief to thrash her head about, hair in her eyes, and wrench at the padded cuffs. You wait until the next time I have *you*, Vince Russell!

As if he could read every thought fulminating in her mind, he gave her another grin. 'Now, darlin'. Here's what I've got for your pretty little pussy . . .'

He took a black latex dildo out of the carrier bag.

Nadia knew her eyes widened. It must be five centimetres in diameter, eight inches long; it looked massive.

With an expression of thoughtfulness, Vince thrust his fingers between her thighs, probing into the warm wetness under the strap.

She wriggled, grunting, as his blunt fingers pressed between the rubber strap and her labia, and dipped up into her cunt. He nodded to himself. Before she could do more than whoop and whimper around the cock-gag, he parted her legs, positioned the dildo under the first hole in the crotch-strap and thrust it straight up her.

Nadia was already wet. She knew that was why he had investigated her so unceremoniously: to see whether he needed to use lubricant. That he didn't –

that being cuffed and stripped and bound was enough to make her dripping wet – made her squirm with shame and fury.

The blunt head of the dildo glided in, pushing her easily wide open.

The indignity of that – of being opened and stuffed with no consent overtly given – made her throb and clench on the thick rubber.

She felt a twist and click as the head of the dildo locked into what was evidently a ring-socket in the strap.

I can't get it out, she realised. I can't move it. And every time I do move, the belt pulls up between my legs and I just push it further up myself . . .

Vince, his voice sounding unbearably self-satisfied in her quiet room, remarked, 'And we mustn't forget your arse, girlie . . .'

Blind red rage blotted out her vision.

She wanted to kill him. To wipe the smug smile off his face; to smack his cheek; to have him on his knees at her feet and begging for her mercy. Most of all she wanted to tell him that he couldn't do this to her.

But he can, she thought. Oh, he can.

He got out a shorter and thinner object, which she saw was a butt-plug with a flared end. Pulling her forward by the shoulders, he bent her down over his knee. Nadia kicked her ankles. Instantly, and with no apparent effort, he lifted his foot and planted it on the side of the bed, so that she was lifted off the floor, not even her toes touching. His arm wrapped about her waist: all she could do was thrash her legs from the knees down, and make guttural voiceless sounds that only she knew for 'No!'

She felt a squirt of cold lubricant inside the rubber strap.

The shock made her kick her heels, and vainly try to

jerk her hips off his knee. His grip never moved. She had a few seconds of cold, sweating anticipation, knowing he must be positioning it over her arse. The delicate ring of muscle flexed, involuntarily, as she felt the rounded head of the plug touch her anus – and he shoved the butt-plug home with one smooth push of his palm.

Oh! Oh Vince!

If she could have cried out, it wouldn't have been *no* now. It would be *more*! The realisation of that made her hot, both with shame and between her legs.

Filled in fanny and arse, she gasped around the gag. The feeling of fullness made her weak in the knees. Vince put her on her feet, and she could barely stand up. She knew she was standing comically bow-legged, a figure of fun. She couldn't help it. The plug pushed open the ring of her anus, and then thrust its thick fullness up into her, giving her no choice at all about being penetrated.

His thumb was busy at the front of her fanny, but she didn't know what at. Something hard and round was being stuffed into the pouch in the strap ... and pressed solidly against up her clit.

'Remote control,' Vince said.

She couldn't make sense of his words. When he held up a small black radio device, she didn't know what he meant. His thumb pressed against a dial.

The 'lump' in the crotch strap whirred into life. It buzzed, furiously vibrating, directly against her clit. She felt stunned: arse stuffed full, cunt stuffed up to the hilt, and now a remote-control vibrator-egg buzzing in contact with her clit. She felt herself sag against Vince's large body. He grasped her under the arms. Her legs trailed. She didn't know where she was.

'Now,' he said, 'I'm going to dress you. Then we're going to go out.'

Out?

If not for the cock-gag stuffing her mouth, Nadia would have gasped in outrage and panic.

She found herself held up with one hand while he picked among her casual clothes with the other. He pulled a pair of full white cotton panties up her legs, and wrestled her into a pair of expensive and well-cut chinos, which he eventually zipped up.

With that done, he uncuffed her wrists, stripped off her ruined blouse and fed her arms through a T-shirt. It blocked her vision when he pulled it over her head, momentarily blindfolding her – making her knees almost collapse.

The T-shirt jerked down. Nadia clenched her fists and went to hit him.

He grabbed her hands again, in one of his. With one finger, he tapped on the gag stuffed into her mouth, pushing the latex harder into her mouth. 'Naughty naughty . . .'

She wanted to kick him. That must be obvious. He stood her up on the floor again, and stepped back.

Dizzy, almost falling, Nadia spat and swore, as much as was possible around the gag, using language she would not use in business circumstances. She knew she must be amusing him – Vince's face had a widening grin on it.

Because he's looking at tiny red-faced Nadia make a fool of herself, scowling with her mouth stuffed over-full with latex cock.

The second she made a move towards kicking his shins, she knew she had made a mistake.

He dropped his hand into the pocket of his slacks. She felt a sudden shift – and then the vibrator-egg in her clit-pouch began to vibrate faster. *Much* faster.

'Vince!' The sound didn't come out as a name. Her legs sagged, and she grabbed at his arm.

The vibrator in her fanny began to whirr at a higher speed.

Her eyes must have been bugging out of her head in anticipation, she thought, blushing furiously. She was right. The anal plug suddenly buzzed into high speed.

Her legs shot apart. She was clinging to Vince, bow-legged, hoarse grunts and snorts coming out around the fat latex cock.

With Nadia seconds away from coming, his hand moved in his pocket again and all three stimulators fell back down to a mild quiver.

'Now you see what you get if you piss me off.' Vince reached around her, his solid, sweaty body in her face. His fingers moved up to the back of her head. She felt him undoing the gag. He added, 'Being in public won't stop me either.'

' "Public"?' Nadia snarled as soon as she could speak. 'Vince Russell, don't you *dare*—'

He watched, grinning. His smugness, and her lack of ability to affect it, turned her on yet more – that in itself made her furious. He stood there in his casual clothes, one hand in his pocket, and waited until she ran down.

'Now we're going out,' he announced, grabbing her arm and steering her towards her front door.

'What? No!' Nadia squeaked, pushing back against him, sandals digging into the carpet.

'We can go out like this, or you can wear the gag as well. Which way d'you want it?'

The idea of being forced to walk down the street with her mouth stuffed full of fat cock . . . the vibrator in her pussy squelched in the sudden wet. She tried to stop blushing, and to look as though it didn't affect her. *I had no idea*, she thought.

'But that's a game for another day,' he added. 'Today, I got other plans. Now come on.'

It was just possible to walk with the thick belt between her legs. If she put her shoulders back and kept her head high, it was invisible – as were the pussy vibrator and anal dildo. There was enough fullness in the chinos that the clit-pouch didn't push out too obviously.

Vince planned this well, she thought. She had to walk with a slow, patrician amble. She couldn't help blushing as they left the house and walked down the street. Vince chuckled under his breath. His hand stayed in his pocket.

'You know what?' he said.

'What?' Nadia growled.

'Variable control.'

It took her a moment to work out what he meant – and then it was obvious. The anal plug seemed to expand to double its width inside her, filling her arsehole thoroughly full.

And it buzzed – anyone within a yard of her could have heard it, she thought, though that might have been paranoia. Nadia found herself too busy trying to cope with the weak knees she suddenly had from being unceremoniously buggered in the middle of the High Street.

'Vince! Please!'

'OK, doll.' He did his best East End hard man impression, and linked his arm through hers, almost holding her up. 'You want the other one? Riiight . . .'

The anal plug deflated and stopped moving. Before she could take a breath in relief, the pussy vibrator switched on.

The thick, wide rubber belt kept it stuffed up her cunt, and Nadia thought that was just as well. As soon as it kicked into high gear, her internal muscles wanted to squeeze it clear out across the road. It was thicker than any dildo she owned, and a good bit longer, and she suddenly found herself on tiptoe beside Vince, as if she could raise herself up off it.

He stopped the controls within an instant of her coming in her pants.

'I don't know what you think you're doing!' she snarled, 'but you're going to pay for it!'

'Hope so.' He grinned at her.

'You—!' Words were not adequate, she found. And the glint in his eye warned her.

'I wouldn't, darling,' he remarked. 'Not unless you want me to put you over my knee right here.'

The ache of her desire to come filled all her body. She must be red-faced, even if nothing else was visible. She glanced wildly about, noting that there were not very many people in the street at this hour of the afternoon. Not many parked cars. If they were to turn up one of the side streets off the main road . . .

I can't seriously be thinking of—

'I have to come,' she moaned under her breath, clinging to Vince's muscled arm. 'I'm so – full. I *have* to . . . Please . . .'

'That's what I want to hear.' There was a gleam in his eye as he glanced down at her. 'Now guess what you're going to do . . .'

She looked at him blankly. 'Do? What do you mean, *do*?'

'You want to come.' His hand moved in his pocket, and she twitched at the throb, deep and heavy, in her cunt. Her muscles wanted to trigger climax, needed to – and the throbbing vibration stopped again.

'Vince!' She didn't like how pleading she sounded.

'I'll let you come.' He looked down at her from his greater height. There was a smug, gloating smile on his face. 'First, you get down on your knees, right here, and you beg me.'

'I—' Nadia stared at him. 'I can't do that! Not in

front of everybody!'

Vince gave a superbly casual shrug.

She hated him in that moment. To be standing there as he was, comfortable and at ease – not rigidly erect, in case some drape of the fabric of her clothing should give away the belt under her trousers; not gaspingly full and all but ready to straddle his leg and rub herself to completion . . .

His hand moved in his pocket.

A wave of throbbing power moved from her anus to her cunt to her clit, each vibrator buzzing in turn. Her knees all but gave way. She thought dimly, I *have* to come – and he knows it!

Her fingers were shaking. She glanced around. A nondescript street, not yet near to the main shops; nobody near enough to see. As she felt the vibration beginning again between her legs, up her arse, and against her clit, she staggered.

'Oh God,' she moaned under her breath. 'You have to stop! No, *don't* stop. Let me finish. Vince!'

'I don't have to stop.' He smiled smugly. 'See, I know what you're going to do if I turn it up . . .'

The thick obstruction filling her cunt vibrated in a deep, solid rhythm. She could have kept her presence of mind, except for the shrill fast vibrations in her bum-hole . . . and now the super-fast vibrating pressure against her clit . . .

Vince was right. He was a bastard because he was right. She was rocking her hips gently forward and back, in full view of the street, but she couldn't stop: she wanted – she *needed* – to come.

He shoved whatever it was on his control up harder; then shut it off.

I can't take any more. She reached and caught his arm between her two hands. 'Vince – please—'

'You begging me?'

'Yes!' Her cheeks must have been burning as she whispered it, low and intense; she felt the heat in them.

'You know what you have to do.'

'Not here.' She glanced around wildly. It was not unknown for her to shop at some of the little stores further on; not impossible that they would meet someone she knew. *And then I would have to stand here and make polite conversation – like this.* The thought of it fluttered her internal muscles, and she clung to Vince's hard-muscled arm to keep herself upright.

'There!' she gasped. With a nod, she indicated the opening of a side street across the main road. It was not a throughway. If she remembered it from passing by, it went nowhere but to the back of one of the grocers' shops, and was where they stored their trash skips. No one was likely to come out and see.

And I don't care, Nadia thought, sweat running down her face. She looked up at Vince, pleading. *I have to, I have to . . .*

'Maybe,' he said. 'But if you do that, you still have to beg, and I get to put you over my knee.'

She bit at her lip, nodded with a lack of hesitation that startled her, and clung to his arm as they navigated the road and walked casually down into the side street.

The tarmac was damp, shadow keeping it that way. To Nadia's eyes, the end of the street behind them was a bright square of light, the people crossing it dolls, too far away to make out their features. There were only the high brick walls to either side, and the battered paint of the metal skips that lined the end of the cul de sac.

Vince took his hand out of his pocket, the control almost lost in his fist.

Before she could speak, she felt the plug in her anus

71

swell again, and throb rapidly. If not for the tight rubber belt between her legs, her muscles would have squeezed it out. The thought of that made her blush furiously.

She found herself standing bow-legged again as the vibrator up her pussy buzzed into life – and whirred at such a high vibration that she reached out and leaned one hand against the brickwork to support her. The 'egg' on her clit vibrated: she clapped her palm over it, pressing it against herself – and it stopped.

'Vince!' She heard her voice come out between a whine and a wail.

He was implacable, the glimmer of humour gone from his eyes. 'On your knees.'

'I . . .' Slowly, sliding her hand down the wall, Nadia sank down on to her knees. The wet tarmac stained the knees of her chinos. She looked up at him. 'Please. Please let me come. Please!'

His cold, appraising glare held her motionless. Even though her mind told her it was only Vince, Vince who was a trustworthy friend, Vince who could get a hard-on in his trousers at the thought of being forced to this position – it didn't matter, Nadia thought. His cold gaze chilled her.

She couldn't stand still now. Her thighs moved in a constant friction, as her filled body tried to rub itself against the obstructions in her pussy and arse. The humiliation of that, and of kneeling in front of him, made her bite at her lip.

I could use my safeword, I could run home and satisfy myself, I could do any of those things . . .

The vibrator began the faintest tantalising quiver in her vagina.

But I'm not going to.

'Please, Vince, I'm begging! Look! I'll do what you want. I just . . .'

She lifted her head and found him not even looking at her. Vince prowled along beside the skips and boxes with an absent look on his face. Before she could explode in fury, he snapped his fingers without looking at her, and beckoned her over.

Stiffly, Nadia got up from her knees and staggered across to him.

'Told you what I'd do.' He sat down on a crate, reached out for the front of her chinos, and pulled her to him by the waistband.

'Vince, I . . .'

Without warning he spun her about, brought his thigh up under her thighs and tipped her head-downwards over his leg.

Nadia gasped, choked off a squeal, and flailed to get her hair out of her eyes. She felt her hands grabbed, her wrists forced into the small of her back and pinned. Gravity kept her head-down and struggling; she could get no purchase, her toes not even touching the tarmac. Vince's arm pinioned her about the waist, trapping her arms behind her.

'Please,' she whimpered.

She almost felt the air move as he lifted his hand.

Without warning, the seat of her pants burned as if splashed with liquid fire.

It was only his palm, Nadia recognised after a second in which she couldn't breathe. Only the hard skin of his hand, whacking down on her bottom. Before she could get her breath, he set up a rhythm, spanking each cheek alternately. Even through the fabric of her chinos, it slammed a white agony into her body. Blindly she thought, Never let me ask him for a bare-bottomed spanking!, and then the vibrating egg in the clit pouch, trapped between her groin and his thigh, began softly to whirr.

She abandoned all control, writhing, legs apart,

73

straining to press herself harder against his body. His slaps landed on the insides of her thighs now. She bit the inside of her cheek, heard herself making a soft, high-pitched noise that wouldn't carry more than a few yards – but evidently encouraged Vince.

His leg came up, tilting her; his hand smacked full into her arse.

The jolt sent the butt-plug up her. She gasped. It began to vibrate. Nadia squirmed, thrusting herself against the constriction of the rubber strap, straining not for freedom but for fuller impalement, deeper penetration . . .

Abruptly Vince leaned back; she felt his hand between their bodies. She realised that he was unbuckling his own trouser belt. As he pulled it free, she humped and squirmed furiously, feeling the tension of his muscles as his arm clamped down around her body.

A spark of white pain stung through her body.

The belt caught her again, this time straight across both buttocks and low on the curve. She arched her back, sweating, feeling his thighs hard under her. The desire to scream almost overwhelmed her, but the thought of being caught like this if someone came to investigate—

'Please!' The shame of discovery spurred her; she found herself trying to lift her bottom up to the snapping cut of the belt. 'Harder! Do me harder!'

The white pain intensified; became a glow of sheer sensation. Writhing on Vince's lap, not able to move her body, throwing back her head and gasping, she got out, '*Please*. I'm begging, Vince, I'm begging you!'

His hand scrabbled at the small of her back.

Within a few seconds, the thick latex dildo in her pussy began to throb, and he grabbed the back of the rubber strap and gave it a solid yank, pulling it up tight against her cleft. Penetrated simultaneously at pussy and arse, stuffed full to bursting, she drew in breath so loudly it was almost a scream, felt her knees and spine go limp, sensation gathering at the centre of her body—

Each object jammed up her vibrated at full speed; she came with such violence that her vision blacked out; and what remained of her conscious mind registered, as her cunt clenched and released on the thick dildo, that Vince Russell came simultaneously and copiously in his pants.

The cherry-red MG, parked under low-branched birches, was invisible from the road. Nadia removed her fingers from her panties and buttoned up her dress, smiling to herself. Better than driving without due care and attention . . .

She started the engine and drove out on to the main road again, travelling at a leisurely pace, her body relaxed and at ease.

The 'country cottage' that Vince was minding was, she discovered, pleasingly modern after her experience of the hotel, and not far outside a town that left her still within an easy twenty-mile drive of Jonathan Parnell's estate.

Evidently the 'cottage' had been a vicarage in the days of large Victorian families, which made the leather-clad dispatch rider on a bike on the lawn outside it look somewhat out of place. When she'd taken the keys from Steve and been coached in memorising the security codes for the alarm systems, she entered to find the place had been done up in polished pale woods, in a surprisingly light and airy version of Victorian Gothic. All the furnishings, including the sound systems, wide-screen TV and kitchen, were modern. And the bathroom en suite to the main bedroom had an ivory-coloured corner bath.

As the sun at last set, Nadia relaxed into the hot, scented bathwater, a glass of wine on the ledge beside her, and felt the sweat and tensions of the day leaking away.

Tomorrow I'll find a local newsagent, Nadia thought. Have the *Financial Times* delivered. If I'm going to work out how I want to invest the money from the business ... well, this is an ideal place to stay while I do it.

And for enjoyment ... it's not a long drive back to Jonathan Parnell's estate, or farm, or whatever that land is part of.

She smiled.

And I did get the impression he enjoyed my company.

CHAPTER

6

'You *can't* back out now!' Fern protested. 'We can't make a film with no cast — we'll have nothing in time for the competition!'

As if it had been choreographed, Hope and Tessa simultaneously shrugged. Body language spoke — and what it was saying, Fern thought, was a big 'So what? Not our problem.'

Hope and Tessa, standing beside the open van doors in the long, dusty summer evening, were a picture of opposites. Just *begging* to be used in a scene! Fern thought despairingly. Ice princess, southern beauty. OK, it's a cliché, but it's a cliché because it *works* . . .

Tessa lifted her bags and banged them down inside the back of the van. Her face was set. She shot a prompting glance at the blonde woman that Fern could not interpret.

'We want to take the van,' Hope said, lifting her head and gazing at Fern from under her pale lashes. 'How else are we supposed to get home? We can't pay for a taxi all that way, and there isn't a train. We want the keys.'

Fern blinked. 'You're nuts. You want the van as well? Why don't you just take the bloody cameras, too! You're ruining this project—'

'You can't make a movie here *anyway*,' Hope interrupted. 'Face it, there's no chance!'

Tess nodded emphatically. 'Being seen by those wrinklies ... that was just *gross*. There's no way I'm ever taking a chance on that happening again!'

Fern heard voices in front of her, in the darkness beyond the van. Dani and Linds, she thought, in the barn. If Dani thinks she can direct, why doesn't she come out here and direct these two morons back out of our van?

Before she could say anything, Lindsey Carter appeared around the side of the battered blue Transit van with Danila behind him. The usual casual smile had gone from her face.

Lindsey said, unusually briskly, 'I asked the estate manager here. There's a train station about fifteen miles north of us. Get in, girls. I'll drive you, and bring the van back here when I've dropped you off.'

'Oh, now, wait!' Fern found herself protesting. A hand took her arm; she looked up at Dani. 'You're not just letting those two walk out of here, are you? They promised—'

It was Lindsey who answered. 'What're you going to do? *Make* them fuck?'

Momentarily, Fern lost the thread of her thoughts.

Hope, with her body tied down over a spanking-horse, her light cotton sundress pulled up to her waist, and her sleek silky panties pulled down to her knees – silver-blond hair tumbling dishevelled over her face as she peers up, icy pride cracking. And Tessa on her knees behind the bound girl, Tessa's wrists tied; Lindsey switching her broad golden arse with a leather strap, her breasts bouncing as Tessa leans forward and reluctantly swipes her tongue up Hope's pussy, and the blonde cries out in pleasure—

It would make a good scene if we're going into BDSM, and Lord knows that's popular enough . . .

Fern sighed.

But it's not going to work in real life.

A look to her side showed her Dani, no more pleased with this situation than herself. Fern made a grimace.

'Yeah . . . OK, Linds. You're right. Take them' – she didn't look at either of the students – 'to the station.'

With a clatter, Hope threw her own bags inside the back of the van beside Tessa's, showing more physical strength than Fern would have credited the slender girl with, and strode off around the van to the passenger door, Tessa with her.

Fern spoke as Lindsey turned around, digging the keys out of his jeans pocket. 'Hey. *You're* coming back, right?'

He swiped at the long dirty-blond fringe of hair that fell over his eyes, and gave a curt nod. 'I'm coming back.'

The van's engine coughed into life a few moments later, and Fern stepped back as it reversed out of the barn, turned and drove off down the unmade road that led out of the back of the estate. Dust rose up in the wake of its departure, and she tasted it on her tongue. As the engine noise died down, she heard the *couru!* of wood-pigeons in the distant trees, and a dog barking towards the stables. And then silence.

'Well.' Dani, beside her, stared bitterly down the track. 'That's us fucked. And not in a good way.'

'We tried.' Fern made a face. 'Linds is right; those two weren't going to stay, no matter what you or I said. They weren't ever serious about this.'

Staring after the van as it bumped down the track,

showering more mustard-coloured dust over the grass verges, she added, without looking towards Danila, 'Think Linds will come back?'

A movement in the corner of her vision resolved into Dani lifting her arm, wiping off the dust that showed so palely on her skin. A slight, pleasant scent of sweat wafted towards Fern; she could see the other woman's T-shirt was dark under the arms. Warm summer flesh . . .

'Maybe.' Danila shook her head. 'What does it matter? How are we going to make a film if we've got to have me behind the camera, and there are just two other people? Because, like, I know Lindsey's keen, and so are you, but . . .'

There was an empty granite trough outside the barn, probably once used for horses to drink from, Fern thought. It had an unplugged drain-hole in it, so that it was dry and empty bar a few fallen leaves. She hoisted herself up to sit on the wide lip of stone. It was warm under her bare thighs, holding the heat of the day.

Hunger niggled away in her stomach, although she thought it ought not to: I ought to be too worried to eat.

She looked at Dani.

''K,' Fern said. 'So now there's three of us. And it *is* three. You can teach me and Linds to use the camera. We'll just have to . . . swap round! Be inventive, rather than have a big cast. Come on, Dani. We can't give up now! We can't just go back to London.'

'No. Not unless I go home to my parents.' Dani shrugged and sat up on the stone trough beside her, her thigh warm and sweat-sticky against Fern's leg. 'Student accommodation finished, remember?'

'Shit.' Taking her belongings out of the shared house and putting them into storage had just been a part of the frantic preparation for the trip west. Fern nodded. 'You're right. We'd need to look for another house, or bedsits, or something. And pay the deposit. And there's the film budget gone. And we *need* to have an entry for this competition! I'm not going to give it up, Dani. I'm just . . . not.'

Fern narrowed her eyes against the sinking sun. A warm breeze blew out of the south-west, like silk across her skin. She saw people in the distance in the yard, finishing stabling their mounts. Women, mostly; carrying nets of hay, washing down the concrete with hoses, carrying away armfuls of tack, brushing down their horses.

Another little thing he didn't tell us was going on here.

'Besides,' Fern added. 'Julie Blue and Angel Sin,' – she mentioned their planned stage names in almost audible quotes – 'aren't going to have their arses kicked, right? I'm not going to let that son of a bitch win!'

'Parnell?' Dani nodded slowly. 'Yeah. Oh yeah. "Mr" Jonathan thinks he's God's gift to women, *and* he thinks he's lord of the manor . . .'

'Maybe he is.' Fern surprised herself with a small grin. 'You know? This place? *Look* at it. It's tatty – but he could well be lord of a manor. Even so, *I* wouldn't have a poker stuck up my arse about it if *I* was letting coach tours of crumblies look around the place. Boy, I wish your cousin hadn't gone around with her eyes shut!'

Dani gave an apologetic shrug that lifted the swell of her breasts. 'Eugenie; she's just not really that bright. You know.'

'I know. Like Tess and the blonde cow.' Fern paused, and found herself sighing. After a moment, she said, 'Dani . . . did *you* think those two were ever serious about doing this?'

'I was wrong.' Slowly, Danila shook her head. 'Just thought it'd be a laugh, I guess. And as soon as there's problems – they're gone.'

The sky cooled, darkening at the height of its dome. Fern lifted her head and felt the stirring of the breeze again, against her sweating skin. The shadows of oaks and beeches fell long and dark across the farm track.

Although she knew it was not possible for them to have driven even a quarter of the way to the station yet, she felt herself tense, waiting for the van to reappear.

What will we do if he doesn't come back? Hitch-hike out of here?

'There's a pub down in the village does food,' Dani said softly. 'I noticed it coming in. I'm not going to sort out whether we can use the kitchens here tonight. You want to walk down with me?'

Fern glanced back over her shoulder. Beyond Danila's profile, she could see a few lights coming on in the house, although the golden sun still put a red stripe across the very top of the candy-twist brick chimneys.

'Yeah, I'll walk down with you.' She pushed herself off the stone trough, narrowly avoiding scraping her skin. Turning, she offered her hands to Danila; the dark girl took them and lightly jumped down.

'You know what,' Fern added, 'I tell you now, I'm going to do it in spite of those losers! I'm going to *make* this work.'

It was perhaps half a mile down the road before Danila took her absent-minded gaze away from the hedgerows. Fern realised the other woman was staring at her.

'What?'

She saw Dani grin.

'I had an idea – about what you were telling me?' Danila reached out and, to Fern's surprise, smoothed an errant curl of Fern's fine brown hair back behind her ear. The touch of the other woman's fingers was soft and hot.

'You were telling me what happened at uni?' Dani persisted. 'All that sexy stuff?'

'What, with Professor Mayhew?'

'Why don't you phone her?'

'Why don't I *phone* her?'

Danila's head went back, black curls flying. Her laugh sounded loud between the quiet hedges. 'Why don't you phone her and ask her if she knows anybody?'

Fern came to a halt, and looked over at Danila. 'What . . . you mean . . . to come and take Hope and Tessa's places?'

'Well, it's not like we can hire actors!' Danila looked as if she was spelling things out to a small child. 'You said *you* did some way-out stuff. Maybe she knows other people, who'd do this just because they like the idea of doing it—'

'Most of the people on the experimental programme were older than those two bimbos.' Fern jerked her head towards the nominal north, implying Tessa and Hope. 'I mean . . . is that what we want?'

'Older women are cool and sexy. As for the guys . . . *I* think we want someone who can help us out here! Someone who can be filmed while he's having sex, and maybe manage to repeat a few lines from the script!' Danila waved her hands while she spoke, turning to gesture at Fern as they walked on. 'Fernie, there's no way we can make the movie the way we've planned it with just two people! You'd be staying up all night altering the script . . . We *need* the help. What does it matter if they're a couple of years older than Tess and Hope, if they look good fucking on video?'

'Or even look fucking good on video . . . Well . . . Yeah. I guess.'

The lights of the village were coming into view now. Fern saw a grocery store: closed at this time of night, but with six or seven young teenagers hanging around outside it, smoking. All the houses had their curtains drawn. Parked cars lined either side of the main road.

There were, however, two pub signs within thirty yards, and what looked like another one where the street went off into the distance.

Stepping through the open door of the first pub, pleasantly surprised at the inconspicuous, modern decor, Fern saw that the back door was open too, leading through to an enclosed garden. A welcome scent of cooking from the kitchen made her realise how hungry she had become.

'Order me half of Daisy the cow. And I want fries with that!' She grinned at Dani. 'And then, you know what – I *am* going to phone Vivienne Mayhew. And the others. After all, what have we got to lose? They can only say no.'

'*No!*'

'Aw, come *on*,' Fern cajoled, keeping her voice down now they were back at the barn. She attempted to send convincing vibes down the cellphone along with her voice: 'Alix, you *know* you want to.'

'I do want to.' A tone of regret came into the other woman's voice. 'It would be fun. I know it would! But, Fern, I've got this business trip to the States and I'm not putting it off. You caught me packing. I'm going to be out of the country till late September.'

'That's way after the competition closes,' Fern complained. She sighed. 'Oh well. Joys of being a high-powered computer consultant, I guess. Cool for you.'

'You got it . . .'

The voice brought Alix Neville clearly into her

mind's eye: late twenties, medium tall, slender, elegant, and with a great tumbling mane of ice-blond hair. Unlike the blonde Hope Frost, Alix had no vanity in her character that Fern had ever found, only a wicked sense of humour, and an odd inclination to underestimate her own self-confidence.

In fact, Fern thought, the only thing I have against Alix is that she's a workaholic. Always has been, as long as I've known her. I'm not going to move her on this.

'OK. If you really mean that.' Fern sighed, downcast, then smiled, to cheer herself up as much as the other woman. *Damn, there goes my last chance*. 'Listen, I would have made you a star, baby!'

'Oh, I don't doubt it!' Alix Neville chuckled. 'I'll come and watch the film when it wins the competition, I promise. Hey – have you tried ringing any of the others?'

Fern shifted on the bales of straw that supported her bottom and back. 'The others?' Like many theoretical country idylls, the barn had its disadvantages, she thought; straw jabbing into the small of your back being one of them. She yanked her biker jacket down firmly. Wearing it was keeping her warm during an evening more chill than she'd expected before she thought about sleeping in barns. *Which are basically sheds, and not at all romantic*. She shrugged. 'Sure, I *tried* them . . .'

The gas lamp spread a white glow in the barn, illuminating the side of the van, and Dani and Lindsey where they sat shoulder to shoulder, leaning back against it, their bottles of beer lifted at the identical moment to drink. Fern lowered her voice.

'I tried anybody who was on the project that I could get on the phone,' she admitted. 'No luck. The other students have all gone off for the vacation and I don't know how to contact them. Professor Mayhew's gone off on sabbatical again ... I guess your Sandro Elliott's in the States?'

'I do hope so.' Alix's voice was a purr which painted, in vivid colours in Fern's mind, a picture of exactly what kind of hot sex the woman had planned for Alessandro Elliott as soon as she set foot in the USA.

Fern squirmed. 'Yeah, well, we can't exactly afford a plane ticket to bring him over here! So I was really hoping you ...' Fern shrugged. 'But it's OK. We'll think of something.'

'Have you tried Jordan Axley?'

'Professor *Axley*?' Fern heard herself squeak. She hid it under a cough, and shifted over on to her side as Dani glanced across at her. The leather jacket squeaked too. Cradling the phone close to her ear and mouth, Fern muttered, 'I never even thought of calling him. You think *he'd* ...'

A year-old memory of the surely-under-thirty but very conservatively dressed – and very arrogant – Professor Jordan Axley made Fern blush. She shot a glance up at the wooden rafters, where the camping lantern cast cobwebbed shadows among the beams. Beams from which a man or woman might easily hang, chained ...

That was in a barn, too. When we 'kidnapped' him; Professor Vivienne and Alix and me. And he ... liked that. Or at least, his cock liked it, even if *he* didn't want to admit it ...

Fern swallowed, finding her mouth suddenly dry. 'Um, I don't know, Alix. What do you say to someone when the last time you saw them, you had them tied up and were whipping them?'

'You say, "Would you like to do it again?" ' Alix's amusement transmitted clearly over the cellphone.

'Try him! He was keen enough on Professor Mayhew's research once we ... convinced him. I've got his home number.'

'You have?'

'He's a bit shy about going to BDSM clubs. Sometimes he phones me. And Vivienne. Now we're both away ... I think you'd have to convince him that he'd never be recognised in the film, because of his job, but I wouldn't be at all surprised if he'd help you out.'

'Well ... OK. I was thinking about more girls, really.' Fern stopped. 'Oh *hell*! Alix, you know what? I was thinking about needing more women, and *maybe* a few more men – but this is porn for women. So I guess we need a few women, and a lot more men! Duh ... good idea, Alix. Hang on, I'll find a pen.'

Extricating a biro from her jacket pocket, Fern printed the number on the back of her hand, and, after finishing the call, transferred it into the phone's memory. She hesitated, snuggling back into her jacket, the lining sleek and warm against her bare shoulders. She had replaced the missing shorts with a pair of low-slung combat pants, now it was past sunset, and she thought she might just slide into her sleeping bag dressed as she was, and leave borrowing a bathroom until tomorrow. Ah, the romance of making movies ...

'You getting anywhere?' Lindsey called over.

Fern waved an irritated hand. 'Hang on a minute, will you! I've got one more call to make.'

CHAPTER

7

The night was surprisingly comfortable in the end, when Fern thought of taking her sleeping bag out of the back of the van – away from Lindsey's unexpectedly loud snoring – and settling herself up on the straw bales at the back of the barn.

'I'll consider the matter.'

The sharp tones of Jordan Axley over the cellphone had brought his aquiline features and neatly cut hair vividly back to mind. Had there been a tremor of excitement in that voice? Or ... anxiety?

'I shall call you back, Miss Barrie, at a more reasonable hour.'

Fern, lying on her back with her eyes wide open, staring into the shadows, thought, *I wonder if he will*.

Maybe I shouldn't have asked him. Maybe I just should have ordered him to get his arse down here ...

The surrounding straw was surprisingly warm, if sometimes scratchy against her cheek or scalp. She did, mostly, undress. Unidentifiable rustles in the bales kept her awake for a while, but she found her attention soon drifting away from them, and from her surroundings, and the memory of the phone call.

Out of nowhere, she thought, I wonder what it's like in the 'manor-house'? I wonder if Jonathan Parnell sleeps in a four-poster bed . . .

Fern rolled over, hot in the sleeping bag although she was stripped down to T-shirt and panties.

Imagining Jonathan Parnell taking his clothes off isn't helping any. I wonder what it would be like to put *him* over his desk . . .

Her fingers found the soft hair at her groin, and pushed down between her legs to the semi-swollen bud of her clit, but sleep washed over her before she had done more than visualise his arrogant features in a pleasing expression of shock.

When she next had a coherent thought, it was because Danila – squatting beside her on the straw, in daylight, and holding out a Thermos-cup of coffee – demanded, 'So what happened with this Axley guy? Did you get through to him in the end?'

The taste of the hot coffee was delicious. Fern tipped her head back, draining the last drop, and wiped sleep-tangled hair out of her face. 'The professor said he'd contact us this morning, when he'd had time to think.'

Fern fumbled down beside herself in her sleeping bag, feeling for the cellphone. It had worked its way down to her feet. She recovered it, and squinted blearily at the battery indicator. OK for a bit . . .

'So what do *you* think?' Danila questioned her. 'Is he keen? Will he do this?'

Fern, about to answer, found herself interrupted by a jaw-cracking yawn that put tears in her eyes. She hitched herself up and out, abandoning the sweaty warmth of the sleeping bag for the welcome cool air of the morning, and fumbled her trainers on.

'Don't know,' she admitted. 'I think we shouldn't

worry about it for a few hours. We should do what filming we can with Lindsey and me. I mean, we're going to have to rewrite the script *any*way. If we shoot stuff, then you can be practising editing it on the laptop while I write new scenes.'

The other woman grunted a grudging agreement.

Outside the barn, the dew still glazed the flagstones of the courtyard behind the house.

Fern glanced across the yard, saw the door that – it had been indicated to them – would allow them access to kitchen and bathroom facilities, and staggered across to the cold-water showers.

By the time she emerged, fully awake, hair uncomfortably not-yet-dry, the Victorian-looking kitchen had bacon cooking on the Aga-plate, and Lindsey Carter was giving it a professional flip with a spatula.

'Bacon sarnie for breakfast?' he enquired.

'Linds! Marry me!'

He grinned, wiping a smudge of grease off his forehead with his wrist, and reached to pass her a plate. Fern began to eat with a concentration that stopped her thinking of anything else, only acknowledging Dani with a grunt when she joined them.

Once the coffeepot was empty, Fern suggested, 'You guys go out and find a safe place we can shoot this morning.'

Dani nodded. 'Shouldn't be too difficult. All we have to do is go a bit deeper into the woods. I know what people are like – if there's a car park, they won't go fifty yards away from it!'

'OK. Text me; I'll come out and find you.' Fern held up her mobile phone and waggled it illustratively. 'I just want to check, first, that there really *is* somewhere we can plug these in and recharge.'

'Wonder if they'll ever successfully surgically remove you from that thing?' Lindsey mused, with a gleam of humour in his apparently serious face. 'Most women aren't *that* attached to their vibrators . . .'

'Oh, ha. Ha. Ha.' Fern wrinkled up her nose at him. She couldn't help slipping into a smile. 'Just for that, you get to carry the kit this morning . . . Move your arse, Linds!'

It was still early. Far too early, Fern thought. There were few people about, even after Dani and Linds had spent what seemed an interminable amount of time arguing about who would carry what now, and come back for what else from the van later. Fern shook her head. By the time their amiable bickering vanished into the distance, she was happy to wander around the buildings at the side of the main house.

Estate manager! she remembered suddenly.

Oh man – *that* was what Parnell said to us. I remember now. Find the guy and ask him for a list of places on the estate to steer clear of. OK . . . better do that. Now where do I look?

The house was not that big – in fact, she doubted it stood more than three storeys tall anywhere – but it sprawled. And it looked as if every generation of the Parnell family had decided to add something different to it – outbuildings, garages, dairies (which, when she found them, housed an exhibition of Victorian cooking utensils, rather than any cows); stables; pig sheds; and a mock-Tudor building that looked as though it might be a teashop when it wasn't so evidently closed. A garish red-brick shed did duty for a visitors' centre. Fern found herself worrying about what that implied about the number of people who might be on the grounds in an average day . . .

No, Dani's right. They don't ever go far from their cars. It just means a bit of extra walking for us, that's all.

She discovered a door just inside one Victorian hallway with ESTATE MANAGER hand-painted in small black letters on a plaque. After a second to draw herself up and plaster a smile on her face, she knocked and walked in.

The man behind the desk grunted something unintelligible as he glanced up. He added, 'List?'

He had presence. That was the first thing that hit her. Presence and authority. She thought he must be in his thirties or early forties. He had a stocky and powerful body, a clipped dark beard, and a degree of polish and neatness about his office that made her momentarily wonder if he was ex-military.

'Uh. Yah. List. I guess . . .' Fern hooked her thumbs in the open side pockets of her biker jacket. She tried not to stare too openly.

Ex-Navy? *Or ex-copper?* she wondered as he picked up a manila folder and extracted a computer print-out. But better-looking than most of them!

Much better looking.

His lambent brown eyes were hidden, now, as he looked down at the sheet of paper, and she felt as if a searchlight's attention had been taken off her. She couldn't take her gaze from him. At the back of his neck, above his collar, a sharply razored hairline was visible. The rough tweed jacket sat easily on his broad shoulders. The beard, clipped as it was, still gave him a slightly wild appearance. I could imagine him on a Harley, Fern thought. But he's holding all the wildness inside him.

Aggression and authority, she thought, drinking in the sight of him: his solid cheekbones, rugged face and powerful hands. He's used to giving orders. A man, not a boy. He's got self-control.

It's that same kind of control that makes you want to unbutton somebody . . . with your teeth.

'Miss Barrie?'

'Uh?'

92

'Your schedule,' his rumbling voice added, as he looked up at her calmly.

Fern took the proffered sheet of paper. 'Ah. Thanks.'

She noticed his hands as he put them together on the desk in front of her. Broad, strong hands; the nails clipped down; a hair or two protruding from the cuffs of his shirt and jacket sleeves. *I should get Dani to have more close-ups of hands; hands are sexy . . .*

'I can work this out.' Fern gave the timetable the most cursory glance. There was a scent in the office: a scrape of mud on the tiled floor, and wellington boots behind the door. A heavier coat hanging from the back of it that would smell of the outdoors. *He's not a man who'll spend much of his time indoors,* Fern thought, and looked up to meet his Guinness-dark eyes.

'There are often daily amendments. You should check in.' He gazed at her with a particular stillness. 'Early mornings, or early afternoons, if you want to catch me.'

Fern felt her mouth move in a smile. 'Sure. I'm Fern.'

'Gilbert.' He gave no hint of whether it was first name or surname, only a brusque nod. It was an unmistakable dismissal. She waited a second, disappointed, but he said nothing more.

'OK, I guess I'll be seeing you . . .' She backed out of the office, pulling the door closed behind her as she went, and halted for a moment in the wide, high corridor.

Talk about weak at the knees! I wonder if 'Mr Parnell' has any other hunks working about the place?

The touch of damp, cold hair against the back of her neck reminded her of the less-than-pleasant cold water shower.

I wouldn't show to best advantage, showering in cold water and with a straw or two sticking out of my jacket, she thought.

She glanced each way down the corridor – morning sun shone around the cracks of the Victorian door that led to the outside, and further anonymous white-painted doors lined the corridor in the other direction.

Moved by curiosity and hope, Fern padded down the marble tiles, pausing briefly by each door. They were made of wood heavy enough that, when they were firmly closed, she could hear nothing through them – but some had been left ajar. At the end of the corridor she reached out, cautiously pushing one door slightly further open.

'Yes!' She put her hand over her mouth, grinning. If the estate manager's office occupied what had evidently been servants' quarters back when this part of the manor house was built, then Jonathan Parnell or another more recent owner had done some useful modernising – a small bathroom and shower, in snazzy ivory fittings, gleamed in the sunlight that streamed in through the small window.

'*Hot* water . . .' She whimpered it aloud.

The worst that can happen is that someone comes along and throws me out. And by then I will have had a hot shower, and my hair will be properly clean . . .

The best thing that can happen – she grinned to herself – is that 'Mr' Gilbert decides he needs a bath while I'm in here!

Swiftly she entered, pushed the door lightly closed behind her, and turned on the shower tap. A minute of fiddling with the controls got her hot steaming water showering down, steaming up the tiny window's opaque glass, and filling the room with swirling wreaths of steam. She closed the shower door, stopping the splashing water but not the hot wet fog.

Damn, Fern thought. My clothes are going to get damp. Never mind, though. It'll be worth it.

She slid off her leather jacket and stripped her T-shirt over her head, while kicking off her trainers. In a smooth, single second move, she stripped down her trousers and panties: naked within fifteen seconds.

The steam raised goose-bumps all over her skin, puckering her nipples. She glanced back at the room door, hoping the corridor beyond was still deserted.

On tiptoe, on the ivory-coloured carpet, Fern stepped over to the shower compartment and opened it, easing herself under the hot water.

She pulled the translucent panel closed behind her, stretched her arms over her head, and did a complete slow turn-about, the jets of water playing against her spine and shoulderblades, her flanks and under-arms, her breasts and belly. Hot liquid ran over the upper slopes of her breasts, tickled her navel and slid down between the cheeks of her buttocks. She reached out to the chrome tap and twisted it, standing in suddenly hard-beating water, eyes shut against the bouncing spray.

Oh, that's gooood . . .

Two or three minutes enveloped in blasting water and steam, and she turned the pressure down. A container of shampoo on a plastic corner shelf was not packaged for female use – probably it belonged to Gilbert – but she mentally shrugged, and squeezed out a quantity of the liquid to massage into her hair. The shampoo smelled musky. The sensation of her fingertips pressing and rubbing against her scalp put her into a trance of pleasurable sensation.

What I need is someone in here with me, she thought, eyes half shut, inhaling the clean scent of water and the odour of soap. Someone to wash my back. Hard hands, rubbing down my spine; fingers holding me *tight* . . .

She found herself gripping her small, taut breasts with both hands. Her nipples sent sprays of water off at an angle. She dipped her head, shutting her eyes, and let the streaming water wash the shampoo out of her hair, one hand pushed down to rub lightly over her clit.

The water ran almost clear of shampoo. Fern straightened up, turned the water on hard and as hot as she could bear it; dipping her head and letting it blast the last traces of soap out of her hair. All of her streamed water. She clamped her eyes shut again, squeezing her hair as hot water runnelled through it, one hand squeezing at her pubic mound.

A male voice said, 'Are you all right in there?'

Fern snapped out of her hedonistic trance. Her head came up, she opened her eyes and mouth – and spluttered as the water hit her in the face.

'What!' She groped for the slippery chrome tap at the same time that she grabbed the shower door with her other hand, holding it closed.

Oh shit oh shit oh shit!

Heartbeats pounded in her throat and chest – and in her groin.

I was expecting *Gilbert* . . .

Jonathan Parnell's voice repeated, 'Are you all right?'

His tone was not concerned, Fern realised.

If anything, he sounds amused. Lord of the manor catches the little pleb girl using facilities that she shouldn't. Oh *shit*.

Fern wiped her hanging wet hair out of her face, letting the soft spray of the shower cloak her in warmth, even if water couldn't hide her nakedness. She raised her voice a little. 'I needed a shower – for medical reasons!'

' "Medical reasons"'?' He sounded thrown.

'I'm physically allergic to cold water at six-thirty in the morning!'

There was a silence. Fern briefly wondered if, should she open the shower door, she would be confronted by an empty bathroom.

She realised that the opaque plastic of the shower door showed movement going on on the other side of it. Fern screwed up her eyes, trying to make out what it was. Colours, moving. Some dark, some pale. Black. Pink.

Pink?

Something tapped, softly, on the plastic. She jumped.

This close, she could make it out to be fingers. A hand. Pink flesh. Cautiously, she pushed the door open an inch or so and peered out.

Jonathan Parnell stood naked on the ivory-coloured carpet.

His suit was a tumble of dark cloth over on the clothes-bin, tangled with his white shirt; but she couldn't take much notice of the garments. Her gaze fixed on his tall, lanky body.

Nude body.

She blinked, opened her mouth, said nothing, and closed her mouth again. Her gaze raced up and down him – the dark hair that fell in a carefully barbered fringe over his eyebrows was echoed by the dark curls on his chest, and the line of brown fur that dipped down from his navel, over his belly to his groin.

Out of the thick, bushy cloud of his pubic hair – pearled with water droplets from the shower's steam – his cock jutted up at a sharp angle, already thick and hard.

Fern found her gaze lingering; found herself looking at the blue veins shadowing the shaft, and the pale foreskin half drawn back from the head . . .

It's not like he doesn't want me to look! she thought, dazed. He wouldn't have taken his clothes off otherwise. Oh, wow.

His hips were taut, the line of his body running muscular and hard from his shoulders to his groin. The muscles of his thighs showed he was a man who either worked out or rode the estate's horses. She reached across, brushing the soft fuzz of hair on the skin of his thigh with the tips of her fingers, her hand inches away from the swelling head and shaft of his cock.

Her hand hovered.

Jonathan's voice came hoarsely from above her. 'Inside.'

'Inside. . . ?' She was lost for a second. She glanced up. His hot, solid body blocked the way out of the shower – and as she met his blue eyes, he stepped forward, moving her effortlessly back under the spray of warm water.

His chest touched her breasts, and her nipples stood instantly hard. She felt the skin of his belly against hers. Solid body against solid body. A hot shiver went from her head to her feet. She slitted her eyes against the steam and spray.

He said, 'Turn round.'

Fern held his gaze for a moment.

Slowly, tantalising herself, she turned on the spot. His skin, against her body, was hot satin. She felt her hip touch his erection; felt the smooth rounded curve of her bottom brush against the head of his cock, and couldn't tell if the dampness there was the shower or pre-come.

'Now . . .' His chest and belly fitted themselves against her back, tightly as if he had been glued there, and his arms came around her.

The grip of his hands on her was not tight, but it

guided her – she let him move her hands, until they rested palms-first against the tiled back wall of the shower. Runnels of water cascaded down her body. Her wet hair clung to the nape of her neck. His lips tracked hot and firm down the side of her neck.

She arched. He took it for the invitation she intended, and bit down, hard enough that she knew it would leave a mark. That didn't matter now. It galvanised her; a shock of sensation running from the point where her neck and shoulder joined, down into her breasts, and shivering into her belly and groin.

Jonathan's hands left her wrists, dropping to grip her hips. Fern opened her mouth, catching droplets of water, and gasped as he clamped both hands around her waist.

His cock lay hard between them, pressed between his stomach and her arse-cheeks. She couldn't help but lean back into him, grinding her bottom against him, her crotch aching.

His hands tightened around her waist and lifted.

For a moment her feet were off the plastic floor of the shower. Suspended with her hands on the wall, water cascading over her, and his hands holding her aloft—

One knee nudged at her thigh from behind.

She parted her legs.

The head of his cock brushed up between her legs, just touching her labia.

It was too gentle, too tantalising. She moaned, wriggling in his grip, slapping one hand flat against the tiles. 'Please!'

'Easy . . .' He rested her back against him, and she could feel him leaning, so that she was momentarily supported by his strong body.

'Ask me for it,' he growled. 'Beg me!'

'Oh!' Fern groaned. '*Oh*. Yes. *Please*.'

He chuckled; she felt the vibration of it through his wide chest against her back.

'You want it, don't you? And since you ask me—'

One of his arms slid up and wrapped around her body, over her breasts, crushing them hard against her ribs. His other hand grabbed her at the knee, hauling it up so that she bent her leg. The head of his cock nosed blindly at her cunt, rubbing her inner lips, her outer lips; sliding back to nuzzle at the bud of her anus, and then sliding forward, so that she sat astride the shaft, straining to close her thighs on it.

She felt him push her leg so that it lodged against his, and thrust his hand between their bodies. Her back arched involuntarily. She felt the knuckles of his hand against her as he grabbed the shaft of his erect prick—

With a bare second's groping for guidance, he positioned himself at the sopping entrance of her pussy and thrust up hard.

Quiveringly alert to every sensation, she felt the thick head of it push between her lower lips, and the flesh of her body enclose his shaft. She froze for a moment. His thrust went on, his arm tightening across her to hold her in place, and the tips of her toes touched the floor as he pushed with his hips, driving his cock up her to the root.

Fern gasped, shook her head, wet hair flying in her eyes. Her chest heaved with involuntary breaths under his constricting grasp.

'Fuck me!' she got out, barely able to form words. It was more an order than a plea. 'Do me *now*!'

His arm fell away from her chest.

Momentarily unsupported, she flailed with her hands to feel the wall – and found herself being pushed forward, still impaled thickly on the length of him. A few inches and she finished up hard against the cold tiles: the palms of her hands pressed against them, her breasts flattened against their coolness; belly and thighs both touching the slick, wet ceramic.

Jonathan's hands took hold of her hips, pressing her inescapably up on her toes and against the wall.

That there was no escape from his urgency – that she could see nothing of him behind her; that steam and water wreathed them both – made her even wetter. She threw back her head, moaning. The shaft within her moved.

Very carefully, it thrust forward, and moved back, thrust forward, and moved back . . .

'Faster!' She got it out between gritted teeth.

The base of his body slammed up between her legs.

Sensation melted her. She could feel his fingers digging deep into her hips, and she struggled to push her legs more widely apart, and let him slam himself up into her as deep as he could go. The hot cock in her seemed, impossibly, to be growing larger; she pressed herself against the shower wall and shook her head violently from side to side. The position meant she could exert no control. His glorious heavy weight pinned her. And now his hips thrust in a growing rhythm; slamming into her. Caught between his body and the wall, she could only spread her legs and try to match him, stroke for stroke, her wet and heated cunt swelling and aching with every thrust—

'Now!' she yelled. 'Don't stop, don't stop, *don't stop*—'

She felt his thighs twist, muscles shifting against the inner surfaces of her own thighs. His hips bucked. His wet hair plastered her cheek momentarily as his face was beside hers; then he leaned down, fixed his teeth in the soft skin on top of her shoulder, and sharply nipped. At the same moment, the pounding of his cock increased, slamming up into her, and she met it with every down-thrust of her own, ramming herself hard down on to him, interior flesh swelling, her skin breaking out in shivers, her whole body loosening—

Sensation gathered in her nipples, her breasts, her toes, her groin; built to unbearable pressure; took the last hard surge of his rock-hard cock up into her slick, running cunt, filling her completely. As the first hot wet spurt inside her and his yell announced his climax, she came in a peak of pleasure so strong that it exploded out from her groin to her spine, her finger-tips, her arched neck, her toes – and shudderingly came again, and again, in convulsive waves; so hard that it was almost painful.

The fall of spattering water from the shower-head stopped.

She dimly realised that Jonathan's hand had reached past her and turned the tap. She sagged against the tiled wall, knees weak, not sure if the blur-ring was a remnant of hot water and steam, or her vision.

The sound of someone moving about in the bath-room resolved itself into the noises of someone putting on clothes.

'I . . .' Fern blinked, swallowed; and stiffly turned around to face the shower's door.

It hung open. A dark stain on the ivory carpet must be water, leaked from the shower. Jonathan Parnell had his back to her, facing the partly steamed-up mirror, using it to knot his silk tie.

'Uh,' Fern added. Every muscle and tendon ached, but a boneless relaxation filled her body.

He didn't turn around to look at her. He was fully dressed now, she saw; even down to his shoes. If the expensive suit looked a little crumpled and damp—

It was worth it. She grinned. Oh *boy* was it worth it!

Outside, in the passage, a voice called, 'Are you done yet, Mr Parnell?'

The estate manager, Gilbert, she realised. With a tone of impatience in his voice.

Has he been *waiting* out there—?

What does he think his boss has been doing?

What does he think I—?

Not looking away from the mirror, Jonathan Parnell raised his voice in answer. 'I'll be right out. I told you this wouldn't take long. Go and get the four-wheel drive out; we need to take a look at the top wood.'

Gilbert's reply to the curt order was not intelligible. Fern could only stare at Jonathan.

'*I told you this wouldn't take long*'?

The air struck her, chill. Fern blinked again, becoming aware that her mouth was open. She scowled. Glaring at Jonathan as he turned away from the mirror, she demanded, 'You thought I'd—?'

'I *knew* you'd fuck.' One of his dark brows went up. 'You left the door unlocked. And, I mean, that's the sort of thing you're here to film, isn't it?'

'What?' Uncomfortably aware of her nakedness, and her fury growing because of it, Fern demanded, 'You think I did that *because* I'm making an erotic film? How the hell—'

'Because you're the kind of woman who *wants* to make an "erotic film".' Jonathan Parnell's tone put quotes around the last words. 'If you're doing it for that, why shouldn't you – well – do it on your own time?'

He nodded amiably at her, reaching for the door handle, and left the room while she still stood, staring, open-mouthed.

CHAPTER

8

Danila looked up from the laptop. 'What's bitten you?'

'*Not* the question you should ask right now . . .' Fern found herself scowling. She made the effort to put it out of her mind.

Just me being self-indulgent, that's all. I shouldn't have done it, but I did. *And he can keep his damn stupid opinions about me to himself!*

'Did you give that Jordan guy my email address?' Dani added after a moment.

Jordan? Oh, Jordan Axley. Fern nodded. 'Yeah. Why? He get in touch?'

The other woman sat back, clicking a key or two, and turned the laptop around so that Fern could read the screen.

She skimmed the small font, stopped, backed up, re-read, and began finally to smile. 'Well, hey . . . Good old Professor Axley!'

'Is he that old? I mean, he's not some old fart?'

'Nah.' Fern shook her head. ' "Young fart", maybe. But this is cool. I didn't expect him to write back with a scenario!'

She let her gaze go to the screen again. Reading what Professor Jordan Axley had written brought his narrow, aristocratic, self-possessed face back into her mind. And his expression, when being topped by three women.

And that, she admitted to herself, makes me feel hot. This fantasy that he's written down isn't *that* scene, but oh boy. Oh boy oh boy.

She sat back against the wheel of the van, fanning her face with her hand.

Thoughtfully, Dani said, 'Is this a problem? This scene isn't in our script . . .'

'I don't think that matters. Look, he says it's a suggestion; he'll do whatever we've got in mind. But I think this would be . . . OK. Don't you? Assuming Linds will go for it.'

Dani's mouth curved up at the corners in a sleek smile. 'Linds just wants to drop his pants again. Sooner the better. You know what, I'm amazed this Axley guy managed to come up with something a woman would like.'

'Don't forget, he's a friend of Vivienne. And she will have . . . instructed . . . him in what some women like.' The thought made Fern smile, and shake the image of Jonathan Parnell out of her mind. 'I'll pick him up on the bike; you and Lindsey set up at the site.'

It was two hours later by the time she had got the bike unloaded from the van and driven out to the nearest station. The train was hurling itself out of the station as she pulled up in the car park, but she saw a tall, thin, dark-haired man striding off the platform into the station building with a walk she knew well from the university corridors. She pushed the bike on to its kick-stand and walked into the ticket office.

Jordan Axley greeted her with a slightly aloof air. Despite the heat of the day, he was wearing his tweed jacket with leather elbow-patches; almost an academic caricature. As they walked back out of the station side by side, Fern thought that, with her in her bike leathers, they must present an interesting picture.

'*Oh*,' Jordan Axley said faintly, surveying the large black and red Kawasaki. 'I had rather imagined we . . .'

Fern, pushing his hand-luggage bag down firmly into one pannier, grinned to herself. She looked up, wiping trails of fine brown hair out of her eyes, and held out the spare helmet.

Professor Axley kept most of his academic air outside the university. His casual trousers and brogues would not have been out of place in the classroom, and if his short-cropped hair was beginning to stick up in the humid heat, that was the only indication that he was not perfectly at ease. She watched his eyelids flicker as he stared at the motorcycle helmet.

'Did you receive my communication, Miss Barrie?'

'The email? Oh yeah.' She smiled encouragingly up at him – he was a head taller than her, and his thinness made him seem even taller. 'You don't have to worry about filming, Dani's handling that. You can wear a mask. I understand about not wanting your students to see you on film. And you'll have a stage name in the credits. We thought, maybe, "Ric Shelby"?'

A faint pink colouring crept up his pale cheeks. Jordan Axley at last reached out and took the helmet from her. He held it with both hands, as if he were not sure what to do with something so modern.

'And, I . . . a safeword?' He stuttered very slightly.

Fern swung her leg over the bike and seated herself on the saddle. 'Just yell, "Cut!" That'll do it!'

She put the key in the ignition and looked up from under the clear visor of her helmet.

'If you've changed your mind, professor, that's OK.

Really. You don't have to feel obliged. You'd be helping us out, but if you don't want to, that's fine, no harm done.'

He didn't speak, but he stepped closer to the machine, and after a moment's consideration swung himself on to the pillion, pressing himself up against her back. She could feel his body hard against her leathers; his arms tentatively coming around her waist.

' "Jordan",' his voice said, rather diffidently. 'It would be silly for you to go on calling me "professor". Under the circumstances.'

She caught his gaze in the wing-mirror. He smiled shyly.

'To be honest, Miss Barrie, I'm enjoying this opportunity immensely. I'm just a little . . . nervous. Stage-fright, perhaps.'

Fern nodded, and indicated he should put the spare helmet on. 'Don't worry, Jordan. We've got you set up with . . . Well, let's just say it's going to take your mind off stage-fright!'

There had obviously been tennis courts here at some time, surrounded by a high chainlink fence. The solidly built fence still remained, but everything beyond it was overgrown by scrub and bushes.

'Ideal!' Fern exclaimed as they walked up. 'Dani, this is terrific.'

Danila wiped her shining forehead, looked up from the camera and smiled. 'It can fit in anywhere we want – back-street urban, or somewhere in the country, whatever. I thought we'd do the plain-clothes police officers scene? Considering his email, I'm gonna bet it's something the professor will like.'

Fern nodded slowly. Her gaze went past the Polish-Hispanic woman to where Jordan Axley and Lindsey

107

Carter now stood with their heads together over much-scribbled upon script pages. Evidently Axley had not needed a formal introduction to the shorter man . . .

'Linds!' Fern called.

Lindsey – he was at least a head shorter than Axley; perhaps more – waved a hand in a casual signal. She saw him rest the hand back on the arms of the professor's tweed suit. Jordan Axley did not move away from him. The contrast of their body types showed each to its best advantage, Fern thought.

'Look at those two. They've got real spark,' she murmured.

Dani squinted up at the angle of the sun. 'Then they'd better spark, because we won't have this light for ever!'

'OK. I guess I'm taking Hope's part in the first bit of the script?'

'You wear your leathers.' Danila slitted her eyes against the sun. 'Or just the jacket over those will do, but some leather always looks good.'

Fern hitched up her cotton combat trousers, and grabbed her biker jacket off the earth at her feet. She picked up her boots in her other hand, and made her way barefoot over the dusty earth to where the men's costumes were laid out over a fallen tree.

Sitting on the log and pulling on her boots, she waved a hand at Lindsey and Jordan. 'Want to get your kit on so you can get it off?'

Lindsey sighed melodramatically. 'And you said this was going to be classy!'

'*I* said it was going to be hot. Dani's the one who wants it classy! We going to get moving here?'

Jordan Axley nodded silently, turning to the spare white shirt and black trousers from the prop box that, fortunately, fitted him. Fern watched him for a moment, and – as Lindsey began to strip off too – walked back to Dani and took a position alongside the chainlink fence.

She reached out thoughtfully and rattled it. Still strong, despite the run-down air of the rest of the place. *I hope it can take what we're gonna do . . .*

Jordan Axley – it was difficult not to think of him as professor – shot her a glance from under black eyelashes as he came to stand beside the chainlink fence, on the worn and broken concrete. Lindsey ambled up beside him. All their shadows pooled at their feet. She looked across to the videocam, giving Dani a prompting glance.

'OK . . .' Danila wiped her black curls off her forehead, pulling a baseball cap firmly down on her head to keep them under control. 'OK! Now . . . We'll run through, see how it goes; if you're in the moment, just – go with it. This isn't about big tits and big dicks, it's about *heart*. I want you guys looking like each other are the biggest turn-on you've seen in years. OK?'

Fern suppressed a giggle. Jordan Axley's dark gaze avoided both her and Lindsey, staring past Dani into the green woods with an absent air. He made the least possibly noticeable nod of acknowledgement.

Lindsey Carter brought his hand round with a resounding crack on the taller man's butt. 'Sure! Let us at it!'

Fern snuffled back a giggle at Jordan Axley's expression. At Dani's equally startled yelp of 'Places!', she glanced around, then walked off to the right-hand side of the stretch of fence.

Taking a hint from Jordan Axley's scene in his email, she had rewritten the scenario to take place in some low-rent district, where the streets were dark, unsafe and dangerous. A scene of American urban decay, with a chainlink fence running along the street and a deserted basketball court on the other side.

But all we really need is the fence . . . And this is neat.

Dani nodded. 'Action!'

The scrub and tall bushes behind the fence ate up the sound, and Fern momentarily wondered how the voice recording would function. We can always dub it in, she thought – and Jordan Axley caught her eye.

He entered the shot from the far side, unsmiling, his professorial air giving him a surprising amount of the authority one might see in a plain clothes police officer. His pale throat rose out of the neck of his white shirt, and his black trousers fitted just slightly tight across his hips. The only touch that hinted 'law officer' were the metal cuffs clipped to the side of his belt, and the dark sunglasses that made him anonymous on camera.

He may be a professor, Fern thought, but he's tasty, I'll give him that. And out of that tweed, he looks about twenty-eight, not forty-eight . . . No, nobody's going to say that's Professor Axley when they see this . . .

Abruptly she realised she should be moving.

She reached into the pocket of her biker jacket and took out a folding knife. Not her own, one that had been sitting in the back of the van. The five-inch blade snicked open.

She called, 'Hey!' across the five yards of concrete and dry grass between herself and Axley, and her voice carried perfectly.

'Stop!' Jordan sounded wooden. He made a face – an expression of annoyance with himself – and his head turned as he evidently looked away, collecting himself and pausing on the scenario.

When he looked back, the dark glasses robbed him of any softness. His mouth was set in an expression of rigid authoritarianism. 'Stop *right* there.'

Fern swung on her boot-heels, turning as if to leave. She heard footsteps quicken behind her, catching up. The 'police officer', puffing a little, passed her and stopped in front, facing her.

'You can stop running,' Axley snapped. 'You're under arrest!'

Fern gave a little eyebrow shrug. Behind her back, she made sure the knife in her hand was visible to the camera. She said, in Hope's little-girl voice, 'I am?'

Jordan's thick black brows dipped behind the sunglasses. If his acting was amateur, he did at least seem to be able to relax into a scenario, she thought. And something about the way he held his shoulders told her he might not be entirely useless in a real street-fight.

But that's different, Fern thought.

With rehearsed swiftness, she slashed the folding knife around in a half-circle that, at this angle, would look as though it came much closer to the plain-clothes operative than it actually did.

He jumped back, stumbling awkwardly. Still moving as fast as she could, she swung Jordan around bodily, slammed the 'police officer' back up against the chainlink fence, and – while he appeared dazed, trying to realise what had happened – reached down to his belt and grabbed his handcuffs, which chinked metallically.

With quick, economical movements, she snapped the handcuffs on him; one pair chaining his right wrist above his head, the other doing the same to his left wrist. She gave the chainlink fence a shake at his back: it held.

'Wh—!' he gasped.

Fern stood confrontationally close in front of the spluttering man, just far enough to the side to let Dani move in close on him with the camera.

111

'What the goddamn *hell* are you doing!'

'Oh, now, don't be like that . . . Don't you want to play with me? Little baby . . .' Fern stroked her fingers across his chest. She carelessly popped a shirt button, exposing his bare skin.

'You can't do this!' Jordan protested. Despite the disguising glasses, the outrage on his clear, clean features was obvious. Fern thought it seemed to have genuine feeling behind it. He snapped, 'You're a thief and you're under arrest!'

'Bad baby . . .' Fern said dreamily. She brought her stiffened palm up into the front of the man's pants.

Jordan Axley made a wheezing gasp of a noise. She guessed that, behind the sunglasses, his eyes were bugging out. For a moment she wondered, Did I hit him too hard?

He sagged against the handcuffs, letting them take all his weight, but it was obvious to Fern that he let himself do it.

She improved her role by reaching up and taking off his watch.

'Pretty,' she remarked. 'You get issued these when you join the police, or you nick 'em off some other poor sap?'

'You bitch! You bitch—!'

'Don't you be a bad boy again. I might have to punish you . . .'

The stiff-backed, chained man stormed, cursed, swore, and – although the camera would have to pick up on the subtle effect – flinched. Fern began to smile.

As he ran out of swear-words, she reached up and ruffled his short dark hair, leaving it sticking up in untidy clumps. It brought her close enough to his chest and his raised arms that she could smell his sweat.

Not all of it from the stress of acting . . .

'Baby boy doesn't want to be punished,' she said,

mock-regretfully. 'Does he. . . ?'

She made an obvious telegraphed movement, as if she would have smacked him in the fly again. His body jerked away, the handcuffs and the chainlink fence clashing. She saw a sweat of panic on his forehead, and the faintest bulge at his groin.

'Get me out of these!' The police officer shook the fence above his chained wrists. 'We'll – talk. It's been a misunderstanding. *Damn you, bitch, get me out of here!'*

With that note of true panic in his voice, Fern relaxed. He can do this. In fact, he's *good*.

'Let me out of this!' Axley howled, his dignity abandoned. His chest heaved. His head turned as if, but for the glasses, he would have met her gaze for a brief second. He looked away. He stood, downcast. 'I – apologise. Unlock my cuffs now. Please.'

Fern reached up and undid another button on his shirt. 'I don't think so . . . I think I'm going to leave you here. Maybe someone else will come along to play with you. Will they take your money? Will they hurt you? Poor baby. Helpless . . .'

He made a hard enough jerk at the handcuffs that they bruised his wrists. With her back to the camera, she gazed up, looking at the small contusions, and gave him an enquiring frown. Almost imperceptibly, Jordan Axley pursed his lips and nodded.

Alix said you still liked this. But it's a shame you don't go to clubs. They'd love you . . .

She moved on briskly to the next part of the script.

'Don't worry. I sorted it out. Got a number from your wallet – made a phone call. Someone should be along to help you any time now.' She made a smile for the camera. 'I phoned your station – guy I talked to said he was your partner . . .'

'No!' Above his head, the chainlink fence rattled as

he wrenched at the implacable cuffs. 'You didn't phone that man! Tell me you didn't!'

Jordan Axley's expression was a complex emotion that held panic, embarrassment, fear, anticipation and black rage. Anybody watching it would know his supposed partner to be the last person on earth he wanted to see . . .

Fern became aware of Dani close at her elbow. Fern sighed happily, with a look of malice.

'I know you guys,' she said. 'And I'm sick of you guys chasing *me* . . .'

She pressed herself against his half-naked chest, her breasts against him through the leather jacket, her hips pressed close to his, belly to belly – and reached around behind him to remove his wallet from his back pocket.

And for once it's there! A prop behaved!

She nearly giggled, and suppressed the impulse. Stepping back, she looking up at Axley.

He muttered, 'Let me loose! Please! *Please!*'

'Music,' Fern breathed, smiling up at him. 'Now, you gotta excuse me, it's off-home-and-count-the-cash time. And I guess it'll be a while before you can put a stop on these credit cards . . .'

She turned, took to her heels and slowed down only when she was off the broken concrete and grass, at the edge of the wood.

Turning around, she squatted down. Her mouth felt dry. Her legs shook. *That was nothing, how come it's such an effort?*

Safely out of camera range, she sat down on a patch of dry earth, shedding the biker jacket. Dani had also backed up a little, she saw.

Under the spotlight of the sun, Jordan Axley's pinioned body hung.

'Cut!' Dani rested the camera down.

114

About to get up, she saw Dani put the camera at her feet, reach up and unlock the cuffs. *Now why is she. . . ?*

Jordan Axley, apparently listening to instructions, shuffled a couple of yards further along the fence, reached up with his arms again, and allowed Danila to chain his wrists high. With that done, she reached up and very gently took the disguising sunglasses off his face.

Oh, I get it. Fern nodded in absorbed approval. A slanting line of shadow fell from a branch, and in his new position, it fell directly across Axley's face.

'You're going to have to re-shoot what we just did,' she said, as Dani came back towards her.

'I want to see what he's like when he doesn't have those. If that doesn't work, it might be this part we have to re-shoot later.' Danila fiddled quickly and deftly with settings. 'Let's just carry on, see what we get. You know, I wasn't sure about him, but – wow. You know?'

Fern nodded.

Dani called, 'Lindsey! Action!'

The 'police officer' Axley tried to wrench the cuffs out of the fence. He had been placed too close to an upright metal support for that to work. Fern realised she could heard his sobbing breaths across the bare ground, and stood listening, her lips parted, as they became more ragged, more like plain sobs, and then died away at last to a silence that held all human fear in it.

Trapped. What will get him first? Criminal scum, or a man he really doesn't want to see? *Oh, he can act . . .*

Fern breathed in through her nostrils, scenting the stink of fear that came out of the man's pores. Her mouth curved in a smile. Fear, and – something else. Just the hint of arousal . . .

Fern seated herself quietly on the ground, watching the scene unfold. She let herself take in the picture in front of her, and not purely from the viewpoint of a film-maker.

Jordan Axley swung from the cuffs, kicking at the chainlink fence. The noise echoed back from the broken concrete, and then died against the muffling surrounding of leaves and branches. Sweat darkened the under-arms of his white shirt, and his hair stuck up damply. Fern watched his mouth open as he panted.

Abruptly, Jordan stopped moving. His eyes darted back and forth. She saw him bite his lip to restrain his panting.

A voice out of the shot said calmly, 'Well, Jordan . . .'

The 'police officer' jumped. Fern saw him jerk on the cuffs, and fall back against the fence, which bounced him forward again. He looked around frantically. Then, she saw him freeze.

A tide of heat crept up Jordan Axley's face. She could all but feel it from where she sat. He was genuinely blushing, so scarlet that it was visible from here. Fern wiped automatically at her neck and forehead. *He's in the moment, yeah . . .*

Lindsey stepped forward into shot.

He wore the same 'plain clothes' white shirt and black trousers, but with his own casual leather jacket open over the rest. His brown-blond hair fell over his forehead.

All his attention was focused on the chained man. Fern realised, a brass band could go by without him noticing . . .

'Are you going to get me out of this?' Jordan Axley burst out, sounding furious and petulant.

The short, stocky man prowled forward. When he was within a yard or two of his colleagues, he said levelly, 'No.'

'What?' Jordan stared.

'I said, "*No*." '

Fern, gazing at Jordan Axley with his hands chained high above his head, and all his body exposed and helpless, thought, Alix was right. He is a hottie guy.

'See, I had a phone call,' Lindsey said easily, still walking around the chained man, looking him up and down. 'Said I might want to help an officer who was down here on their own. Since it was my partner. Only, you know what?'

Hardly audible, Jordan Axley said, 'What?'

'I don't want to help you.' Lindsey smiled coldly. The leather jacket made him look bulkier, more muscular; he looked as if he could take the taller man in a fight.

'I'm your partner!' Axley spat.

Fern heard Lindsey chuckle. She had a hard job to stop herself joining in. It is almost impossible to be dignified, or to take the moral high ground, when sweating profusely and suspended by handcuffs, and Jordan Axley wasn't succeeding on either count.

Lindsey stopped pacing. He stood right up close to Jordan. 'You don't act like my partner. You leave me to clear up after you. You take too much credit. And, you know what really pisses me off? The way you always look at me like I'm *dirt* . . .'

As Fern watched, Jordan's gaze dropped. He looked to the side, away from Lindsey. Fern saw his cheeks colouring again.

'Damn you, get me out of this!'

In a tone that Fern entirely approved of, Lindsey said, 'Poor Jordan . . .'

He still smiled. Waiting. Fern saw the dawning comprehension in the other man's eyes. Saw Jordan lick his lips, and look down, painfully, with droplets of sweat running down his face. Dani came in close with the videocam, to get the rumpled and half-open shirt; the desperate expression of a man clinging to his dignity.

'Please,' Jordan Axley whispered.

'Oh, that was *good*.' Something about Lindsey spoke of boundaries crossed, bonds broken. 'Real good. Do it to me again, Ric.'

Fern saw, clearly, the moment when water brimmed on the lower lashes of the man's eyes. His aquiline features were contorted with fury, with helplessness, with humiliation. *Oh, but I wish we could persuade him to let us film that!*

Too loudly, Jordan Axley said, 'Please – take the cuffs off me. Please.'

Without any change of expression, Lindsey gazed up.

Fern saw the tension in Axley's body, saw how he apparently had to force himself to keep his gaze on the smaller man.

'Please,' Jordan finished, 'I'll do anything you say.'

'Oh yes. *Oh* yes.' Lindsey's grin became demonic. 'You give good grovelling, don't you, Ric? Must be all the practice you get with the bosses . . .'

Axley flinched as if the name were his own. His chin sank down on his chest. He rolled his head to one side, as if looking for assistance.

'What do you want?' he asked, his voice cracking. His shoulders and arms shook now, and she could see a quiver of muscle tension in his long legs. 'Just – tell me. What you want. You got me. I'll do it.'

Lindsey put one hand either side of Jordan, making the fence bow and shake where he leaned on it. 'Suppose I don't want anything?'

'Everybody wants something.' A gasp that might have been pain or a painful laugh. 'Right now, I don't *care* what I have to do—'

Fern nipped her own lip, almost hard enough to draw blood. Jordan Axley looked up, his eyes catching the light, and they were limpid, luminous with unshed tears. His lips were quivering.

Lindsey said, 'You tell me.'

'What?'

'What do you want to do,' Lindsey persisted, 'to get out of here? You tell me, Ric. What will you do?'

'Any – anything.' Jordan licked dry, cracked lips.

'No, you don't get it. You gotta tell me,' Lindsey said. He smiled, lazily, shifting position so that he showed off the breadth of his shoulders and the strong body under the leather jacket to the camera. 'You make me an offer, Ric.'

The chainlink fence creaked. Jordan's knees had sagged, Fern realised, and almost all of his weight was hanging on his hands. He didn't seem to be able to take his eyes off Lindsey's face.

'Oh . . .' Lindsey's nostrils flared slightly. He glanced down. 'Oh, Ric. Oh dear.'

Axley's face heated like a beacon.

'And there I was,' Lindsey purred, 'thinking you were afraid . . .'

Plain to Danila's camera, plain to Fern's view, a growing bulge pushed out the fabric of Axley's trousers. She felt herself hot with arousal, watching him.

'I'm not – you don't – I can't—' Jordan Axley's voice broke with tears. He seemed to get a little control of himself, fixing his gaze on Lindsey's face. 'I have – I have a lot of paying to do . . .'

'Sure,' Lindsey purred. 'You sure do.'

'Let me go,' Jordan whispered. 'I'll suck you off.'

There was a silence.

'Well, I don't know . . .' Lindsey's lazy, mocking voice. 'How good are you, Ric? How good are you at sucking cock?'

'I—'

As Lindsey moved again, she could see Jordan's

body clearly. Below the white, sweat-stained shirt, below his Italian leather belt, the material of Jordan Axley's suit pants jutted out with a rigid erection.

'I could be good,' Jordan whispered.

'Better than the fun I'd get watching you gang-banged by the next group of homeboys that come down this way?'

A flash of white as Jordan's eyes moved, shifting to Lindsey, and then around in panic. The chainlink fence jingled softly.

'Victor . . .' Jordan spoke as if it were Lindey's real name, and choked up. He shook his head. It was evident from the way he held himself that his raised, chained arms were in agony. 'You,' Jordan said, no louder than a whisper, but steady. 'I told you. I'll do anything. You fuck me, Victor. You fuck my ass. You *know* you want to!'

The short, stocky man lifted one of his hands away from the fence and ran it down Jordan's cheek.

Fern saw the sweat run down Jordan Axley's face. He pushed the side of his face into Lindsey's hand, as if he couldn't help it, biting his lip; and the bulge in his pants grew bigger.

'What do *you* want, Ric?'

Jordan's chest rose and fell, rapidly.

'I want you to—' Jordan stopped. He looked at Lindsey, whose muscular arms enclosed him on either side. 'I want *you* to want me. I want you to think I'm hot, the way I always think you . . . You drive me crazy! Every day. Victor – fuck my ass. Please?'

Fern noted that Lindsey let it go to the very limit before he moved. Let Axley colour up, clamp his eyes shut, try desperately to turn his aroused body away in the small space between them. Reality and movie blur-ring: the bite of rejection evidently went deep enough to make him feel abject humiliation.

Lindsey slid his hand down from the police officer's face and put it over the bulge in Jordan's pants.

When Jordan's eyes flew open in shock, Lindsey bent his head down and put his lips on Jordan's mouth, and pressed him back against the fence in a long, deep, thrusting kiss.

Lindsey put both his hands under the man's arms, and despite being shorter, hoisted him up until only the toes of his shoes touched the ground. In a low growl, which might have held a laugh in it, Lindsey said, 'Do *I* think you're hot?'

Fern chewed at her lower lip. Suspended, helpless, Axley swallowed hard as he gazed down.

Abruptly, Lindsey flipped him bodily and let him down again, the cuff-chains crossed now, the 'police officer' with his face pressed against the chainlink fence.

'Victor—!'

'You asked me a question,' Lindsey purred behind him. 'Is this an answer?'

Fern saw Lindsey reach out and put his arms around the man's waist. Jordan's body went rigid. She saw him struggle to get his face away from the wire enough to look down.

A flash of white. Naked flesh – what Lindsey had been doing, Fern saw, was unfastening Jordan's belt and trousers. They slid down to his knees. Sunlight illuminated his white thighs, and he quivered at the mobile air. Lindsey reached up and slid his fingertips under the waistband of Jordan's boxer shorts.

'Oh my God,' Jordan half-sobbed. 'I'll kill you if you leave me like this!'

The younger man made a purring, chuckling sound. Carefully and very slowly, he eased the black silk boxer shorts down. Fern gazed at Jordan Axley's white rump, naked to the sunlit air.

'What, leave you like this, you mean? Bare-ass? With your cock hard enough to hang my jacket off?'

Jordan's forehead thumped against the links of the fence. Fern could see his shoulders slump. He was not thin – he was well-made, all in proportion to his height, and strong – but for a second he looked skinny, rumpled, and blatantly undignified in his arousal.

His face was turned away. 'Victor, please!'

'Please what? Please don't leave you here?'

'Please fuck me!' Jordan got out, his voice dry and breaking. 'Please say – you want me.'

A change went through Lindsey. It was not evident to Jordan, who couldn't look that far over his shoulder. A small smile touched Lindsey's lips. He moved forward, until his body was touching Jordan's back – touching all of it – and he dipped his head forward and put his teeth down on Jordan's exposed neck.

Fern, leaning forward a little, could see that Axley's body shuddered from head to foot.

Lindsey said, 'I want you. And I want you to beg. You're not going to look down your nose at me any more. You're not going to leave me with my hand down my pants at the end of the day, wondering how I'm ever going to crack you open . . .'

Axley shuddered, with a sound that might have been a laugh or a sob, or both. 'I never intended—!'

'I looked at you every day.' Lindsey spoke in the taller man's ear, pressed to his back, Danila squatting three yards off and getting them in close-up. 'I wanted to touch you right there in the office . . .'

He slid his hand down and wrapped his sun-browned fingers around Jordan Axley's pale cock.

'Oh God!' Axley swallowed. 'If you had, I would have come right there in my pants—'

'You know what I would have done to you?' Slowly,

Lindsey's hand began to slide the soft skin up and down Jordan Axley's cock. Fern found herself rocking on the earth. She put a hand down her waistband, pushing her fingers under her panties and feeling for the swollen nub of her clit.

Lindsey's voice, almost hypnotic, crooned, 'I would have taken your pants down, Ric. In front of all of them ... I would have touched you, like this ... I would have made you come, helplessly—'

Axley's breathing peaked; he thrust hard into the other man's enclosing hand. Lindsey didn't let go of Jordan; his free arm went about the taller man's waist from behind, clamping Jordan's narrow buttocks firmly into his groin.

'You would have begged me not to do it,' Lindsey whispered in his ear. 'But I wouldn't listen. I'd have put you face-down over your desk, with everybody looking at you ...'

Fern saw him take his hand from Jordan's cock. The other man thrust his hips, helpless, squirming. Lindsey made as if to spit into his hand.

At Dani's rapid direction, he reached into his jacket pocket at an angle the camera could ignore, and Fern guessed him to be squeezing lube into his palm.

He rammed his hand up between Jordan's legs.

The other man's mouth fell open, his head dropping back against Lindsey's behind him. His loud gasp of shock echoed around the clear patch of ground.

Fern pushed her finger further down, into the wet, the heel of her hand pressing against her swollen clit. She spread her booted legs wider, supporting herself on her other hand.

Lindsey's voice was soft but clear. '... And I would have held you down ... and I would have said, "Ric – you don't get it until you beg." And what would you have said?'

Raggedly, brokenly, Jordan Axley stuttered, 'Fuck me! I would have said "Fuck me, right here, right now – make me squeal like a girl!" I would have begged you. Please, Victor. *Please!* I would have given you my ass and begged you to stick your cock right up me – right there—'

Jordan broke off, inhaling sharply.

His back formed a precise curve. With his hands chained above his head, he could do nothing about the bobbing prick that jutted away from his body. Lindsey had one arm around his waist, the other on the white bare cheek of his arse.

Lindsey unzipped his trousers, pulled out his stiff cock, rubbed it briefly to full erectness with his hand – and thrust it hard and without warning between Jordan's arse-cheeks.

'Ahh—!'

Fern saw Jordan fall back to rest in perfect equilibrium against Lindsey's body, impaled on his cock. Jordan's fingers gripped through the links above his head. The cords of his throat tautened.

'Do me,' Jordan whispered. 'You hate me. I'm your enemy. Do me till I can't stand. Punish me, Victor – hurt me like I deserve!'

One of Lindsey's hands went under Jordan's sweat-soaked shirt, reaching again for his cock. Fern saw his hand clamp tight about it. His other hand went across Jordan's chest, half-turning his body so that he could reach up and put his mouth over Jordan's. He began to thrust.

A low growl sounded in the back of Lindsey's throat, even while his lips stayed glued to Axley's. He thrust in a quickening rhythm.

Fern put her hand down her panties, her eyes fixed on Jordan Axley's huge and still-growing erection. She felt herself open, begin to convulse—

124

With an incoherent shout, Lindsey buried himself to the hilt in Jordan's arse. Its white cheeks shone. A white arc of cum jetted out into the air from Jordan's cock and fell across the dusty concrete.

Jordan Axley spurted, coming, coming again, his face slack in absolute ecstasy. Lindsey thrust again, groaned, and came for the second time. Fern clamped her other hand over her mouth to keep in her squeal as she came simultaneously.

For a long minute they hung against the wire . . .

'*Oh* yeah!' Fern whispered under her breath, slumping back on the concrete, feeling as if every bone were loose in her flesh. 'That's showbiz. . . !'

CHAPTER

9

Nadia Kay paused outside the small, single-storey brick-built building, listening to the thumping noise that came out through the open doorway.

It's a gym, she realised.

The thumping was recognisable as boxing gloves rhythmically meeting a punchbag, and she could detect, beneath that sound, the clink of weights being put back on the rack. She looked around her, back towards the 'visitors' centre' – which had evidently been built at much the same time, by the same untalented architect – and the manor-house beyond it.

Is this the best place to 'accidentally' run into Jonathan Parnell again? And when? When he comes back out?

She had caught sight of him by genuine accident – having expected to need to search the farm estate before she found out where he was – carrying a fencer's mask and foils and walking into this building. Perhaps stopping work for an hour to play hard;

perhaps holding a business meeting while working out . . .

No one went in with him, Nadia reflected. I wonder how crowded the place gets?

Squinting, she could make out a dusty foyer behind the glass doors, but there didn't seem to be a great number of people currently using the gym. As she stood, hesitating, two men came out talking, carrying gym bags, neither of them Jonathan Parnell.

As they passed her on the way to the untarmacked car park, they didn't break off their conversation, but she registered how their gazes flicked to her and stayed for a noticeable moment.

Nadia smoothed the tailored blue silk dress down over her hips. The hem finished halfway between hip and knee, but she knew she still had the thighs to carry it off. A summer look, but semi-formal; her best guess at something that could carry off any situation in which she might find herself, once she found her 'Jonathan Parnell' . . .

It had not been difficult to track him down as the owner of the estate where she had met him – a few days of enquiry, and another few days before she glimpsed him in the local market town and confirmed the identification. And she confessed, privately, to being impressed by the fact that he had given his real name.

And impressed by the house, now that she had driven up and parked in the visitors' car park, and spent some time wandering about in the grounds.

However. She cast a cursory glance down at her heeled Italian leather sandals. I'm not dressed for *this* kind of a workout . . .

She began to smile. She couldn't resist it, could feel the corners of her mouth curving up.

Now wouldn't *that* be a surprise for him? And I

think perhaps Jonathan needs a little surprise – he was just a touch too offhand in the aftermath of our encounter.

Nadia felt in her handbag for the soft roll of notes that she kept there in addition to her credit cards.

The change from the sun outside to the dimly lit interior blinded her for a moment, and she found herself meeting the gaze of a rather young man behind the counter in the foyer. His gaze fixed on the draped neckline of her silk dress, and the thrust of her rounded breasts under the fabric; red colour suffused his cheeks. Patiently, Nadia waited for him to meet her eye.

'Good afternoon,' she said sweetly.

She paced across the foyer's carpet tiles as if they were the catwalk of a model show. A quick glance showed her three sets of double doors that led off into the rest of the building. One, by the sounds, was the weight-lifting gym; no noise came from behind the other two doors – *no*, she corrected herself.

The nearest set of doors had caught, not quite closed, and from beyond she could hear the slide of footwear on waxed boards.

But no click of foil meeting foil.

Nadia put her manicured finger to her lips, careful not to smudge her subtly shimmering lipgloss, and trod silently over to the door under the boy's startled gaze. She reached out, easing one of the doors open a fraction, and gazed through.

Practising on his own. Probably prefers it to weights, or running on a treadmill. A smile curved her lips. And the risk of being interrupted is . . . there, certainly. But what's a little risk?

Turning, Nadia put her hands against the sides of her breasts, smoothing her dress down her flanks, over her hips and down the tops of her thighs. She saw the teenager's eyes widen as he sat behind the counter, and he unconsciously squirmed.

Nadia walked back to the counter and leaned her arms on it, inclining her body a tiny bit. The silk curved, holding her swelling breasts. She looked the young man in the eye.

'I wonder if I might hire some gym equipment?' she said brightly.

Ten minutes saw her kitted out in a borrowed fencer's suit, close enough to her own size that the slight tightness across bust and hips wasn't a problem. She finished putting on the shoes in the cubicle next to the foyer, the boy watching her with undisguised interest. She had left him a comfortable amount to cover the deposit on the face-mask and foil; he shoved it under the desk without looking at it, continuing to watch her move.

As she straightened, picking up the mask, and his gaze left her arse, he said, 'You done this before?'

Surprised 'my friend Mr Parnell'? Nadia wondered. Not exactly . . . She saw the young man nod, indicating the foil in her other hand.

'Oh – this.' She whipped it up in a salute, smiling at his wide eyes. 'I'm afraid I was often champion in my year, at college. One doesn't lose the touch.'

Unless, of course, one is fighting a bout one intends to lose . . .

The boy broke out in a grin. Conspiratorially he looked out into the foyer, and made a show of checking the doors to the other parts of the gym before beckoning her forward. He moved a little awkwardly, Nadia saw.

The feel of the fencer's one-piece white suit clinging to her body made her nipples stand up under the fabric, and she couldn't resist swaying as she walked towards him. His tracksuit trousers bulged at the front.

'Under other circumstances . . .' Nadia allowed regret into her voice, smiling up into his eyes. All elbows and knees, not a day over nineteen, and with a hoarse croak now as he muttered something completely unintelligible. The soft black material of his pants outlined a massive cock straining up towards his waistband.

As she reached for the door, and moved to go through it, Nadia turned so that she slid between the boy and the door, her slim buttocks brushing against his groin as she glanced up over her shoulder, into his wide eyes.

His mouth went momentarily shapeless. She kissed one finger and dabbed it against his cheek, and darted into the gym, letting the door swing closed behind her.

Now he's going to be busy, either entertaining himself, or changing his trousers . . .

She lifted the fencing mask quickly, and had it on before Jonathan Parnell finished turning round.

This small gym was all but bare: nothing but a waxed golden wood floor, and sunlight streaming in through high clerestory windows. A couple of small vaulting horses and a mat had been pushed into the far corner. In the middle of the empty space, Jonathan Parnell, in plain white polo shirt and shorts, lowered his foil and reached up to remove his own mask.

For a long moment he stared, puzzled. Nadia took in the sight of him. The tailored white casual sports gear showed off the line of his body from shoulder to thigh: how it narrowed down to his muscular hips, and swelled a little with the muscles of his thighs. A stray beam of sun gilded his dark hair, and picked out the clear gaze with which he watched her.

Nadia brought the foil up in a simple salute and took her first guard.

The movements were enough to let him know this stranger was a practised fencer: she could see that in his face. His gaze swept over her, and she saw him register the taut material across her flat tummy, and the strain of the cloth where it enclosed her breasts. One foot advanced, the other turned a little to the side, she regarded him through the mesh mask, over the hilt of her foil.

Curiosity showed on his face. The slight frown eased. She thought, for a moment, Does he recognise me? Then the tip of his foil flashed up and he feinted and struck, and she was moving back before she realised it, reacting purely to his strength and speed.

The hall was silent except for the thud of trainers on waxed wooden floorboards, and Nadia's breath in her own ears.

Jonathan brought up his mask and put it on again, in the second before she could close the distance. Her thrust was met by an arrogant counter; the tip of his foil all but grazed her chest as she darted back out of his reach.

No – he did touch me. Nadia didn't look down – didn't take her eyes off the figure in front of her – but she could feel a cool touch of air against her collarbone.

Whether by accident or design, the tip of his foil had scored across the weakened fabric and cut it.

Now he'll see I'm not wearing a chest-guard. Nadia bit her lip in frustration. And as for what else he might be seeing – given that I took my bra off because this suit is too tight . . .

Still with her gaze fixed on his mask, her point countering his second thrust, she reached up with her free hand. Her fingers encountered torn cotton canvas, and naked flesh. Tracing the rip, her fingertips let her know that it began just above her left collarbone and terminated between her breasts. Where her breasts stretched the too-small garment, it gaped open. The shadow of her cleavage must be fully visible to him . . .

It's what I wanted, Nadia thought, switching the placing of her feet and moving swiftly to a higher guard.

Annoyance none the less made her flush. It wasn't supposed to be this easy for him!

His faceless figure drove her up the hall, away from the entrance doors.

The click and whisper of foils touching filled the air, and behind her mask Nadia felt her face covered in a thin film of sweat. Her lips pressed together. Narrowing her eyes, and recovering the concentration that she had practised long ago at university, she whipped up her point, bound his foil, touched him squarely on the chest, and disengaged.

The mask hid his face. She wanted to see his expression. Reading his body, she saw him hesitate, reassess—

The tall man lifted his foil in salute, and sprang forward.

It's a long time since I exercised like this! Nadia reflected, meeting his attack. But I believe one never quite forgets . . .

The next few minutes were a blur. She felt the foil become an extension of her hand, and her feet move automatically into the positions for thrust and counter, guard and retreat and attack. Instinct took over from thought. She found herself grinning savagely behind her mask as she pressed him back a full pace.

Except that I came here to lose!

Her chest lifting and falling with exertion, Nadia

slowed her thrust. She couldn't see Jonathan Parnell's eyes, nor the direction of his gaze.

But I think I'm getting through his guard because he's looking at – what shows.

Nadia smiled to herself. The rapid movement had widened the tear and pulled the fencer's suit further back, by the feel of it; air cooled the skin above her breasts, and she felt cool, also, between them. When her free hand lifted to her chest, she brushed the naked curve of the side of her breast, and realised everything was uncovered except the nipple.

And a sudden movement might see to that, she thought, glad of the mask that hid her smile.

He attacked.

He caught her in mid-thought, and she reacted purely by instinct, parrying the thrusts that came from above, below, right hand, left hand – moving swiftly backwards as she did so, no attack touching her, but driven all the same.

Let it happen!

Nadia let her hand slow very slightly.

It was not enough to show. Not to Jonathan Parnell, she thought. He's a good fencer, but not superb.

She was not sure she would have detected such a move in an opponent either. But it was just enough.

The foil left her hand, wrenched from her grip by an accurate fast twist of his blade.

She heard it clatter on the floor, bouncing away from them. His foil came up again, fast, and she stepped back—

The gym's wall touched her between her shoulderblades. She froze, coming to an abrupt halt before she slammed painfully against the hard surface.

Now! she thought. Now, Jonathan!

Poised, anticipating, she waited for him to reach up, pull the fencer's mask from her and disclose her face.

The button of his foil came down and settled on a point precisely between her breasts.

She flinched involuntarily at the touch of cool metal. *What. . . ?*

Jonathan Parnell reached up with his free hand and took off his own mask.

She stood with her back to the wall behind her, not able to move forward. Knowing she could brush the light foil safely aside with her hand didn't incline her to do it. *What will he do now?*

'You . . . attacked me,' he said softly. 'Didn't you – girl?'

A sense of relief flooded through her. She thought, At least he recognised me.

'Jonathan—'

'No.' He stood gazing down at her, his dark brows pinched in a frown.

Something other than displeasure was present in his expression, Nadia thought. For a sickening moment she thought it was disappointment.

No. Something . . . darker than that, she thought, suddenly more conscious of the obstruction at her back. What is it that he wants to make of this?

The scent of beeswax filled the room, and a faint tang of sweat, and under those scents something else – arousal? she thought. His loose-fitting shorts showed a faint bulge at the crotch.

'Did I attack you?' she said softly.

'I think so.' His voice rumbled. For a second he glanced away, looking at the exit doors. He turned back, raising a brow in a plain question.

Nadia didn't reach up to push the foil aside.

'That was . . . bad of me,' she murmured. 'Was it?'

His foil button lifted, tracing a cool passage up between her breasts, over the dip at the base of her throat and up her neck to rest under her chin.

Nadia couldn't lower her head; he was lifting her chin uncomfortably high. She found herself standing up on her toes a little. The helplessness of her position put a warmth in her crotch, and she squirmed against the suddenly constricting garment, hoping he wouldn't catch the movement.

What is it he wants to . . .

'Are you afraid?' Jonathan Parnell purred softly. He smiled.

Nadia managed to swallow. The tingle of apprehension that went through her at his smile made her hotter. She felt the brick wall behind her pressing into her back, and realised that she was trying to push herself back through it, away from the foil-point and away from the large, tall man.

'I think you are.' He smiled again, the light from the clerestory windows catching in his eyes. It robbed him of all expression but a flat, gloating cruelty. 'I think you're just a little girl who's in way over her head. Who's scared, now. Scared enough to pee in her panties . . .'

Nadia moved by reflex, attempting to step forward from the wall. The foil button against the underside of her chin moved as she moved: she was in no danger of impaling herself. But it didn't stop pressing against her flesh. As she froze, the foil in his hand eased her back against the wall. Away from escape.

'Am—' Nadia found her mouth too dry to speak. She swallowed. 'Am I that scared? Would you . . . let me go, if I were that scared?'

She couldn't stop her squirm and wriggle at the thought. She found herself moving from one toe to the other, her groin aching with heat. This isn't what I'd planned; not this humiliation! Oh God, did he realise this would get me hot? Or does he just want to play this scene for himself? Or for both of us?

135

The pressure of the foil button against her throat interrupted her thoughts.

'You thought you could beat me,' he whispered, leaning forward to speak, his eyes fixed on her mask. 'And now you know you can't. You're here. Helpless. I can do whatever I like to you—'

The spurt of hot liquid caught her by surprise.

She fought against it, but the position she was in, backed up against a solid wall, and with a threat in front of her, touched a deep chord inside her. *Oh, Vince would love to see this!*

Urine spurted between her lower lips. The heat of it startled her. She tried to restrain herself, biting her lip and whimpering, and his foil urged her chin up, the back of her head against the wall.

His other hand grabbed the front of her fencer's suit, knotting it in his fist, pulling it tight across her breasts. He lifted.

The damp crotch of the garment cut up between her legs, forcing her up on to her toes. The humiliation of it triggered a helpless release: she realised she was losing control of her bladder completely. A further spurt of piss soaked her crotch, and she knew it must show on the outside.

Jonathan Parnell looked down and grinned.

A jet of urine flooded her panties.

She couldn't help the stream, couldn't stop it. Hot piss filled the crotch of the garment, and – being treated cotton – held it for a second. She felt the seat of her suit flood and fill; felt the liquid run down her inner thighs, trickle over her knees, fill the legs of her suit, and flood and overflow her trainers. Panties, trainer socks, the lower half of the fencer's suit: sodden and sopping with hot piss that cooled in the air . . .

Nadia whimpered, her eyes clamped tight shut, her

hands clenched into fists. His grip on the front of her suit still hoisted her up on to her toes. She felt the material drain, pouring down her legs, and she squirmed against the heavy seam of the garment where he pulled it up between her legs.

Clammy and cold, the material clung to her bum and belly, her hips and thighs.

She squirmed. Her labia swelled, the lips aching; humiliation and shame fired a furious desire in her to lie down and be fucked in the ruins of her clothes—

Light touched her eyelids. Startled, they snapped open. She found herself looking directly at Jonathan's face.

His foil leaned discarded against the wall. In his now-free hand, he held her fencing mask.

'You peed in your panties.' He smiled, crookedly, not letting go of his grip on the front of her suit. 'You were so scared, you filled your suit . . .'

'Fuck me!' Nadia gasped, both at her own bluntness and at the strength of her desire. '*Fuck me!*'

'In your wet panties?'

'*Yes!*'

Her face must be scarlet: she could feel the heat radiating from her cheeks.

'You want *me* . . ' he put a slight emphasis on the word, 'to have you now. The way you are.'

'YES!'

Her mask hit the floor as he tossed it aside. His other hand came up, he gripped the front of her suit between his fists and wrenched the cloth apart. The sound of ripping cotton echoed from the gym walls. It parted; the suit split past her waist; Nadia found herself half naked, breasts exposed, the lower half of her body still enclosed in clammy wet cloth.

He grabbed one of her breasts in each hand and squeezed, his fingers clamping hard.

137

Nadia reached down to pry ineffectually at her torn clothing, trying to push it down off her hips.

The tall man grabbed her hands, put them together and held her wrists easily in a single hand. She felt them lifted, and came up even more on to her toes as he pinned them against the wall over her head.

'Please—' She could do no more than gasp.

His strong hand caught the front of the wet, ruined suit and yanked it down past her knees.

Her ivory silk panties still clung to her, transparent with piss. Nadia writhed helplessly in his grip, lifting her knees alternately, trying to rub herself against the wall and push the tight wet pair of panties down. They didn't move.

'Jonathan—!'

Her head hung forward; she could see now what he was doing. He reached forward, hooked his finger under the leg of her panties and pushed his hand inside. He didn't pull them down. She felt his hot hand against the soft flesh of her belly; then his fingers dived between her legs. Her cleft ran hot and wet with her juices and with the last of her piss.

Nadia groaned. 'I want your cock!'

'You don't deserve it . . .' His finger thrust deeply into her heat.

She found herself spreading her thighs to accommodate him, thrusting at him as he held her pinned. One finger was joined by another, by a third – she thrust against him—

The realisation swept over her: that she was standing with the ruins of her clothes round her knees, and the cold uncomfortable wet pair of panties clinging to her stomach and hips and buttocks, and a man's hand frigging her off with no regard for her dignity or her desire for his cock—

Heat gathered in her groin, her knees sagged, she

hung helplessly in his grip, and the expert thrusting of his fingers seared hotly against her inner flesh, rubbing, pressing, diving deeper, deeper, harder, faster—

He hit the spot inside her and all the ache of her body, her straining flesh, zeroed in on that one spot and exploded out again in a ferocious blast of pleasure.

He stripped her, a few minutes later, as she lay bonelessly content on the floor, and wiped her damp flesh with his cotton polo shirt, which he took off for the purpose.

Languid, on her back on one of the gym mats, Nadia stretched her arms up and grasped his shoulders, bringing his body down against hers. His heavy flaccid cock, resting between her thighs, began to swell and lift. She raised her legs and clasped them around his waist, and let his strong thrusts into the heart of her carry her over the brink again, shivering as if all her skin turned into hot velvet.

The angle of the sun had changed and still they lay together on the mat, naked and side by side, talking inconsequentially.

I might as well mention it now, Nadia thought, warm and content. What better time to talk about a good idea?

She turned the conversation deftly to the manor-house and the estate, by way of a question of how she had known where to find him.

'This is an interesting place you have here. You have a number of' – Nadia paused, trying for a tactful phrase – 'facilities with potential. The visitor centre; the café . . . and this gym,' she added with a smile.

Jonathan wiped the sweat from his forehead. It had darkened his already-dark hair to the same deep brown as his eyebrows, making his features even more positive. The brows dipped slightly. 'What about the gym?'

'I was walking around, before, outside . . .' Nadia shrugged, rolling over off the mat and on to the warm wood of the waxed floor. She rested on her stomach, breasts pressed against her folded arms. She lifted her chin, so that she could gaze at the tall man where he sat cross-legged now. 'It's very like the other things here – the tearooms, the nature walks, the Victorian displays . . . You've got so much possibility here, but it's all . . ' she sought for the right word, 'diffuse.'

Now Jonathan Parnell definitely frowned. A tingle went through her groin at that. She put it aside. It's never wise to mix business and pleasure that closely.

'If you have any objections to the way I run my estate—'

'No! No. Goodness, no . . . Jonathan.' She smiled, and reached to stroke his forearm, the hairs of it feathery under her fingertips. 'You have a wonderful place here. In fact, you have no idea how much I'm impressed.'

He gave her a reluctant smile. 'I don't?'

Unselfconsciously, Nadia switched her legs around and sat up, supporting herself on one arm. With her free hand, she pushed a falling lock of her hair back from her face.

'I've recently sold up my business,' she said, 'and I've been abroad for a while. Now I'm home, I've been looking for something to invest in—'

The dark-haired man laughed. It did interesting things to his body, and the half-swelling cock that lay on his white thigh, but Nadia felt herself irritated. 'You're amused?'

'What "business" were you in?'

'Antiques and ephemera. I had a shop near—'

His deep voice interrupted. 'I hardly think running

some little local shop gives you an insight into running as estate of this size.'

Nadia met his dark gaze. 'A shop near Neil's Yard, in the West End of London,' she completed her sentence mentally – but not aloud. Hardly a 'little local shop'.

Jonathan Parnell extended his arms in a stretching motion that showed off the flex and swell of his muscles, and sprang to his feet in one smooth movement. Nadia tilted her head back to look up at him. If he was self-conscious about his nudity, he didn't give that away – And I like that, she thought.

I don't like the rest of his attitude, however.

'I have some money to invest,' she persisted, hearing her voice flatten with stubbornness. 'I had considered talking to you, with a view to—'

'Good grief!' he broke in. He shook his head, gazing down at her, and as he casually picked up his boxer shorts in an easy movement she thought she glimpsed him grin. He added, as he turned back to her, 'You really ought to be more careful. There are unscrupulous men who'd love to rip off your couple of thousand, or whatever it is. Look, it's really nice of you, but—'

'You're not taking advantage of your assets.' Nadia stood up, finding herself irritated at being unclothed now that he was pulling up his boxer shorts and unselfconsciously tucking away his cock. 'Even I can tell that, two hours after walking into the place. You have livery stables, you have tours around the house, you have shabby little tearooms; it's all . . . *bitty*.'

She scowled. Not the right word; not professional enough to convince him – why am I *trying* to convince him?

'Jonathan—'

'Look.' He interrupted without attempting to soften

his voice, and pulled a polo shirt over his head. 'Nadia – it is Nadia, isn't it? Nadia. This has been very pleasant. I've enjoyed it.'

He combed at his hair with rapid fingers.

'Let's not spoil it, OK? Let's not think about investments, or money, or any of that stuff, all right?'

Nadia felt her lips press together. Her hand clenched at her side, her nails digging into her palm. 'And why should we not think about that?'

He sighed. It had the effect of shaking his body back into an everyday stance. A man in white gym kit, his hair a little dishevelled; nothing else to show that he had been doing what he had been doing.

'Don't *worry*.' He smiled, too stiffly, emphasising the word. 'We've had a great time, we've enjoyed ourselves; you should carry on enjoying yourself. I've got to go, but I'll get Gilbert or Suzy to show you over the gardens – you'll like them. And come back any time.'

Nadia stared at him.

She realised her lips were parted; that she was staring at him open-mouthed.

Jonathan said, 'You're too pretty to worry yourself over money. Nadia, you're a terrific lady. You shouldn't worry about stuff we leave to the accountants, OK?'

He turned on his heel, and the gym door swung closed behind him before she could find her voice, or even shut her mouth.

Don't worry my pretty little head over it.

Nadia gritted her teeth as she walked. She glanced down, stopped, and tried unsuccessfully to brush the creases out of the silk dress.

And I can 'come back any time'.

'Who does he think he *is*!' Nadia spoke aloud, relieving part of her outrage. If she had been less well

142

dressed, and not in open-toed sandals, she might have kicked the flint pebbles that littered the earth of the car park.

He makes me want to throw just the kind of tantrum that would convince him I am an empty-headed woman!

' "Your couple of thousand".' She snorted. 'Who does he think he is – and what does he think I *am*? An idiot?'

Just because I like to switch sometimes and submit in the bedroom, that does not make me someone to be led around by the nose outside it!

Between the shop, sold on with stock and goodwill, and the items that she had carefully chosen to go to Christie's or Sotheby's, and the results of an equally carefully chosen investment portfolio, she thought that what she had available to invest in a business or buy a new one amounted to considerably more than a couple of thousand pounds.

'But it won't be *that man* I invest with!'

She swung about on her heel, turning away from the red MG and walking with quick easy steps towards the oak trees, the cattle-mown lawns and the Victorian kitchen gardens beyond them.

I need to walk this off first, or I shall drive like a maniac!

She walked and fumed, not thinking much of where she was going. The grass flicked past beneath her elegant, expensive sandals, succeeded by grey flagstones, and eventually by a soft woodchip-covered path that led her into woods where insects danced in golden shafts of light, and the water of the lake occasionally flashed between the tree-trunks.

A kicked-up woodchip caught under the toe of her sandal, and Nadia stopped; supporting herself with fingers against the smooth bole of a beech tree, shaking

143

the fragment loose. Her temper, muzzled by exertion, rose again as a hot sourness in the back of her throat.

How *dare* he!

A flash of colour interrupted her fury.

CHAPTER

10

I'll say this for Jordan Axley, Fern thought to herself with a grin: he's not afraid of hard work . . . In fact, with him here, and Lindsey, we might actually get a film made! Not the one we scripted, but a hot one. Maybe hotter than our script . . .

Dani lifted her gaze from the videocam on its tripod and squinted through the sunlight at the two men.

'Cut?' she suggested.

'That would be one way of stopping them.' Fern strolled over to stand beside the other woman, watching, and leaned a casual elbow on Dani's bare shoulder. 'Bit drastic, though. Bucket of cold water might help.'

'I wouldn't mind, but we need them for the *next* scene as well as this one.' Dani stretched, letting Fern's hand slide down off her shoulder, down her back and over her rump. With an explosive *wuff!* of breath she relaxed, all gangling energy. Fern felt the girl's muscles shift under her skin, and under the skimpy pair of shorts she was wearing.

Fifteen feet away, cradled in the photogenic

haystack that Lindsey had found in a corner of the estate, the dusty-blond man sprawled face-down, glued with sweat to Jordan Axley's back.

As the man under him grunted and attempted to rise, Lindsey Carter reached out and rumpled the dark hair until it fell into Jordan's eyes. Jordan glared up at him, dishevelled, but his hips still moved under Lindsey's pounding.

'You two!' Dani put her fists on her hips and bawled at them. 'Save *some* of it for the next take!'

Fern moved a step to the side, which took her behind Dani, and put her arms around her. Dani, after a moment, leaned back into her embrace. Fern reached a hand up and rubbed her palm feather-light over the nipple that pushed up, a hard bud, under the thin, soft cotton of Dani's T-shirt.

'I can be a fluffer.' She breathed the words into Dani's coffee-dark ear, with a grin at how the other woman shivered. 'Without even touching them. Hey, guys . . .'

Lindsey knelt up between the older man's thighs, one hand planted unceremoniously between Jordan's shoulderblades, pinning him face-down on the tumbled bales of the haystack as he withdrew his limp member. 'Not if you were to suck it *off*, Fernie! I'm done here.'

It was, Fern had realised when Lindsey brought her to the location, straw rather than hay; but it looked golden enough to be impressive on film. Though her experience sleeping in the barn had told her that straw was more prickly than hay, she had decided to let the boys find that out for themselves. And Professor Axley's yelps had provided an interesting addition to the soundtrack, she reflected, smothering another grin.

Dani, breath audibly catching in her throat, said, 'Then *you* can operate the camera! Or you, Jordan?'

Jordan Axley mutely shook his head, just able to get it up out of the enveloping straw. Naked as he was, his pale-as-cream skin now held the palest pink scratches over his back and buttocks, from the straw. She thought that, despite his evident desire for pain, he was probably going to be glad of their insistence on all-over sunblock.

Seeing the apparently uptight and high-buttoned Jordan Axley with his legs apart, anus shining with the last of Lindsey's cream, made Fern press herself even harder against Dani's back. She ground her hipbones into the woman's backside with a bump that made Dani gasp.

'We can move into those woods.' Fern extended her free hand, pointing beyond Dani. 'It's going to be way too hot out here soon. There's places in there we can shoot by natural light, so we won't have to go back for the lighting kit.'

'Sure. Suits me.' Dani's voice sounded clipped. The tension in her body was plain. Fern eased herself back a fraction, and ran her hand down Dani's back. The woman arched like a cat.

'Oh, what the hell.' Lindsey stood up, hauling up his jeans and zipping them, squinting against the sunlight. 'I can operate the camera. You girls going to hog the limelight?'

' 'Bout time we did some hot girl-on-girl action,' Dani said dreamily, pushing her rounded buttocks back against Fern's groin.

Fern mimed a moan. 'Oh yes. Yes, it is. It really is . . . So let's get going, shall we? Professor, you coming?'

'*Again?*'

He spoke with such deadpan precision that Fern was caught unawares, and spluttered off into a peal of laughter. She noted how the very corner of his mouth

147

twitched, betraying his amusement.

'If it's acceptable,' he murmured, 'I find myself in need of an immediate shower. Will it be sufficient if I return and meet you in an hour?'

Fern nodded, stepping back from Dani and giving him a smile. 'Oh, sure. We'll be more than an hour filming a girl-on-girl scene, the way things are going. You want to meet up back at the Victorian kitchen garden? If we could borrow the Victorian costumes the staff use, I've got an idea about that . . .'

She noted Lindsey and Jordan exchanging a long-suffering look, but since she was evidently supposed to see it she confined herself to an amiable smile, and helping Danila pack up the equipment.

By the time Jordan Axley had dressed and strolled back towards the house, everything was packed for transportation. Fern swung two of the heavier cases off straps on each shoulder and staggered off after Dani and Linds.

The shadow of the oak and beech trees cast a pleasant cool over her as soon as she stepped into the wood. The tall trees towered above, leaves still in the windless noon. She heard a crack, far off, and wondered if a branch had fallen somewhere in the forest, or whether someone else was walking there. She stopped, head lifted, but caught no further sound.

There were paths through areas where the under-brush was tall, brambles blocking out a view of anything at ground level. In other areas, only brown leaves carpeted the wood's floor, and the smooth boles of beeches soared directly up from the earth to the canopy.

Putting down the cases, Fern glanced around – a string of yellow plastic tape looped between trees towards the top of the slope; that would be another prohibited area. But here . . . She hauled the flattened sheet of paper out of her back pocket and studied Gilbert's timetable.

This ought to be OK. I don't want another coachload of wrinklies. Once was more than enough.

Dani's voice interrupted her thoughts. 'Why don't you go back too, Linds? It's not like you couldn't do with a shower. And I can set two of the cameras up on automatic, so we can intercut the finished shots, and you can do some takes with the small cam when you get back . . .'

'You mind?' Lindsey Carter scrubbed his fingers through his dirty-blond hair. For all his cat-like ability to return himself to a state of neatness, he looked, Fern noticed, irretrievably hot, bothered and sweat-soaked.

He added, 'It's *got* to be a bad day – I don't even wanna catch Jordan in the shower.'

'Poor baby,' Dani crooned, grinning. 'Did we wear you out, then? Poor ickle boy.'

Lindsey grabbed the crotch of his jeans, jerked his hips towards the dark-haired woman, and winced.

'That's the trouble with guys,' Fern noted helpfully. 'One shot and it's all over.'

All over Jordan, if we managed to keep the camera in focus . . .

Lindsey gave her a grin, turning to go. 'Keep it hot for me! If you're so go-all-night, girl, we'll go again when I get back.'

'Promises!' Fern waved and walked over to Dani, to collect the equipment.

The prop case was no lightweight thing to get over tree roots and brambles, and she was glad enough to halt in a glade some twenty yards further on. The ground was leaf-strewn, and clear of all but a few clumps of ferns, curling over on themselves, rich green and gold in the sun. In two or three places under the hornbeam and beech, there were piles of logs daubed with paint – perhaps marked for cutting and thinning out the woodland, she thought.

'How about this?' Fern dropped the costume case by the side of one of the woodpiles, a barricade of weathered silver logs.

Dani squinted at the location. 'Yep, I'm good to go. Let's get changed.'

The barricade of logs would make a good backdrop to the shot, Fern thought. With the usual amount of fiddling done as they set up the equipment, she came back to rest her hand on the warm texture of the wood, and glanced around at the cameras for a last check up.

'Looking good . . .' Fern opened the prop box. 'Are you going to be packing, or am I?'

The curly-haired woman grinned. 'Both of us. You first, then me.'

'Cool . . .'

The T-shirt and cut-offs came off easily, although it was not until she discarded the body-warmed clothing that Fern realised Jordan and Lindsey had not been the only people in need of a shower. She paused for a moment, the warm air blowing like silk over her body, and then groped in the props case for a harness made of black leather with steel D-rings. With practised ease, she snapped it tight at her hips and eased her thumbs under the leather to make the straps more comfortable in the crotch.

She reached into the box again, and chose one of the shorter and thicker latex dildos. We'll do a face-to-face first, she thought. And I can switch to something longer and thinner if she wants me to do her arse . . .

A squirm of heat went through her crotch at the thought. Fern settled the dildo into the socket and turned about, fists on naked hips, to give Dani a grin. ' "Suck me off, bitch!" '

'Which kind of movie are we making again?' Dani's teeth flashed in a white answering grin. She bent to squint through the viewfinder on one of the cameras, and her muffled voice added, *'Bull-Dykes of the Jungle?'*

Fern cast a glance up at the determinedly English beeches and oak trees. 'Either we need a better budget, or your computer generated effects will win an Oscar!'

'Nah, that'll be my performance . . .' Danila leered, and put her fingers over her mouth in a giggle. 'OK, we're rolling!'

'Then come and do what I said . . .'

The sun cast a faint heat through the trees, stinging her shoulders. Fern thought her flesh must look ivory-pale in the shade of the woodpile; Dani's merged into the dappled shadows of leaves as she walked forward.

With a soft crackle of leaves, the naked brown woman went down on her knees.

Fern grabbed the shaft of her dildo and guided the head to the woman's lips. She ran her other hand through Dani's hair, which flowed like liquid silk between her fingers. The scent of warm woman-flesh surrounded her, and she closed her eyes for a moment.

By feel, she touched her strap-on dildo to Dani's lips. A thrust of her hips pushed it forward very slightly. She drew back, thrust forward again, opened her eyes, and found herself looking down at the top of Dani's head.

The woman's lips enclosed the moulded shaft of the dildo, saliva streaking the surface as she swirled it with her tongue and leaned forward, deep-throating all of it until Fern felt Dani's forehead against her belly.

That there was no physical connection – that it was only shaped plastic in a leather harness – made no difference; Fern felt as if the girl sucked *her* cock. The base of the modelled cock thumped back against her clit as she thrust forward, and heat began to grow between her legs.

Dani leaned back, the thick shaft sliding from between her lips. 'I can think of somewhere better to put this ...'

Fern, breathless, nodded. I should have insisted on us both packing at the same time: we could do one hell of a sixty-nine! Well, maybe next take—

'Get down,' she said roughly, pushing at the brown-satin shoulder in front of her.

Danila slid gracefully down on to her back beside the silvered wood, leaves crackling under her, and stretched up her arms. Fern knelt between the other woman's thighs. Supporting herself on one hand, she reached for her crotch with the other, guiding her strap-on. The softness of Dani's skin against her own thigh made her shiver, sensation running all through her body—

A voice a yard above her murmured, in an awed, devout tone: 'Wow – rug munchers.'

Fern shot upright – up on to her bare feet, without noticing; glimpsed faces; realised, *I'm naked!* and dropped back down, grabbing for her discarded clothes.

Six or seven young men in green camouflage jackets stained with pink paint leaned over the log barricade. Three of them were loudly complaining and swiping at the one who had spoken. All of them carried weapons. *Weapons.* Fern blinked. Their odd shape told her they were not rifles, or farmers' shotguns; it took the distant *crack!* of something firing, and one of the men taking out a whistle and furiously blowing it, to draw her attention to the masks they wore, shoved up on the tops of their heads.

So they could see.

So they could *watch*. Us.

Dani's voice, between bewilderment and disgust, exclaimed, 'Paintballers?'

Fern heard herself give an embarrassed yelp. Without thinking about it, she snatched up Dani's shirt, holding it against her, trying to stretch the fabric to cover her from crotch to nipples. There wasn't enough material; the leather and D-rings of the harness showed, and the dull grey latex of the dildo felt slick and heavy, resting against the skin of her thigh.

In the wake of the whistle, more men with guns came running through the woodland. One of the ones with Dayglo marshal's clothing on was accompanied by a man in a Barbour jacket.

Jonathan Parnell.

He met her gaze – and said nothing. His eyebrows lifted.

'They're *not*—' Fern glared at the paintball players, hauling in her temper. '*Not* supposed to be here! Not now!'

With freezing politeness, the tall man remarked, 'Bookings are often revised. I suppose that you might phone into the office and talk to Gilbert before you set up for filming? It would have been the more – obvious – way of doing things.'

Fern's cheeks flamed.

Nudity had never bothered her. Being surrounded by young guys while half naked – and wearing a strap-on – *That's something else again*, she thought, fighting to keep tears out of her eyes.

'So, ah, we'll be going, then.' She shot a glance at Danila. The naked girl huddled, clutching a cluster of ferns to her. It gave her a little shelter. She didn't look as if she wanted to move. '*When* you clear the area!' Fern snapped at Jonathan Parnell.

The arched brow lifted again, with supercilious

avoidance of any comment. He turned his back, speaking to the paintballers in quiet tones, seeming to shift them back and away into the woods by sheer force of personality.

Not just paintballers, Fern noted, catching a glimpse of one or two non-camouflage colours among the crowd as they began to retreat. Tourists, too. Oh, hell.

Dani snorted, making the thick fronds of the green ferns quiver. 'If it goes on like this, we'll be able to sell tickets to public performances!'

'If it goes on like this,' Jonathan Parnell spoke over his shoulder, 'you'll both be arrested for indecent exposure. May I suggest that, since you do have a contract to be here, you try to act with *something* like a degree of professionalism?'

An unexpected female voice broke the silence in the barn. 'I wonder if I could speak to you for a moment?'

Fern jumped, spun around, and almost lost her balance. She hopped on one foot until her flailing hand grabbed the back door of the van and she steadied herself.

At least I had time to get my clothes back on.

Dani coming in wouldn't have been a surprise. Lindsey might well have come to cheer her up – he not being that good at offering condolences. But a stranger's voice, and a woman's— *That's trouble.* Probably wants to bawl me out for the *total* mess I just made of everything. I *so* do not need this.

'Go away!'

'I really don't mean to cause a problem . . .'

The voice was feminine, with a distinct tone of Sloane Square, but Fern could detect nothing patronising in it. That puzzled her. If it's someone come to complain about what just happened, they'd be madder than she sounds.

154

Fern lifted her hand to shade her eyes. The sun coming through the barn's doorway was a bar of molten white light. Against it, a figure gradually came into focus as it – she – entered the shadow and approached the place where Fern stood by the van.

'What do you want?' Fern spoke bluntly, but was appalled to find the swollen feeling of tears in her throat.

The voice's tone shaded into concern. 'Are you all right?'

'No!' Fern clenched her fists, driving her fingernails into her palms. 'No I fucking am *not*, since you ask, and why is it your business anyway?'

The last of the sun-dazzle left Fern's vision. She saw a woman no taller than herself, dressed in an expensive silk summer dress, azure in the barn's gloom. A stray sunbeam, let in by a chink in the roof, struck fire from the woman's pageboy-cut red hair. Fern took quick and successive note of Italian leather sandals on the woman's neat small feet, an unusual absence of tights or stockings, a small leather clutch-bag that also spoke of Italian style – and then a neat, oval face with permanent laughter lines embedded at the corners of concerned dark eyes.

The woman had one of those faces that might have been anywhere between thirty and late forties, Fern thought; and, if not for the bright hair and summer outfit, something in the ease of how the woman's body moved, almost slinking across the barn floor with catwalk poise, reminded Fern of *film noir* heroines.

The woman looked at Fern with open concern. 'He had no business to speak to you in that way. No business at all.'

The pain of fingernails in flesh proved ineffectual. Fern swallowed at the lump in her throat, choked, and burst into tears.

She stood with her hands pressed up against her eyes, her palms slick with hot wetness, completely unable to stop crying. Her chest jerked and heaved.

A cool hand touched her skin as an arm went around her shoulder.

Fern rested her hands against the older woman's shoulder and wept into her fingers.

A few minutes later – shaky and hiccuping, but getting her grip back – Fern straightened up. She wiped her bare wrist hard over her eyes and the rest of her face. 'Sorry. I just— Sorry.'

'Here.' The redheaded woman took a very small tissue out of her clutch bag and unfolded it, offering it gravely.

The scratch of absorbent tissue over her eyes made Fern feel the heat and swollenness of her skin anew.

She took a deep breath, scrunched up the tissue, and looked at the woman again.

'My name is Nadia,' the woman said. 'Nadia Kay. Are you sure you don't need a cold drink? Or an aspirin, perhaps?'

'No. I'll be OK.' Fern sniffed again. She put her hands on her hips, stretching her spine; that sensation serving to anchor her back in her body again. 'Well, that was embarrassing. I guess it's my day for embarrassing. I'm sorry. What was it you wanted to know?'

If the briskly businesslike tone failed to impress the woman, she wasn't impolite enough to let it show. She glanced around the barn, evidently noting the van and the piles of equipment, and then returned her gaze to Fern's face. Fern saw her pure green eyes, which stood out with unusual clarity against the easy lines of her face and the slightly age-blurred texture of her skin.

I wish I had that kind of poise, Fern thought, aware of her internal voice sounding, for once, forlorn.

She's easy in her skin. I bet *she* doesn't—

Fern cut off thought of the too-raw recent memory.

Nadia Kay said, 'I saw what happened out there, and I saw Jonathan Parnell's behaviour towards you. I wanted to extend my sympathies. And—'

She paused momentarily, and Fern met her clear gaze.

'Well, to be completely honest, I doubted that was the first bad experience you'd had with Jonathan. I wondered if we perhaps had something in common?'

Fern stated bluntly, 'He's been a shit since we got here. But we don't have anywhere else we can go in the time. We – you said something in common. . . ?'

Fern halted, looking past the other woman and catching sight of Danila and Lindsey at the barn entrance.

In answer to her hesitating glance, Nadia said, 'Bring them in, by all means. What we have in common is being badly treated by that insufferable man. Would you like me to tell you more?'

Fern lifted a hand, beckoning Dani and Lindsey.

'Yeah,' she said. 'You know what? Yes, I would.'

CHAPTER

11

'He wants his *arse* kicked, that's what he wants,' Fern said flatly, after Nadia Kay stopped speaking.

The elegant older woman folded her hands in her lap. She nodded delicately. 'I can't help but agree. If any man needs his bottom kicked, Mr Parnell does.'

Nadia Kay looked out of place in the barn, Fern thought, seated as she was on the bale of straw that Lindsey had gallantly reached down for her (taking the opportunity to show off his gym-cosseted muscles). The cobwebs that greyed the top of the support posts, and the unnamed old agricultural implements hung on the walls, all made an incongruous context for this very well-dressed redhead in the high-heeled shoes.

For a moment, Fern found herself imagining Nadia's hands in snug leather cuffs, the small woman forced to stand on tiptoe as a chain pulled her wrists up towards the barn's heavy crossbeams. Silk dress riding up to show the soft flesh of her thighs. Maybe the green eyes wide with apprehension or fury, with the small full-lipped mouth stuffed with a gag . . .

Or – I wonder how she'd Domme.

Fern found herself squirming on the van's cold metal floor, imagining her naked body tied firmly to one of the wooden uprights, and Nadia Kay sliding the very tip of a riding crop down her spine, over her buttocks, into the wet hot flesh of her cleft. That upper-class voice mouthing the filthiest words; the sleek red hair with not a strand out of place as her arm rose and brought the crop down in a whistling *crack*.

'. . . Fern?'

'Uh? Oh. Sorry.' Fern focused her eyes. She glanced up, and realised that not only Nadia, but Linds and Dani, were staring at her. 'I was miles away.'

Tartly, Danila said, 'Can't wait to read it in the next screenplay. Fernie, *look*. OK, the guy's a pain. A serious pain. But we've already lost the girls, and we really, *really* need to keep a place where we can shoot. I don't think we should annoy Jonathan Parnell.'

Fern glared. 'I can't believe *you're* saying that!'

Nadia Kay cut in. Lifting her head to look up at Danila, she said, 'Jonathan Parnell. Who apparently leased you the right to film here, without telling you that you'd be running into tourists everywhere on the site. That Jonathan Parnell? He's the one you don't think has something coming to him?'

Danila's satin shoulder lifted; dropped. The sun called out bronze and blue highlights from her tumbling black curls. Her white tank-top vest was already smeared with dust over her breasts; Fern found her gaze sliding into the warm shadowed darkness of her cleavage.

'*Damn*, you should get in front of the camera,' Fern repeated, irrelevantly, and then got herself together. 'Dani, you're saying that just because we need the place to film, we should bend over and take it?'

'Yeah.' Dani shrugged again, rubbing one palm over her pale-coffee skin. 'That's what I'm sayin'.

Look, girl, that's just what we have to do – bend over, grab our cheeks and spread 'em. Cos what other choice do we have? There isn't time to sort out anywhere else. We already don't have our full cast—'

Fern cut her off with a wave of acknowledgement, looking down from the back of the van. 'Linds? What do you say?'

His expression was unusually serious. Fern saw him glance at Danila and then at the older woman before he turned back to her.

'Sorry. I say, "Bend over, girlfriend"!' Lindsey spread his hands. 'But you know what? If someone's going to pull my pants down and stick it up me, I like them to *ask* first.' A brief grin flickered over his face. 'Mostly.' He became serious again. 'So, if we get to the end of this, and we're done – *then* I'm all for giving Mr Parnell an experience he won't forget.'

Fern raised a brow. 'I was thinking more that we should sue him or something . . .'

Nadia Kay looked up from studying her subtly pearled nails. There was a wicked glint in her eyes. 'Where's the fun in going through the courts? Having Jonathan Parnell literally arse-upwards would be extremely satisfying, don't you think?'

Fern smiled for a second.

Yeah, the fantasy appeals. Snotty bastard getting what's coming to him.

But it's just fantasy.

She stood up from the back of the van. She looked at Danila, and at Lindsey. 'So. What you guys are saying is: we've got just the two choices. Crash our chances of filming here, because we're making a fuss about compensation or whatever; or carry on with the shoot, and just suck it up. When Parnell hands out crap, we smile and take it. That about right?'

'That's it.' Lindsey Carter shrugged. 'And I don't

160

like it any more than you do, but, hey, it's your film.'

Danila broke in quickly: '*Our* film. You stood by us, you could have gone off when Tess and Hope did.'

Her dark brown eyes moved, and Fern caught the glance intended for her. It was not difficult to read the unspoken message. Linds has acted like he's committed to this, as much as we have. Don't mess up this gig without thinking about that.

Nervously Fern paced the straw-covered concrete.

She walked as far as the barn entrance, and stood gazing out of the wide doorway at the concrete sheds doing duty as extra stables on the far side of the courtyard. A teenage girl groomed a chestnut mare outside one shed. The hollow clop of the mare's hoof, rapping occasionally on the hard-packed earth, echoed through the still afternoon.

Fern turned around. The sun had filled her eyes with dazzles: she stood in place, frowning, trying to make out the silhouettes of her friends. She spoke into the black void, not able to keep the frustration out of her tone.

'I guess we're stuck, then. We do what the man says. And hope we get done here without too many more fuck-ups.'

Nadia Kay emerged from the shadows. Against the black of the barn's interior, her red hair and sky-coloured dress made her stand out as if she were limned in fire. Dani and Linds stood, less distinct figures, behind her. The more mature woman, in her cut-glass accent, said, 'I can't blame you for that decision.'

Contrary to what Fern expected, there *was* no blame in Nadia's tone. Not even a hint of it. Fern bit her lip. An accusation might have swung her into being defensive – 'We've got a film to make!' – but the woman's rueful, understanding nod made Fern fill up with burning anger again, and all of it focused on Jonathan Parnell.

How he's behaved to her, how he's behaved to us . . . and there's no reason for it!

'He's a shit,' Fern said bluntly. 'What he said to you. I'd want to rip his balls off, if it was me. But . . . I hate having to ask this, but, *if* this is what we're agreeing, then – if you're going to have a row with him, can you wait until we're done? It's only going to be three more weeks, we *have* to get a cut done before the deadline, and—'

The red-headed woman held up a hand, as if to stem the flood.

Fern found herself panting. She shoved her hands deep in her pockets, hunching the biker jacket up around her shoulders, and hacked at the barn floor with the heel of her sandal.

Dani put in: 'We don't want to ask, Nadia. But I'm going to. Please don't rock the boat. Not until we've finished the filming. If Parnell pitches a fit and throws us all off-site, then that's it. We're done for.'

Nadia Kay stepped delicately past Danila and paused, chin up, scenting the air. To all appearances she savoured the scent of sun-hot dust, and the ripe undertones of earth, horse and flowers in the garden. She looked at the distant chimneys on the skyline, and then back at Danila and Lindsey. Fern saw her eyes sparkle.

'Well.' Nadia glanced at Fern. 'I'm on holiday at the moment. I have little to do. Rather than wear myself out fretting about this and that – and since Mr Parnell has seriously annoyed me – I wonder if I might help you?'

Fern blinked.

Dani's head came up. 'Do you mean, help with the shoot? Do you, ah, know much about movies?'

'Not very much, no . . .' Nadia Kay smoothed her dress down over her hip with an absent-minded gesture.

A lock of her jaw-length red hair slid forward, out of the elegant style, to drape across one finely shaped eyebrow and sultry green eye. She shot Fern a glance from under it, something wicked moving at the corner of her mouth.

'No, I can't say I'm a film expert. But I do know a reasonable amount about fucking. And I *am* absolutely shameless.'

She is, too! Fern thought, watching Nadia Kay. Despite herself, a broad grin spread across her face.

Jordan Axley stood spread-eagled between two of the barn's wooden supports, his wrists and ankles tied so that his body formed an X. Kneeling in front of his unzipped trousers, Nadia Kay nibbled with scarlet lips down the length of his shining-ivory cock, swiped her tongue back up it, and slid the glans into her mouth.

Jordan groaned. His head fell back. The second camera must be catching Nadia's red-nailed fingers, digging painfully into his bare arse. He whimpered with pleasure.

'Go Nadia!' Fern murmured.

The lighting equipment cables were a trap for the unwary, looped across the barn's floor and over the rafters; the cameras themselves made an intimidating presence – and Nadia Kay flawlessly avoided obstructions, giving the impression that she hadn't the slightest idea that she was being filmed.

Dani muttered under her breath, her eyes fixed on the laptop screen and the videocam output: 'The camera loves her . . .'

'I don't think Jordan is objecting, either.' Fern tried

to suppress her grin. 'Maybe we've discovered a star . . .'

'Miss Blue,' Nadia Kay's voice purred across the expanses of the barn. 'Perhaps you'd care to assist me.'

There's my cue . . .

Nadia had chosen a stylish costume from the props boxes: a short cocktail frock in black satin that showed off her creamy, gold-dusted flesh. She needed no stockings on her smooth legs. Her small slender feet were encased in black shoes with six-inch spikes, upon which she walked with a confidence that made Fern sure she had worn such things before.

To complete the outfit, the older woman had picked out a tiny hat – no more than a scrap of black felt – with a black lace half-veil that shadowed her wicked, smiling eyes.

Fern, walking into shot, felt the high heels of her own evening shoes – and how they made her walk, emphasising the sway of her hips and the tilt of her breasts. They make you stick your tits and bum out, she reflected, moving up beside Nadia. Can't help but look slutty – and feel it, too . . .

Whereas Nadia's black satin merged her into the ominous shadows left in the corners of the shot, Fern knew she must stand out. She wore a sheath-dress of gold satin, tight over her breasts at the deep neckline and ending twelve inches up her thighs. She had made sure her hair was pinned up with half a dozen glittering crystal clips. *Class and tart. Always works*.

Nadia bent over, legs together, her smooth, rounded arse pointing towards one camera, and put her mouth back over Jonathan Axley's cock.

Fern picked up a ready-lubed latex dildo from the unobtrusive props stand and walked around behind Axley. The thin man stank of fear and of arousal. A swift flick of her gaze assured her her toes were on the chalk-mark on the floor. Fern reached out and put her hand on Jordan Axley's left buttock.

He jerked in his bonds, for all the world as if he weren't expecting her. Straining to look over his shoulder at her, he whimpered, 'Please . . . *no!*'

Fern held the well-greased dildo where he and the camera could see it. 'Well, now, you get a choice. You can take this. Or my *other* girlfriend can help you out . . .'

His lips framed a repeat of the words. Fern nodded towards the figure entering on cue.

A sleek figure in a close-fitting scarlet cocktail dress swayed across the barn floor and turned to lean back against the wooden pillar at Axley's side, chest thrust up, one foot placed delicately in front of the other in traditional model position.

Nadia lifted her head from where she knelt, sucking cock, and dabbed delicately at her smudged lipstick. She gazed at Lindsey. 'Now you do look absolutely delicious, darling.'

The cameras might as well have not been present, Fern saw, catching the smile that went between the older woman and the boy in a dress.

Nadia reached up, plucking a strand of the boy's long wig. Blond hair fell to his narrow waist. She let it run through her fingers. Her green eyes glinted, her fingers clenching softly but immovably in the long tresses. 'I like your hair . . .'

Fern slid her hand over Jordan Axley's warm, smooth buttocks – and caught him watching Lindsey, and the slight bulge that was spoiling the line of Lindsey's dress at the groin.

She pushed at his flesh before he could clench, and the thick moulded head of the dildo popped open the muscle-ring of Jordan's arse. She saw Dani zoom in one camera for a close-up on Jordan's expression of appalled but desired humiliation.

Fern caught sight of a pink flush on Lindsey's cheeks, under the subtle make-up that gave him a sharp, doe-eyed, luscious-lipped face, as he grinned down at the kneeling red-head.

Nadia wrinkled her nose in a kitten-grin. 'Now . . . I wonder what else you have that I'd like.'

With a neat economy of movement, she put the sides of her hands against the outsides of the boy's thighs and slowly slid the scarlet silk upwards. The flimsy material did not disguise the raging hard-on under Lindsey's dress.

A long shaft of bright light cut across the set.

Fern groaned, and simultaneously heard the same annoyance from the others. She squinted against the sunlight coming in from the now-open barn door. 'What the . . .'

The black silhouette of a man resolved itself into that of Jonathan Parnell.

He stared at them.

The tall, broad-shouldered man said nothing, only watched them silently for what seemed the longest minute of Fern's life.

Without a change in expression – or an apology – he turned on his heel and strode away. The light struck his face as he did.

What I'm seeing, Fern realised, is an expression of . . . disgust.

'I think . . .' Nadia looked across the deserted car park towards Jonathan Parnell's house. 'I think I may be beginning to understand something.'

Fern hooked her thumbs under the waistband of her denim cut-offs. She felt the soft skin of her waist under her knuckles. The evening's warm wind whipped tendrils of fine hair into her eyes. She glared through it.

'Understand *what*? Something . . . about him?'

The older woman shrugged. 'Perhaps. He appears to be very keen on the, shall we say, "woman-inferior" scenarios. But when I . . . when he and I . . .'

A pink flush warmed her cheek.

'There was a moment. He looked at me, I almost thought, with disappointment.'

Fern frowned, confused. 'Disappointed about what? Nobody's going to be "disappointed" to find you . . .' she hesitated, then grinned, '. . . on the menu! Are they?'

'That's very kind.' Nadia gave her a glintingly amused look from under dark-copper eyelashes. 'In fact, I didn't have that in mind. I merely thought – well, that our Mr Parnell may not be such a Dom as he likes to give the impression of being.'

'Nah.' Fern scowled, and let her arms hang loose again, and kicked at the gravel, sending dust up and small stones scattering. 'Wish I thought he *was* a sub. I'd give him something that— No. Never going to happen. Because, firstly, he's too uptight to ever submit to anyone; and secondly, he's just a smug, self-satisfied git who likes to be on top!'

Nadia Kay's laughter pealed across the car park.

Fern watched the woman's elegantly cut hair swing back, and the soft line of her throat in profile; her head tilting up as she laughed without restraint. Fern nodded, not able to stop herself smiling with the older woman's amusement.

She is *such* a find! Her, Jordan – and Lindsey and Dani – if we can *ever* get any shooting done, we're going to have a stunning film.

But that bastard . . .

'I'm going to have a talk with Dani.' Fern shrugged off her other thoughts, and met Nadia's cool green gaze. 'She says she wants to do some classy soft-focus stuff in one of the gardens here. But I think that if we can't keep people from finding us out in the boonies, we might as well sell *tickets* if we try doing it close to the house!'

'Tickets? What a perfectly wonderful idea!' Only the glint in Nadia's otherwise straight face gave away her humour. 'Far better than "soft focus" fucking . . .'

The sound and sight of the classy Nadia Kay saying 'fucking' out loud sent an arousing shiver down Fern's spine. She grinned to herself.

'I've *got* to put you and Jordan together again,' she said aloud. 'When you Dommed him, he just about crapped himself.'

Nadia's answering smile was unequivocally wicked. 'I'm not sure you have enough film stock for *everything* I'd like to do to the estimable Professor Axley . . .'

'Yeah, well. The script rewrites are getting more kink in them all the time.' Fern bent to pick up her bag, and shouldered it. 'OK, I'll catch you again tomorrow, after I've talked to Dani – you will be here, won't you?'

'Oh yes,' the woman said. 'When tomorrow comes – I'll be here.'

Back at the cottage some hours later, her strained muscles further relaxed into boneless, sensual pleasure by a long soapy bath and a glass of red wine, Nadia was just wrapping a long silk gown about herself when the doorbell rang.

She lifted a brow, looking out of the window at the descending sun. It must be past ten! she thought. Who would call at this hour of the night?

'Nadia?' The estuary accent beyond the door mangled her name in a very familiar way. ' 'S only me, darlin'. You can put the shotgun away.'

Coolly, Nadia drawled, 'A shotgun's rather more your style, isn't it, *darling*?', but she was grinning as she said it, and rapidly undoing the chain on the door.

He does sound like an East End gangster, even if he is in reputable security work . . .

'Vince!' She threw the door open. 'How lovely. But why didn't you *call*? You frightened the life out of me . . .'

'Come up here on the spur of the moment, didn't I?' The large, shaven-headed man on the doorstep shrugged. His smile mirrored her own. 'Missing you . . . I shoulda called, I spose. Didn't worry you, did I?'

'You did, rather.' Nadia held her silk robe around her with one hand and stood back to let him in.

Vince Russell stepped into the hall, taking a quick look around, and then glanced back down at her. His smile faded. 'Didn't mean to do that.'

'I know.' Nadia rested her hand momentarily on his arm. The leather blouson he wore was cold under her fingers, with the late evening's chill. She moved to close the front door.

'Shoulda thought, all the same,' his voice said behind her. As she turned back to him, she saw the self-reproach on his face alter, becoming a kind of hopefulness.

'Yes . . .' Nadia hid a smile and made a theatrical moment out of looking him up and down. 'Yes, Vincent. I believe you should.'

A slight flush showed on his unshaven cheeks. He hung his head, staring at the hall floor in front of his shoes, all but shuffling from one foot to the other.

Nadia couldn't help her voice warming. 'It *is* lovely to have you here. I hope you can stay – for a few days, at least. I have some friends here who'll love to meet you.'

He gave a silent nod. Without raising his head, he

looked up at her from under his brows.

'But in the mean time . . .' Nadia snapped her fingers decisively, and pointed.

Vince Russell fell to his knees on the floor before her.

CHAPTER

12

The sounds of harvest hung in the air; white-gold fields being mown down to stubble by distant machines. Fern, striding back up the hill from the village, glanced back from the view and caught sight of her forearm: faint hairs shining gold against a now-perceptible tan.

We've been here longer than I thought.

We've only got a few weeks more – and most of that ought to be back in London, editing the film . . .

There were few people about as she came back to the estate, and the barn and the van were both empty. Fifteen minutes of frustrated searching failed to uncover Lindsey or Jordan – *And I bet I should have looked in the village pub!* she reflected – but she caught sight of Danila down past the Victorian kitchen garden.

Dani walked out from among the greenhouses and sheds with a wave back over her shoulder – to a woman, Fern realised.

I don't recognise her . . .

She raised a brow as Dani came up to her.

'We can use the garden!' Dani beamed. 'Suzy says

it's fine, as long we stay on the paths and don't damage any of the plants.'

' "Suzy"?'

The Polish-Hispanic woman's teeth shone against the clear coffee-coloured skin of her face. She looked so bouncy that Fern couldn't help feeling energised herself.

'Suzy designed the scented garden, over past the Italian courtyard?' Dani added, 'And – *she* said I should call her Suzy – she's . . . guess who she is?'

'Who?'

'Suzanne Parnell.' Dani paused, before adding: 'Mr Parnell's mother.'

'His *mother*?' Fern shot a startled glance after the middle-aged woman disappearing in the distance.

With her sleek white hair and green boots, the woman could have been any one of the middle-class horse owners who frequented the estate's stables. As she vanished into the distance, Fern thought, A garden designer – well, that's not so unusual. But that she's Jonathan's mother . . .

'She's a cool old lady,' Dani added. 'If we're going to make another film, maybe we should make one for, like, older women?'

Fern made a face. 'Maybe. I'll still be happy if she doesn't walk in on filming, even if it *is* her garden!'

'She's kinda vague. I'm not sure she'd notice.' Danila held up the box-file she carried. 'So – what are we going to have in this next scene?'

'For the garden? Something tasteful. As to who's in the scene . . .' Fern shook her head, momentarily irritated. 'We really did need to have Hope and Tessa here. I mean, I do want to do another scene with Jordan and Lindsey – they sizzle – but I don't want the movie to be *all* boys doing boys.'

'*I* like boys doing boys,' Dani protested, with a grin.

'And boys doing girls, and girls doing boys. *And* girls doing girls,' she added dreamily.

'Dani, *you'd* watch *stick-insects* shagging!'

The other woman pretended to consider the thought. 'Yes. But I wouldn't film them.'

'Gah!'

'Going to check on costumes,' Dani added cheerfully. 'See if we've got anything classy. You seen Linds anywhere?'

Fern sighed. 'Not yet. You carry on. I'll see if I can track 'em down.'

Dani gave an absent nod and walked on. Lost in visualising the composition of shots? Shaking her head, Fern glanced down towards the greenhouses.

She frowned. Movement. That's what caught my eye. What . . .

Squinting against the white sunlight, she thought she made out Nadia Kay – and a man's figure beside her, down where the greenhouse glass flashed back light at the sky. Not Lindsey Carter, not Jordan Axley; she knew their silhouettes too well.

Is that Jonathan Parnell? she wondered.

You know, I think it just *might* be . . . Now how come he's talking to her, and she isn't knocking his head off?

Fern hesitated, unsure whether or not to walk on down the path towards them. The older woman, self-possessed as ever, looked perfectly capable of rescuing herself from any situation. And Parnell . . .

Aw, shit. Fern scowled. *No. Don't tell me she's thinking about sleeping with him again. Just cos he's a hottie guy . . .*

Have some self-respect!

As Fern watched, the tall, dark-haired man dipped his head, speaking with a degree of intensity to Nadia. The woman hesitated. After a brief moment, she turned on her high heel and vanished through the gate leading towards the stables, and Jonathan Parnell followed her.

A knock on the office door found her Gilbert, but the estate manager was not in the mood for conversation. He grunted assent to Fern's request to borrow the bathroom, and she spent the better part of an hour washing off the dust of the countryside in a shower that was regrettably uninterrupted.

Damp, but drying quickly in the heat, Fern took the opportunity afterwards to walk through some of the house's upper rooms. Panels, paintings, portraits, she thought, bored within minutes, and made her way back to the main stairs. She trotted down the steps – and came to an abrupt halt.

Nadia Kay, evidently just having entered through the front door, lifted her head and caught Fern's eye.

'Ah. There you are. I have something I think you should see,' said Nadia, halting in the hallway.

Fern raised a brow, jumping down the last step and landing neatly on the black and white tiles. 'What, now? I think I need to talk script with Dani—'

'Now.'

This is the beginning of something, Fern thought suddenly. *But – what?*

That it was not the way in which Nadia usually spoke to her, or to anyone for that matter, was a clue; but what settled it was the combination of dress and attitude. Nadia was wearing an ivory shirt, open at the throat, with clip-fitting jodhpurs and neat brown knee-high riding boots.

And by the look on her face, that's not because she plans on going out riding with the horsey people.

'Come here,' the small, red-headed woman said.

The tone of her voice made Fern's stomach lurch.

She hesitated for a moment, catching her lower lip between her teeth and nipping at it painfully. Do I want to. . . ?

Yes. Yes, I think I do.

Nadia pointed at the door to the outside.

Fern walked towards it, hesitated – and stepped out of the door into the courtyard. Nadia let her move past. Fern felt hands touching her hair, her shoulder, the side of her cheek. She hesitated again.

'No, keep looking forward.' Nadia's voice from behind her came as a purr.

From over her head, a folded silk scarf came down across Fern's eyes.

She flinched; made herself stand rigidly still. *So . . . Nadia wants me blindfolded.* The soft, cool material pulled snugly against her brows and temples, brushing her cheeks. Her vision was a glow of light at the edges, and soft black at the centre.

Nadia's voice came again. 'Walk forward . . . I'll help you.'

Fern groped the air in front of herself.

It's an empty courtyard. I know it is. So there's nothing that can harm me . . . is there?

The soft touch of Nadia's hand on her skin became a grip as the older woman's fingers encircled her wrist. Pulled forward, feet uncertain on the flagstones, Fern found herself led on in darkness.

'Step. Step up.'

The lip of a stone step caught the toe of her shoe. She stumbled – and Nadia's arm was an iron bar, holding her from falling with unexpected strength. Fern got her foot under herself again, felt her way cautiously up a kerb—

No, it is a step, she realised. It's the way into the Italian courtyard garden.

The hand left her wrist.

She drifted to a halt, finding herself tilting her head to listen, and to catch the drift of warm summer air across her face. Knowing that she could reach up and pull the blindfold down at any time disinclined her to do it.

An insect buzzed near her, then droned away. Something moved on stone: a shoe? The sound of cloth on cloth: someone moving?

We're not the only two people here, Fern thought, just as a small hand touched her shoulder from the front, easing her gently back a step.

'Steady . . .'

Something hard touched her back. Fern stopped moving. The point where it touched her arm conveyed texture. Tree-bark, she thought.

Nadia's hand left her shoulder. A second's pause, then it touched her ankle, above her sandal; Nadia's fingers and – something else.

A loop of silk rope slid snugly tight around Fern's left ankle; inside seconds, another loop slid tight against her right ankle. Silk rope against skin. She flinched, made to move forward – and was caught as she fell.

The ropes are around the tree behind me! Fern realised.

Hands held her, gripped her shoulders and arms, helped her upright.

The hands did not let her go.

There were too many to belong to Nadia alone. Besides, she smelled the soft odour of Dani's skin; didn't need the give-away chuckle that was muffled by a hand.

'Dani, what *is* this?'

'You'll like it. Trust me . . .'

The hands did not let her arms go. Fern felt her arms smoothly and firmly moved back behind her, her wrists being brought together way behind the tree.

Now I *can't* take the blindfold off.

Ropes looped her wrists; pulled snugly close. The plaited cords didn't bite in – but she would chafe if she pulled against them to free herself, Fern could feel that.

A spurt of almost-safe anxiety made her swear. 'What the *hell*—!'

A tug at the silk scarf. She felt it pull free of her hair, her forehead: light returned to her world in a brilliant blast, so that her vision ran.

Blinking her eyes, shaking her head, Fern got her vision clear.

'Surprise!' Dani sang softly. She stood beside Nadia, the videocam tucked under her arm. Her dark hair hung loose in ringlets, tumbled beside Nadia's sleek elegance. Her shorts and crop-top exposed a smooth brown area of her tummy, and a navel-stud winked silver in the sun. She grinned, meeting Fern's gaze.

The two women stood so that she had to twist her head around to see them. Fern, frowning, glanced away, looking straight ahead.

In front of her, a heavy wooden garden bench had been placed out on the flagstones, and a man tied face-down along it.

A white silk scarf filled his mouth – and, by the way his cheeks pushed out like an undignified chipmunk, it covered an effective ball-gag. His dark hair hung dishevelled into his eyes. His wrists were tied down at ground level to the bench's ironwork frame, his ankles to the frame's other end.

It left him just about able to lift his chest and hips an inch or four above the flat wood of the bench, and he did it as Fern's gaze fell on him. He pushed himself up, wrenching at his bindings, his cheeks working behind the gag and his eyes blazing.

Jonathan Parnell.

From Fern's left, another man stepped forward. Back against the wall, he had a stillness that had made him invisible until now, in the way that birds of prey or big cats are invisible. She could imagine him out early, in the dews and fogs, moving soundlessly among the estate's animals. Gilbert. He stroked his short beard as he walked up to the bench, his gaze on the bound figure of Jonathan, ignoring Fern as if she weren't there.

Fern shot a glance wildly around.

Dani bent her eye to the viewfinder of the videocam. Nadia bent over, rummaging in a bag – it was like a sports bag, but longer and thinner; Fern recognised it as a case for martial arts weapons.

The older woman straightened up, holding a riding crop.

Jonathan's body jerked; a muffled 'Mmmph!' issued from behind the gag. She saw him gripping the iron-work of the bench with both hands. For purchase, Fern thought. He wrenched at his feet, and the bindings on his ankles.

Gilbert walked up to that end of the bench, reached casually under the other man's lifted body and ripped down the zip of Jonathan Parnell's trousers.

Jonathan froze.

In that moment of shock, the burly estate manager took hold of the younger man's jacket and flipped it up, caught a fistful of the expensive suit trousers at each of Jonathan's hips and dragged down trousers and pants in one smooth, apparently effortless movement. Leaving the man in front of Fern's startled eyes, bare-arsed under the summer sky.

CHAPTER

13

'Well,' Gilbert's deep voice remarked. 'There you are . . . sir.'

Fern's stomach quivered. The resonances in the bearded man's tones were amazing; she felt her toes curl. And being bound – she tugged her wrists experimentally apart, and felt the silk rope dig more snugly into her flesh – being bound just made his dominance more unavoidable.

I can't help watching this. How can I help it? It's not my fault . . .

The dark man put his hands behind his back and surveyed his employer. His formal dark suit contrasted strongly with Jonathan Parnell's exposed white buttocks, made the younger man if anything more naked than naked.

Jonathan glanced back over his shoulders with difficulty. Fern saw his feet shift on the ground, although his shoes were shrouded by the tangled mass of his trousers and underpants.

'Gilbert—'

'That would be "Mr Gilbert".' The estate manager

spoke firmly and without a moment of hesitation.

Fern shot a look at Dani. Her eye never left the eyepiece, but her hand came up in acknowledgement: Yes, I'm getting it; whoever would have thought this guy could do improv like this?

Fern cleared her throat with a squeak. 'Do we . . . Are we. . . ?' she managed.

Nadia spoke. 'You'd better do what he says.'

Jonathan Parnell turned a face of outrage towards her. 'You never said anything about another man!'

Fern felt Nadia's soft-skinned, strong hands resting on her shoulders where the woman stood behind her. Equally softly, and with an undertone of iron, Nadia's voice said, 'Nobody was ever going to *ask* you, Parnell. Now I suggest you be quiet – and take what's coming to you.'

The dark-haired man's lips shaped the word 'Please,' but no breath of it got exhaled into the air. His pale gaze held Nadia's, above Fern's head, his body still in its bindings over the bench.

'What—' He managed to speak aloud. 'What have I got coming to me?'

The silken caress of Nadia's hand dipped down from Fern's shoulders, sliding into the V of her shirt. The cool fingers touched Fern's breasts, and pinched her nipples, sudden and hard. Fern gasped.

As if it were not happening, the red-head looked towards Gilbert. 'That's rather up to you, I believe. Would you like him' – a casual inclination of the head towards Jonathan Parnell – 'to beg for it?'

'Yes.' Gilbert grunted. There might have been a smile hidden in the neatly clipped beard. He squared his shoulders and reached down to the front of his trousers, casually unzipping himself. 'Yes, I believe Mr Parnell ought to beg. He's got a *lot* coming to him.'

Her nipples still stinging, Fern watched him take

out a thick, pale cock, seven or eight inches long without being fully erect. Gilbert roughly encircled it with his fist, yanking at it – it grew no longer, but it swelled more thickly in his hand.

'Jonathan?' Nadia said, her gaze not shifting from Gilbert's cock. 'I believe you should beg to have your arse or your mouth filled.'

The calm and casual way she used the words, and her cut-glass accent, made Fern's groin ache.

It must have had much the same effect on Jonathan Parnell. Even bent over the bench and tied as he was, he hoisted his rump into the air, and she caught sight of his erect cock curving from his bare belly.

'You can't let him bugger me!' he protested, his voice high. 'And I won't have him *near* my mouth!'

Pacing as evenly as a model on a catwalk, Nadia moved past the enigmatic Gilbert – the estate manager frigging himself casually as he watched the older woman's neat, swaying bum – and picked up the riding crop where it lay on the flagstones.

Fern all but whimpered.

Dani might have the camera on her, but Fern felt herself past noticing. To be tied so that she couldn't bring her thighs close, to rub them together . . . to have her hands behind the tree's solid trunk, so that she couldn't reach around and stuff her fingers down her knickers . . .

'Oh *Jesus*!' she moaned out loud.

The lens of the videocam glinted, turning in her direction. She was dimly aware of it taking in her writhing frustration. Parting her legs, she ground her buttocks back against the trunk of the tree: any vibration better than nothing—

'Beg him.' Nadia raised the crop and brought it down smartly across Jonathan Parnell's exposed arse.

The bound man jerked and screamed. Across the

white skin, a red weal began to make itself visible. As Fern watched, Nadia reached out with her elegant finger and traced the mark.

Jonathan hissed between his teeth.

Nadia's cold voice said, 'You *will* do it.'

The thought of that chilly authority directed at her, instead of at him . . . I'm creaming my panties, Fern thought. Which, by the way, I shouldn't be wearing; oh God, I want to shove something up me!

The crop went up, sharp against the blue sky, and lashed down.

Jonathan Parnell lurched, catching a stripe across his naked flank; threw his head back, sweat-damp hair flying, and bellowed, 'Yes! All right! I'll beg! I swear it – please—'

'Do it!'

It was a strain for him to look behind himself: Fern could see the tendons and muscles standing out in his throat. His tie was askew now, and the top button of his shirt gone. His jacket covered him to the small of his back, but below that there was only skin: his muscular arse, thick thighs, and the comic spectacle of his trousers and pants around his expensive Italian shoes.

'Put it in my mouth,' he said sulkily, his gaze fixed on the bearded man.

Gilbert exchanged a glance with Nadia.

'No,' Gilbert said, as if the elegant redhead had spoken, '*I* don't call that begging, either. And you know what, Mr Parnell? I really think I've had enough of your mouth. Much as I'd like to shut you up with this–' he gave his cock a hard stroke '–I want your arse more.'

Oh Jesus! Fern thought, her eyes wide.

That isn't the best way – a long thin one's best for fucking the arse. Long and thick is going to *hurt*.

Except ... that's what Gilbert wants, isn't it? To hurt his boss – to humiliate his boss.

Jonathan Parnell stared at his underling with wide eyes.

We can't film this. We have to stop this.

Fern turned her head to where Dani was just taking her eye from the video's viewfinder and straightening up.

The same thoughts were evident on the Polish-Hispanic woman's face. There's a scene, and then there's raping him, and we can't—

Jonathan's voice interrupted Fern's panic. 'Are you going to fuck me, Gilbert?'

Fern jerked her head back around, staring.

The dark, bearded man straightened, bouncing on the toes of his polished shoes. She saw him meet his employer's gaze. In that moment, some unspoken communication went between them.

'Mr Gilbert.'

'Are you going to fuck me, Mr Gilbert?' Jonathan Parnell sounded both meek and panicked. Fern watched his hips squirm against the bench. He yanked his hands, but the ties binding him to the bench's legs didn't loosen. 'You're not going to have me up the arse, are you?'

'Yes. I am.'

'You can't do that. I'm your employer.'

The estate manager smiled.

It was an expression on two levels, Fern realised as she saw it. Part of it was within the scene – the smile of a man who has his enemy at his mercy – and the other part ... that was pleasure at the result of the negotiation, she thought.

Because I did just see a negotiation here. And Jonathan is about to get – what he wants.

Nadia – I guess she guessed right.

Gilbert enclosed his cock in his fist and pumped it; it swelled to a thickness his hand could barely hold. Fern found her gaze fixed on it. As he took two steps forward to the bench, she found herself tensing her thigh muscles rhythmically, as if she could come merely from that. The emptiness between her legs was a frantic hunger.

'You can't!' Jonathan's voice was wobbly. He pulled his wrists against the silk ties; jerked his ankles. The only result was to lift his arse a few inches above the wood. His head thrashed from side to side. 'Please – no – don't—!'

He can't see Gilbert any more, Fern realised. He knows what's going to happen to him, but not when. Or how—

Nadia, turning around from something on the garden wall, clapped a cupped hand between the bound man's buttocks.

A high-pitched squeal split the air, followed a second later by a deep guffaw from Gilbert.

A handful of cold lube, Fern realised.

Squirming, undignified, Jonathan Parnell writhed on the bench. Gilbert put his fists on his hips, staring down at the prone man in front of him. As Fern watched, Nadia squirted more lube into her hand and began to caress and stroke Gilbert's now-purpling cock.

'Steady . . .' The bearded man raised a hand, almost absently. As Nadia stood back, he stepped forward, putting himself between Jonathan Parnell's bound ankles.

I wish I had a cock! Fern thought frantically. The ache between her legs was becoming unbearable. I wish I had one in me; I wish I had one to stick in somebody – maybe I could come just from watching this—

'You don't dare, Gilbert!' Jonathan Parnell said thickly.

'You've been asking for this. For a long time. *Sir*.' Gilbert bent down, grabbing the elegant man's hips, and pulled him sharply back.

It left Jonathan in a half-squat, his arms extended in front of him, stretched to where they were tied. It was a position of comic indignity, Fern thought. He looks like he's going to squat and shit. But then, what's he's going to get ain't coming out, it's going in . . . .

Digging his fingers into Jonathan's thigh muscles, the bearded man hoisted him up on his toes. Fern saw every muscle of the half-naked man quiver with the strain. Gilbert, completely dressed except for his open zip and jutting prick, seized the fleshy globes of Jonathan Parnell's buttocks and parted them.

He dropped a hand to his cock.

'Feel that? Sir?'

'You can't do this!'

'I'm going to ram my prick up your bum-hole, sir. And there's nothing you can do to stop – me—'

'No! *Please!*'

Gilbert's fingers sheathed his cock. Fern saw him press the head of it against the puckered bud of Jonathan Parnell's anus; saw the younger man squirm, wriggle, try to shift forward—

'No, not up me, not hard, *no*—'

Glistening with lube, the thick cock popped open the muscle-ring of his arse and glided straight up him, deep to the root.

'*Oh!*'

The expression on his face – the startled round O of his mouth, the sheer discomfiture – moved Fern to throw herself side to side, as much as her bonds would allow. Her swelling nipples peaked against the friction of her shirt. Her shorts felt tight against her belly and bum. She tried to rub herself against the crotch-seam.

With a baritone shout, Gilbert shoved his hips

forward, his thighs hitting Jonathan's arse, and froze, jerked, froze again and jerked again, spending the contents of his balls up the other man's bum.

'Oh *shit* . . .' Fern heard herself whine.

'Somebody's not happy,' a male voice murmured in her ear.

Fern barely jumped. A haze of arousal drowned everything except the frantic desire to come. A few yards away, she heard Nadia exclaim, 'Vincent! How nice!' but she ignored it.

'Oh God, give me cock!' she moaned.

'Is that what you want?' Now that he came around to stand in front of her, she saw he was a big man, with a shaven head; broad across the chest. Nadia's friend, she remembered through the haze of wanting.

He wore a plain white shirt, and a large bulge poked out the front of his black trousers. 'You want this, honey?'

'*Yes!*'

'You're gonna have to tell me what to do . . .' A broad grin spread across his face. 'Cos, you know, I don't want to make a mistake . . .'

On the bench behind him, Jonathan Parnell lay impaled with a cock up his arse. Gilbert's strong, thick fingers still bit deep into his buttock-cheeks. Fern fixed her gaze on Jonathan's expression: his sweat-soaked dark hair all askew, his eyes wide and shocked, his mouth loose with unadmitted satisfaction.

She whimpered. 'Pull my shorts down!'

Hands at her waist popped the button there. Fingers slowly, slowly pulled down the zip.

'Faster!'

Cool air touched her hips; cloth whispered softly against her thighs, sliding down. It rucked at her knees; she felt it when she tried to widen them apart.

'And my knickers, damn it!' She was half sobbing.

186

'Get *on* with it!'

'Very pretty.' The stranger's voice was thick, but he picked delicately at the waistband of her pink satin knickers, and let them snap back against her softly rounded belly. 'Very pretty . . .'

'Get them out of the way!'

' "Please".'

Fury and desire made a red haze in her head. Fern gritted out, '*Please* take them off me!' thinking at the same time, I'll make sure he gets what's coming to him later. But for now – for now—

'*Please!*'

The drag of silken cloth roused her skin. She shivered across her belly and hips. Her knickers caught around her knees but she parted them anyway, stretching the material.

Looking over the man's shoulders as he moved in close, she thought: I'm Jonathan, undignified, going to get a prick right up me, whether I want it or not, humiliated because I *do* want it – and at the same time I'm Gilbert: wanting to come, come *now*, just needing one shove—

The hot velvet-hard head of a prick touched her lower lips.

She moaned, trying to squat in her bindings and push it up into her.

A voice at her shoulder grunted, 'Hold on!'

The man's hands grabbed her arms, locking her motionless to the trunk of the tree; his legs parted her thighs; his thick, hot cock rammed upwards, stuffing her instantly, completely full; and she came hard enough and wet enough to soak him and wipe out her vision in black dazzles all across the brilliant sky.

CHAPTER

14

The scent of coffee drifted across the Italian courtyard.

Fern's nostrils flared. She realised her mouth felt dry.

She opened her eyes, hearing the chink of cups, and saw Nadia carrying a fully laden old-fashioned tray in both hands.

Borrowed from the estate manager's office; the little kitchen next to it, Fern thought, aware of her mind fuzzily guessing.

And now I think about it: Gilbert – Jonathan—?

She pushed herself upright where she sat – on one of the courtyard's marble benches, she realised. The stone felt cold beneath her hands. And her thighs, she realised. *And my bum* . . .

' 'Ere.' Vince Russell held out a cotton gown.

One of the ones she and Dani had bought for Hope and Tessa to wear between takes, Fern realised as she reached up for it and wrapped it around and under herself. The shaven-headed man grinned down at her.

'Um . . . thanks.' Fern felt her face heat.

'My pleasure. And it was. Nadia, girl, let *me* do

188

that—' Vince moved forward, and Fern saw him reach out to take the tray of coffee cups, cream and sugar from the elegant redhead.

'No,' another male voice interrupted. 'Let me.'

Fern turned her head and stared at Jonathan Parnell. The dark-haired man stood by the wooden bench, and had evidently just stopped rubbing at his wrists.

Whoever tied him is good, Fern thought. They didn't leave a mark.

Jonathan had evidently no more desired to put his sweat-soaked and crumpled clothes back on than she had hers – but he, unlike Gilbert beside him, was not wearing one of the cotton robes. He stood stark naked, his shrunken, spent cock visible, nestling in the almost-black curly hair at his groin.

And, naked, he stepped forward as Vince gave an acknowledging wave, and took the tray from Nadia.

Jonathan Parnell inclined his head, as if to show respect.

'May I?' His voice was husky.

Nadia surveyed him, her chin raised. Fern frowned. *This is about more than who dishes out the refreshments . . .*

Aware as she spoke that she was sounding plaintive, Fern said, 'Can you guys sort it out later, and can I have some coffee *now*? I'm pooped!'

Dani's broad laughter echoed in response from the other side of the courtyard.

'Well I am!' Fern glanced across, and saw her – with Jordan and Lindsey leaning over her shoulders – watching something on the screen of the laptop notebook as she squatted cross-legged in front of it on the sun-warmed flagstones.

'Can't think why,' Dani called. 'It's not like you were doing any of the work . . . But, hey, I've got some really good footage of you here. Girl done by boy while watching two boys ... We can *use* this.'

Fern swivelled around on the marble bench and also sat cross-legged, so that the sun fell across her lap and feet, warming her skin under the voluminous robe. Leaning against the courtyard's brick wall at her back gave her a good view of everybody.

And of Jonathan Parnell's naked arse as he bent over to offer the tray of cups to Nadia, who had seated herself elegantly on a recliner by the canework garden table. As her elegant hands came up to enclose the cup, she raised her eyes to Jonathan over the rim. Fern caught an almost imperceptible nod from her to the dark-haired man. 'Go and serve Fern.'

'Yes.' Jonathan turned away instantly, and walked across the courtyard towards her.

Fern let her gaze roam over him: the wide shoulders and the curves of the muscles of his upper arms; the cords of his throat where anxiety showed in their tension; the flex of his thighs as he walked. And his naked chest and belly, and his deflated prick, and balls – *not on display*, she realised. It's not that he's boasting about what a hottie he looks. It's that he's naked and the rest of us are dressed.

Jonathan stopped in front of her bench and sank down on both knees, still holding the tray in front of him.

'Why?' Fern said simply.

He looked up from under dark lashes.

What was in his eyes was not part of a scene, Fern realised. Too private to be filmed. Remorse, perhaps even guilt ...

'Is this an apology?' she blurted, before he could speak.

'I ...' Jonathan's mouth twisted in a wry smile, briefly, and then he looked at her with a raw seriousness. 'I haven't been very – tactful – in what I've been

190

saying recently. I've been judgemental. Rude. I can only say that I'm sorry.'

Fern flicked a glance at Nadia, and saw that her face showed no surprise. 'You and Nadia – you talked about this?'

'I made an apology, yes. This— Well. This is part of it.' He inclined his head slightly, as if to emphasise his position below her, kneeling naked on the flagstones.

'You want to sub for Nadia. And . . . for me?'

He nodded. 'I owe you.'

Fern bit her lip.

She covered a moment's furious thought by reaching out for coffee. A red workman's mug, and fresh-brewed coffee, strong and sweet and black. The taste lingered on her lips, and she licked at them with the tip of her tongue.

'What about—?' Fern nodded at Gilbert, who had joined Jordan and Lindsey in watching the rushes over Dani's shoulder. As she did, Gilbert said something, inaudible at this distance, and both the men and Danila broke out laughing.

'Submitting to him,' Fern persisted. 'Was that *punishment*? Because, if so, that's so *wrong*—' She broke off. 'I thought you were enjoying it. That it was what you wanted. Even if you were *pretending* it was a rape. But—'

Jonathan Parnell put the tray down on the flagstones, and didn't look up as Vince Russell came to remove the last mug and walk back to Nadia. His gaze was fixed on Fern.

She found herself lost for words.

'It would be . . .' Jonathan paused, 'humiliating . . . to have to admit that I wanted to be tied up and buggered by a subordinate. An employee. Even if you could say I owe him, in real life – I haven't been easy to work for this year.' Jonathan shrugged, and a touch of red burned in his cheeks. 'But – Fern. Does Gilbert seem the kind of man who'd . . .'

'Without an invitation?' Fern found herself firmly shaking her head. 'No!'

The heat in Jonathan Parnell's face increased. He looked away, at the sunlight falling warmly gold on the Italian brick. 'So, it therefore seems – likely – that he had an invitation.'

She couldn't help a grin at his squirming embarrassment.

'So it was arranged?' At his nod, she let herself slump back against the brick wall behind her, giving way to relief for a moment. 'I *thought* Dani wouldn't. And Nadia wouldn't. Not if you didn't consent—'

'I didn't consent.'

A jolt of alarm shot through her. Jonathan held her startled gaze.

'I *offered*,' he said.

Fern took a sip of the coffee, not breaking eye contact with him. The liquid was on the brink of too hot. The heat and flavour flooded her mouth. She swallowed.

'Why? And . . . Dani can bounce up and down with as much enthusiasm as she likes. It's not like we can *use* the film. Your face shows.'

He gave a shrug, the movement of his shoulder affecting his body, making her newly aware that a naked man knelt before her and that she was clothed. Imbalance in the power exchange – it's not like the normal 'between-takes', Fern thought. But this isn't a scene, either.

She added, 'This is no different from all the takes we messed up. We've been here for weeks, and—'

Jonathan Parnell's voice broke in, tone becoming harsh. 'Maybe you *should* use the film footage, if you want it.'

He's not being harsh because of me personally, she realised. And that tone isn't anger, or disgust, it's . . . What is it?

She prompted him, finding herself speaking without malice. 'What? How could we use that film?'

He shrugged. 'It's not like it's going to matter. I've explained to Nadia. I should make my excuses to you – although I know it doesn't excuse what I did.' His gaze was clarity itself, looking up at her. 'I implied something about you that isn't true. I'm sorry. This is partly an apology. I was – I was in a foul temper; I lashed out at everybody. What I said isn't true. That's all there is to it. I'm sorry.'

Fern put down her mug on the marble bench beside her and reached forward, taking Jonathan's broad fingers in her hands. His skin was cool against her fingertips. 'Now tell me why it doesn't matter.'

Bleakly, he said, 'Because I'm going to lose the estate anyway. There are debts. I can't make it pay, whatever I set up – whatever business I bring in. God knows I've tried! This last year— But nothing's enough. So . . . use the film, if you want; it's the least I can do.'

CHAPTER

15

'Maybe he could be a porn star?' Danila suggested.

Fern bundled up the robe she'd discarded when she dressed, and threw it at the other woman's head. '*Honestly*, Dani!'

Lindsey gave a sardonic grin. 'And get paid as much as I do? Yeah, *that'll* keep this place going . . .'

'Linds, if we paid you what you're worth, we couldn't afford you!' Dani caught the robe and dropped it on to the pile of sleeping bags on the barn's floor.

Fern watched as Lindsey sat down in the back of the van, inside the open doors. The light from outside the barn caught highlights in his hair, which flopped down into his eyes. Fern found her gaze drawn to the swirling straw motes in the golden air, and the open collar of Lindsey's shirt, and the base of his throat where a pulse beat.

That would make a shot. Then pull back: show him just in a shirt, naked from the waist down . . .

Lindsey Carter pulled up his jeans, as she mentally framed the opening of the scene, and zipped them. He stood. She felt her hand twitch, wanting to touch the sun-faded denim, worn white and silk-soft over his hipbones, thighs and crotch.

'I don't see anything we can do,' he said.

Fern shrugged. 'I guess. But . . .'

Danila straightened up from the camera bags. 'I feel sorry for him too. But I don't know what we can do. Hey. You want to look at the rushes here, or shall we go in the kitchen where it's cleaner?'

'Let's go inside.' Fern picked up her biker jacket and slung it around her shoulders, and the heat of the sun as she stepped outside made sweat spring out under her arms.

She walked quickly around to the rear of the house, the others following, and entered by the door that led past the estate manager's office.

Fern gave Lindsey a nod. 'Knock on his door, will you? He might want to take a look at these.'

An eyebrow went up. 'How come you don't ask him?'

'Because I think he likes pretty boys more than he likes pretty girls?'

Fern watched illumination dawn on the young man's face. He grinned.

She added, 'Even if we could use the film with Jonathan in it, there's still Gilbert . . . and I think he'll mind. I don't know; maybe we can CGI a mask in or something. Dani . . .'

She walked on down the corridor to the kitchen, deep in conversation with the Polish-Hispanic woman – whose response to most of the suggestions was 'But we can't afford that quality of computer-generated image, and I can't do Paintshopping!' It kept her attention, so it wasn't until she walked into the Victorian kitchen itself that she realised she was hearing voices.

Nadia Kay and Jonathan Parnell sat at the pale,

scrubbed wooden kitchen table. A half-bottle of wine stood open beside two still-full glasses. A folder of forms and printouts occupied the table between them.

'– still know some very good accountants,' Nadia was saying, as Fern entered the room. 'But all these little enterprises that you've got trying to bring money into the estate ... Unless you have one guaranteed major source of income— Fern: hello. Danila. Is that the computer with you?'

Jonathan's strong, manicured hands closed the papers inside the folder before Fern could get a look at them. But I don't need to see, she thought. Debts. Business plans. More debts. Like he was telling us ...

'You're gonna want to see this!' Danila's rich voice echoed off the kitchen's white-plaster walls. 'I've done a quick cut of that scene. Couldn't resist it. And I've rescued some footage from some of the other screw-ups – if you'll pardon the expression. If there's a power point, I can show you.'

Dani began to set the laptop up on the table near Nadia. Fern watched Jonathan until he met her gaze. He gave her a self-deprecating half-smile then stood and moved to her side. Speaking quietly, he said, 'Do I take it that even my starring role isn't going to give you enough of a film to enter in your competition?'

'Not just you, is it?' Fern jerked her head, indicating the corridor outside.

'Ah. Yes ... You're right.' His broad shoulders moved in a shrug. His eyes, meeting hers, were clear. 'I still owe you. Perhaps you should reshoot the scene with your male actor – Lindsey, is it?'

Fern found herself frowning. 'You really are sorry, aren't you?'

'I've messed up a lot of things.' Jonathan frowned. 'It looks as though I've lost the big match – though that doesn't mean I'll give up on everything. And I do feel somewhat responsible for the débâcle your filming has turned into – conceivably I should have warned you more emphatically about other people on site, and non-exclusive use.'

'Oh yeah.' Fern nodded. 'Yeah. But . . . look, I don't know how you're going to take this, but – I don't want to film guys *really* doing what they don't want to do. Some people like that. It's not my thing. And I was thinking that with Linds and Jordan and maybe Vince Russell, Dani and I could still shoot some cracking stuff before the deadline – assuming me and her and Nadia take turns in front of the camera. So . . . I guess what I'm saying is, yes, having you in the film would be cool. Especially a hot scene like that one with Gilbert. But only if you want to do it . . . Even if it doesn't *look* that way.'

She looked up, meeting his gaze.

Jonathan Parnell's smoothly shaved cheeks flushed a dark red, and he blinked, looking at her from under surprisingly long lashes.

'You mean that . . .' He paused. 'Basically, I'd have to admit to liking acting as a slave. To other men. Maybe to you and Nadia.'

Fern couldn't repress a grin. 'Well, yeah, you could put it that way.'

Jonathan Parnell blushed furiously.

'I suppose so,' he muttered.

'Pardon me?'

'Maybe. All right. Yes.'

'Sorry, didn't catch that – louder?'

'I said *yes*, all right! YES!'

Both Dani's and Nadia's heads jerked up from the laptop's screen at the kitchen table. Fern confronted two identical expressions of bemusement. It was evident that they hadn't been following the conversation.

'Nothing,' Fern said cheerfully. 'Nothing at all . . .'

'Uh huh. Tell me later.' Dani went back to hitting keys. One of Nadia's pale hands rested on her bare, olive-coloured shoulder; Fern mentally framed it as a close-up, and nodded to herself.

'If I were you, I should wear a mask or something, all the same,' she said, turning back to Jonathan and speaking in an undertone. 'I mean, you don't want to shock Mum and your relatives, now, do you? Which, incidentally, is the problem with – oh, hi, Linds. Hi, Mr Gilbert.'

The bearded man, entering the Victorian kitchen in the wake of Lindsey Carter, gave her a nod of acknowledgement. He followed it, a split second later, with one to Jonathan Parnell.

' "Gilbert" will be fine,' he said, the bass tones of his voice giving Fern a familiar slight vibration down in her chest. He was wearing a suit and green Barbour jacket, and boots; evidently Lindsey had just caught him coming in. 'I understand you wanted to speak with me, Miss Barrie?'

Fern shot a glance at Lindsey, who grinned at her. He looked a little ruffled. Making out, were we? she thought.

Oh thanks, Linds. Leave it to me to explain things, why don't you!

'The film we're making . . .' She hesitated, groping for words, not helped by Lindsey's too-innocent attentiveness. 'Well, it's . . . it'll be going in a competition, a nationwide one. And if it wins or places . . . I mean, even if it doesn't, the *judges* will still watch it. And. Well. I mean . . . you get a really good look at your face if you're watching the footage . . .'

Mildly, the bearded man said, 'You think they'll be looking at my face?'

She wasn't sure if she imagined a faint emphasis on the last word.

Lindsey snuffled behind his hand, muffling a snort of laughter.

'I don't have any relatives or associates who would be concerned by that kind of thing,' Gilbert said gravely. 'And while it's possible that my employer might object on moral grounds, I feel it's equally possible that he won't.'

His expression was perfectly deadpan.

Fern found herself grinning widely. His tone of innocence matched Lindsey Carter's – and is just as false, she thought. At her response, a faint flicker of appreciation showed in Gilbert's eyes.

'Do I take it there's something worth seeing?' he added.

Fern, flashing back on the stocky bearded man's casually powerful buggering of the helpless man beside her, felt momentarily as if her T-shirt and cut-off denims were too tight.

'You might say that.' She grinned again, turning to the two women at the kitchen table. 'Dani, you going to run the rushes for today, so these guys can have a look?'

'In a minute . . .'

'Aw, come on.' Fern walked around behind the chairs that Dani and Nadia had drawn up close together. She put her hands on their shoulders, peering down at the screen. 'I thought you were watching them already. What's this one?'

Dani, absently thumbing the trackball, said, 'The scented garden.'

'Oh, right.' Fern was vaguely aware that the men had followed her; taller bodies crowded in behind her, and she felt a hipbone solid against the cheek of her bum.

Or maybe not a hipbone, she reflected, with a private grin. Because that's one hot scene . . .

The bodies behind her shifted, and a brief glimpse up showed her Vince Russell, moving to a point where he could see the screen without needing to do anything as overt as shoulder his way there. She gave him a quick smile.

Pressed between Lindsey's thigh, as she was, and with Jordan's ectomorphic height behind her, she had a sudden physical appreciation of them all – Vince with his hair grown out into baby-fuzz, having not shaved his head today, and half-moons of damp under the arms of his shirt; Jordan a picture of prissy elegance, but she could feel his erect prick against her back, through the fabric of his suit; Jonathan Parnell with his jacket off and top shirt button undone, taller than any of them except Jordan Axley; and Lindsey with his corn-fed yellow hair and wicked blue eyes, pressing himself back against Gilbert.

All of them in a scene with one woman, Fern thought suddenly. *That* would be something. Especially if it was me . . .

'What do you think?' Dani spoke with her gaze still fixed on the computer screen and the moving flesh there.

Vince gave a wide grin. 'Nice garden, darlin'.'

'*Thanks.*'

'Yeah, well, "tasteful" ain't really me.' Vince put his broad hands on Nadia's shoulders from behind, and grinned down at her and Dani. 'Like a bit of kink, me.'

Dani's lips folded together. 'It's not *for* you, it's for the girls—'

'And girls don't like kink?'

Fern took her eyes off Dani and Lindsey on-screen, where the camera showed their flesh dappled with shadows of bamboo canes and night-scented stocks. She began to straighten up. Conciliatory, she began, 'We've got something for everybody, I reckon—'

'*I've got it!*'

Nadia's slim, elegant hand thwacked down on the kitchen table and the discarded manila folder. Dani grabbed reflexively at the laptop as it jolted, yelping:

'Got what?'

'Got the answer.' Nadia reached out and turned the screen around so that it faced her again. She pointed, jabbing a pearl-nailed finger. '*Look*. Jonathan. Look at that. That's your answer.'

Fern spluttered, put her fingers over her lips and nose to muffle the noise, and looked apologetically at the red-headed woman.

'Sorry,' she got out. 'But, "the answer" is Dani swallowing Linds's prick?'

'*I* think it's a good answer,' Lindsey said dreamily.

Fern hit him on the arm.

'Fern!' Nadia Kay's schoolmarm tone snapped across the air, quietening the rumble of conversation among the men. She glared.

Fern made an effort, which she hoped was invisible, and repressed laughter. When she could trust her voice to be steady, she said, 'What's the answer to what, Nadia? I don't get it. What do you mean?'

'There.' The older woman all but tapped the screen, impatiently. 'If it's handled right, that's what will keep Jonathan from having to sell the estate.'

What had been a dirty giggle at the expense of Nadia's phrasing died before it got out, faced with Jonathan's expression of hope – and how rapidly he concealed it. Fern said, 'What, you mean . . . you're not saying he should make dirty films here, are you? Because I don't think they pay well enough—'

'*Not* the fucking.' Nadia's exquisitely made-up lips shaped the last word with absolute precision. That, and the snap in her tone, made Jordan Axley's prick quiver to attention; Fern could feel him behind her, against her bottom.

Into the silence, Nadia said, 'The garden.'

There was a pause.

Fern frowned, squinting at the small image on-screen. 'The garden?'

Dani added, 'We shot it there so we could do a bit of classy soft-focus stuff, you know? Olde English garden softcore. I don't know what . . .'

'Look at *why* you could do that.' Nadia's pointed nail indicated the swelling banks of flowers, either side of the winding paved walk; the raised beds; and the waterfall trickling noisily into its pool. 'Different levels. Structures. Balance. Most of the shots you're using here were almost composed *for* you.'

A look of insult faded from Dani's face. 'Well . . . yeah . . . I guess.'

'Design.' Nadia snapped out the word. '*Design*. There's real talent there.'

Beside Fern, Jonathan Parnell's puzzled voice said, 'Suzy designed the scented garden. I don't think my mother would appreciate that use of it—'

Fern saw Nadia's eyes brighten with determination as she interrupted him.

'I'm not suggesting it for filming purposes, Jonathan. In fact, I'm not suggesting merely the scented garden – *or* the fishponds. Suzy designed them too, yes?' At his nod, Nadia rapidly continued, 'I mean *gardens*. It's no use trying to run this estate with a bit of the land leased off for this and that. You can't turn it into a health farm: the countryside is stiff with them. What will people come *here* to see? Gardens.'

Fern saw the men glance at each other: a look went between Jonathan and Gilbert, a slightly puzzled shrug between Jordan Axley and Lindsey, and Vince Russell bit at his lip, his hand closing more tightly on Nadia's shoulder, and slowly nodded.

202

'Classy,' Vince said. 'Your mum, she want to do any more of these?'

Jonathan, looking helplessly at sea, managed to say, 'Well, yes, she often hints that she'd like more ground – and she's shown me designs. And— Yes. It could work, I suppose. But,' here he glanced again at Gilbert, 'these things don't happen in a season. Even if we transported in mature plants. From design to garden, it would be a year at least, and these debts—'

'I'll cover them.'

Nadia stood up. Fern watched how her words echoed off the faces of the men around her. Jonathan Parnell looked down at the small woman, his mouth open.

'You?' he blurted.

'You know I've been looking for a project to invest in.' She smiled. 'I'll invest, cover the debts and the start-up costs; then I'll get my money back as your mother designs and implements more of her gardens. Honestly, Jonathan, I don't know *how* you could have had this talent under your nose all the time, and not noticed it!'

Fern caught a side-glance from Jonathan. The dark-haired man's mouth moved in a self-mocking grimace. Addressing both her and Nadia, he said, 'I seem to have missed a lot lately. I can only apologise.'

Fern grinned, looking at his stunned expression and the beginning of joy in his eyes. 'Hell, no, you can do a lot more than that!'

He looked at the garden on-screen, and then back at Nadia. 'You're serious?'

'I'm serious. In fact . . .' Nadia turned around to face them, putting her bum against the kitchen table and resting one foot elegantly over the other. '. . . In fact, I have another announcement to make, too. Fern. Danila. I don't know whether you'll win this competition you're entering for, but I should certainly like to invest some of my money in an independent film company – if, that is, you intend to make any more films of this nature?'

'Oh, *shit*, yeah!' Fern exclaimed.

She sprang forward a second after Dani, and threw her arms around both women. An arm thumped her, and she found Lindsey attempting to embrace all three of them simultaneously.

She bounced on her toes in the hug, all but dancing on the tiled kitchen floor. 'Yes, yes, *yes*! Nadia – look, I'm going to say what Jonathan just said.' She stopped bouncing, breathing hard, and gripping Nadia Kay by her slender shoulders. 'Are you sure?'

'Yes. This looks like fun. And that's what I've been looking for since I got back to England. Fun.'

Dani, in Fern's ear, carolled a long, 'Whoo-HOOO!'

Fern reached forward and stroked her hand across the flies of Jonathan Parnell's trousers. He gasped, and his cock leaped under her hand.

'Get the camera!' She grinned. 'I have this idea for a scene...!'

CHAPTER

16

'Woah! You all need stage names to use, first!' Danila glanced around at the group. 'I have to have *something* to put in the credits. At least the arts foundation isn't insisting on real names on the actual video . . . Fern?'

'Don't look at me!' Fern protested. 'It was bad enough coming up with names for *us*.'

' "Dinky Stretton",' Gilbert said aloud, gruffly.

Fern stared.

'It *is* my porn-movie name.' He sounded defensive. 'First pet, plus the street you were born in. That's the rules.'

Vince Russell grinned. 'Bugger the rules! That's *scary*. And besides, I'd end up as "Scamper Fleetwood". Or "Puss High Street", which is even scarier. Dunno about you, mate. What about "Susie Van Siclen" for Nadia? Or "Sweet Valentine", or "Afro Dyete"?'

Fern eyed him, between admiration and doubt. 'Where do you *get* stuff like that? We need something – normal. Like . . . like . . .'

' "Victor Steele" for Lindsey?' Jonathan Parnell put in.

Danila sighed loudly. 'We're changing that! Could we *be* any more obvious?'

'DeeDee Dicks?' Lindsey suggested. 'Wee Willie Cummings?'

'Shut up, Lindsey!'

'Minka. Seka. Desirae. Jewel.' Vince shrugged at the look Danila gave him. 'I'm better at girls' names, OK?'

'You *think*?'

'Guys' names are easy.' Fern couldn't stop herself starting to giggle. 'Richard. Jack. Roger—'

'I object to being a verb!' Jordan said.

'You want to be a Dick?'

There was very little coherent speech for the next few minutes. Jordan sprawled on a kitchen chair in a fit of undignified giggles.

At the end of a quarter-hour, Fern sat on the table's edge and read aloud from a much-crossed-out list. 'OK, these are the sensible suggestions. "Jack Roland".'

Jonathan Parnell nodded.

' "Ric Shelby".'

Jordan looked down his nose with exaggerated hauteur, and then gave her a shameless wink.

'. . . "Louie Wolff" . . .'

Vince Russell smiled.

'. . . "Thomas Gatto" . . .'

Gilbert nodded.

'. . . And "Dick Babcock".'

Lindsey grinned at her. 'It's either Dick or Randy!'

'And I like "Jewel" – I'll be Jewel Rose.' Nadia stretched, cat-like. 'That has the right amount of classy sleaze, I think. And now – shall we begin?'

*

'Tease me, would you?' Fern remarked, gazing up at the solid, muscular form of Vince Russell – at the moment a far less prepossessing figure than he had been an hour or so earlier.

'Not me, girlie—!' He bit at his lip, mortified, and glanced at Nadia, who stood at Fern's shoulder. 'Sorry. I mean, no, *ma'am*.'

'You certainly do,' the red-headed woman remarked dreamily. 'But, unfortunately, Vincent, that isn't what you *said*. And I believe that Fern here has every reason to wish to inflict a spanking on you . . .'

The Italian courtyard made a remarkably good area for filming, Fern thought, with cables running out of the house to the lighting equipment, and a number of huge Victorian carpets thrown down on the flagstones to deaden the sound of footsteps. Vince Russell, standing on the carpet, still in his street clothes, shot a glance at Danila, checking the camera focus – and the other men, watching from behind her. Fern saw his face flush a dark red.

'Ma'am, it isn't fair! She wanted me to . . .' Vince's voice trailed off. He looked down at his shoes. Mumbling, and as if he were entirely unaware of his audience, he said, 'Does *she* have to do it, ma'am? Can't you?'

'I'm afraid not, Vincent.' Nadia gave Fern a distinct wink. 'But you won't be lonely, I assure you. Fern, this was a very good idea of yours – a last set of BDSM shots before you need to start editing the film. And . . .' she glanced back past the camera as Danila started filming. '. . . so many men in need of adequate punishment . . .'

Fern caught Vince's gaze and moved forward.

The front of his trousers rose.

'You're going to take it bare-arse,' she said, distinctly enough for the microphones to pick it up. With his soft brown eyes gazing anxiously at her, it was easy to forget the cameras. She smiled. 'I'll let you have one choice, though. Hairbrush, or my bare hand.'

She could see the thoughts flash across his face: A brush will hurt, but this little girl – what harm can she do? She's going to flail away and she'll just embarrass herself . . .

'Your hand,' he rumbled, wiping his wrist across his mouth and shifting his broad shoulders as he shucked his leather jacket off.

Fern nodded, walked over to the straight-backed chair that Lindsey had brought out of the kitchen and seated herself on it.

The large, scruffy man in white shirt and black slacks followed her. At her signal, he began reluctantly to unzip his trousers.

'One extra for every ten seconds I have to wait,' Fern said, letting her voice become flat and cold.

Stumbling with haste, he pushed his trousers and underpants down together, and stood bare-arsed. Fern patted her knee. He moved to stand at her side, kneeling down, and she felt the weight of him come down across her thighs as he stretched himself over her lap. He was a large enough man that his hands and feet rested easily on the carpet. The golden sunlight fell on the white globes of his arse as she carefully drew back his shirt, exposing them.

'Give me your hand.' She watched Vince Russell crane to look back over his shoulder, met his gaze and snapped, '*Now.*'

Still supporting himself on one hand, he lifted the other arm back and up. She caught his wrist and pinned it in the small of his back. Before he could struggle, she wrapped her arm around his waist, lifted her other hand and smacked it down squarely on the seat of his butt.

'*Yahhh!*'

Fern grinned. 'I've done this before . . .'

His surprised yell echoed off the Italian garden's brick walls. She tightened her embrace around his trim waist, lifted her arm and brought it down full-strength. Her fingers walloped a scarlet impression into one arse-cheek and then the other.

Vince Russell yelled again.

He squirmed, as if he would have tried to move away. Fern lifted one knee, tilting him forward towards the carpet. He slid down on to his forearm, his knees lifting, gravity now doing the work of pinning him over her lap.

'Please!' he yelped. 'Please! Don't! Not so hard!'

Fern, feeling the swelling of his trapped cock against her thighs, grinned down at him. 'I wouldn't talk about "hard" if I were you . . .'

'*Arrgh!*'

Methodically, Fern lifted her hand and brought it down, covering every square inch of his arse-cheeks with red imprints, until his skin turned from a glowing pink to a deep red and his squirming yelps began to give way to groans and sobs. She could see the tears running down his cheeks as he tried to look back and up at her.

'Please!' he whimpered.

His thick, throbbing cock twitched; she felt it. Before she could move, his body shuddered and convulsed, and she felt the spurt of hot wet come against her leg, trickling down her thigh and dripping to the ground.

He lifted himself up, half turned on one hand, and

met her eyes. His aghast expression almost made her spoil the take by bursting out laughing.

'Oh God, what did I do?' he moaned. 'Julie – ma'am – I'm sorry – *please . . .*'

'Please what?' she prompted.

Heat sparked in her groin in reaction to the absolute submission in his expression.

'Please, miss,' Vincent said. '*Please*. Punish me again.'

Fern watched from the side of the carpet, beside the cameras, eyes wide.

In the centre of the open space, Gilbert stood at parade rest, his wrists pulling a chain taut between them.

She saw the estate manager's muscles flex under the cuffs, and his shoulders stiffen. A solid erection pressed against the flies of his trousers.

Jordan Axley's hand descended with a solid whack on Vince's bottom. The thick-set man wailed loudly.

Gilbert jerked.

It was a tightly restrained movement of his hips – but not restrained enough, Fern saw.

He came in his pants.

Fern got up and walked towards him, aware of Lindsey swinging around, training one camera on her. She stepped up behind Gilbert and put her arms around him, feeling his whole body stiffen. She could feel the heat coming from his burning cheeks. Grinning at his discomfiture, she reached around and put her palm flat on his belly. The wet cloth of his trousers slid over his skin, and she carefully and deliberately rubbed his sticky come into every crevice of his pants and his flesh.

'Oh God!' he moaned.

'Serves you right for not coming to see me in the

shower.' Fern grinned wickedly.

He could have broken free: nothing restrained him from walking off. Fern felt something twitch under her hand – humiliation bringing his cock upright again, swelling in her grip through the wet material.

'Say please.' She stood on tiptoe to whisper into Gilbert's ear.

His deep voice growled, 'Please!', and cracked.

' "Please make me come in my pants." '

Something like a sob sounded in his throat. The solid heat of his body, and his sweating humiliation, had Fern humping her crotch against the back of his thigh before she realised what she was doing.

'Please,' Gilbert whispered, 'make me come in my pants . . . oh God I have to come! I have to— Aah—! Oh, you're going to pay for this—!'

'Yeah, sure!' Fern squirmed against him, her eyes tightly shut, her hand clenching on his throbbing cock through his trousers. She slid one hand back and grabbed the short chain between his cuffs, so that she held his hands still. He thrust his hips into her other hand, and she didn't follow her impulse to yank down his zip – she circled her finger and thumb around his cock, amazed that he could be so hard again, so soon. Fretting it with the material, increasing her strokes, harder, harder—

'*Please!*' Gilbert whimpered.

She clutched hard, wanked furiously at his rock-hard cock, and felt his body thrust forward into her hand and begin helplessly to spurt, soaking the front of his trousers again as he came.

The desire to come herself made her shift from foot to foot and rub her cheek against his back and the rough cloth of his jacket.

'Going to pay, am I?' she murmured, after a moment.

211

His raw, deep voice gasped, 'Yes!'

'You don't dare.' Fern felt for the keys to the cuffs, barely able to get the metal shank into the lock, her hands were shaking so much. The click of the manacle opening seemed loud enough to fill the world. As the chain clattered to the ground, she lifted her chin and looked up at him defiantly.

Nadia Kay crawled across the carpet on her hands and knees, wet hair hanging down into her eyes. Sweat turned it from bright copper to dark bronze, and behind the slicked-together strands of her fringe her green eyes grinned at Fern.

She reached out and made a long arm, past Fern.

And I'm too worn out to even look—

'What are you doing?' Fern got out, hitching herself up on both her elbows and looking down the length of herself at the older woman prowling like a big cat.

'Oh – I have just a little something I'd like to give you . . .' Nadia sat back on her heels. The light shone on her sweat-slick breasts, their taut nipples still jutting with arousal, and the trails of come across her belly and thighs. Her lips curved up.

Fern realised the red-headed woman had one hand behind her back now.

'What?' Fern managed.

Nadia looked up. Fern realised, a moment too late, that Nadia was looking at someone behind her – and two shadows fell across her as a solid body knelt down, with a thump hard enough to shake the ground, behind her left shoulder, and a second person knelt down softly at her right.

Fern looked wildly from side to side, her hair flying. Shifting her weight to get up, and lifting herself off her elbows, she found herself caught –

the solid bulk of Gilbert caught her left hand, a white grin splitting the darkness of his beard. She barely had a moment to realise what he was doing when a tight, strong set of fingers closed around her right wrist.

Jordan Axley gently but inexorably pulled her right arm up, lifting her hand above her head, and then eased it back as Gilbert did the same with her other hand.

The ground touched her between her shoulderblades. It was automatic to lift her legs, to kick—

Both her ankles were seized.

Fern just managed to lift her head off the ground, and spit out, 'Fuck, what are you *do*—'

Vince Russell, his bare buttocks still a warm crimson, had hold of her ankles. She tried to draw up her legs, and found she couldn't bend her knees. He caught the glance of someone beyond her, and nodded. Hands and an obstruction came down in front of her face.

'Open wide,' Lindsey's voice said cheerfully.

Fern opened her mouth to protest, and realised a split second too late how bad an idea that was.

The rubber ball-gag slipped between her lips, settling deep into her mouth. She thrust at it with her tongue, all but retched – and found that Lindsey had taken the opportunity to buckle and tighten the strap. He let go of her head and stepped past Jordan, and she threw her head from side to side, screaming past the thick obstruction in her mouth.

The strap didn't slide. All that came out was a muffled yelp.

' 'Ere, 'ave this.' Vince unceremoniously lifted her right ankle and thrust it into Lindsey's hands. He was naked except for garter belt, stockings and heels – and the heels didn't make him likely to overbalance,

Fern realised grimly, trying her best to kick out with that leg.

The two men at her feet knelt down. She felt herself flat against the ground. They began to exert a pressure – pulling her legs apart, she realised.

'Mmpph!' she protested, frustratingly inaudibly.

'I'm so sorry,' Jordan Axley's cultured tones murmured at her ear.

Fern got her head up, for one startled moment thinking, *He's going to let me out of this.*

With his free hand, Jordan settled a small cushion under the back of her head.

'Wouldn't want you to miss the show,' he added, eyes gleaming with amusement.

Damn, he remembers when I had him strung up in that barn . . . Fern twisted her hips, her bare bum sliding on the ground. Strain every muscle as she might, she couldn't get free. *What are they going to do to me?*

Nadia Kay's smooth tones said, 'And here's the winner's prize . . .'

Fern blinked. The naked woman, now standing, was holding something up. As she squinted, Fern managed to make out what it was – a chocolate bar. A thick, solid chocolate bar.

Oh, you're joking!

Nadia, mock-sorrowfully, continued, 'But it seems that you won't be able to eat it. Never mind. I'm sure we'll be able to get it into you *some*how . . .'

Bitch! Cunt! It was no use trying to shout, with the ball-gag filling her mouth to capacity, but Fern glared with all her might at the slender, small woman, and wrenched herself in the grip of the four men.

'Jonathan.' Nadia's voice crackled with authority. 'Come here, please.'

The big man stepped past Fern's supine body and

she saw him drop down on his knees at Nadia's feet, his head bowed.

'See if you can fuck Fern with this,' the older woman said, with no change in her tone – as if it were a perfectly reasonable thing to say. 'Oh, and, no hands. And I shall be here with – encouraging discipline, for you.'

Fern, with the ground solid under her shoulders, back and bottom, glared up at the faces around her. Neither Gilbert nor Jordan seemed to be exerting any force to hold her wrists pinned to the earth. Vince knelt on all fours, rather than sitting back on his heels – plainly the weals on his arse still stung. Lindsey—

Lindsey, holding her ankle still with one hand, drew a fingertip up the sole of her foot.

'– Eeek!' Fern heard herself through the gag. Her hips involuntarily bucked off the floor. She landed hard on her bottom, feeling cool air on her sopping-wet pussy.

Jonathan Parnell turned around on his hands and knees, naked but for the leather cock trap that now painfully enclosed his swollen dick. He was holding the chocolate bar between his teeth.

She would have laughed – if she hadn't been gagged, she might have had hysterics. His head vanished down between her thighs.

The first touch of a solid object came. Slick against her thigh. Slick, but hard underneath, and sliding down the soft interior skin towards her labia, touching her inner lips—

Fern gasped, her mouth opening in a silent, gagged wail. The solid chocolate bar slid up her, feeling thicker inside than it had looked in Nadia's hand. Nadia stood with her arms folded, stark naked, crop carried in one hand, and smiled down at her.

'I think Jonathan's going to have to *work*, isn't he?' Without warning or change of tone, her gaze locked with Fern's, Nadia unfolded her arms, lifted the crop and slashed it down against Jonathan's arse.

Fern heard his muffled yelp. His face mashed up against her, between her thighs; she felt his nose and cheeks, his forehead and lips, his warm sweat and hot breath.

She wriggled, as if she could push herself down on the inadequate obstruction.

'That isn't working too well, is it?' Nadia bent forward, her small breasts swinging in front of her, and peered with mock interest at Jonathan's face in Fern's groin.

Fern growled. If I could say no, I'd say a lot of other things!

'Men never know what to do . . .' Nadia pushed the dark-haired man back and fell on her knees between Fern's thighs. Fern saw her bend gracefully forward.

The indignity of knowing what she must look like, spreadeagled and with a chocolate bar stuck up her fanny, made Fern try to twist and writhe. The combined strength of four grips meant she couldn't move her limbs an inch. She felt an odd security in that fact. Her rapid breathing slowed. She found herself still moving, but in a slow grind, as if she could push her hips up and get something inside her pussy.

Nadia reached between her legs.

Fern felt the thick, sticky obstruction between her legs begin to move – to slide backwards and push forwards; to thrust and withdraw, thrust and withdraw . . .

Faster! Fern mewed through the ball-gag, rolling her

eyes and squeezing them shut. She concentrated on the feeling that centred between her legs; the slow, sticky thrust, the sucking withdrawal, the brush of Nadia's knuckles against her labia.

Not big enough. Fern's eyes flashed open. She met Lindsey's cheeky grin, and blushed. *I don't dare look at the others! But I want – oh, I want—*

'Oh, will you look at that?' Nadia lifted up a chocolate-stained hand and moved it this way and that in the air, staring with apparent fascination at her own fingers. 'It melted . . .' Nadia brought her hand near to her mouth, and extended a small pink tongue, licking delicately at the crevices of flesh between her fingers.

'Mppphh!' *Then give me something that won't melt! Oh God, please! Now, please—*

Nadia's cool hands seized her thighs, sticky fingers biting in. She bent delicately forward, so that Fern had a view over her bowed head and shoulders to the smooth globes of her arse rising up.

Warm air vibrated against the lips of Fern's pussy.

'Jonathan,' Nadia's voice said, 'you may remove your cock cage and fuck Fern's arse, but *you* may not come until *I've* pleasured Fern.'

Fern's eyes met Jonathan's over Nadia's prone body. His fumbling fingers were yanking at the buckles and steel rings. When they came free of his cock, Fern saw that he was holding a straining, thick erection in his grasp.

Without a word, Lindsey held up a tube of lubricant.

Fern pulled at her arms and legs, trying to get some purchase, some movement – but the grips on her were too strong. With a nod at the younger man, Vince Russell shifted his grip on her leg. Fern felt both her legs being lifted and her knees were suddenly crooked, one over the shoulder of each man. They still held her ankles, tight against their chests. She couldn't kick, couldn't flail—

'Now . . .' Nadia's breath vibrated warm and wet against Fern's labia. Fern saw her shift to one side as Jonathan moved forward, standing between Vince and Lindsey, his glistening cock in his hand.

Before she could do anything – move, try to cry out, protest, beg for more – a hand slapped cold lube up between her bottom cheeks.

Fern jerked. A tongue flickered across her clit. She moaned, muffled by the gag. As she was distracted by the swirl of Nadia's tongue – the redhead moving around beside her hip and leaning over her – a cock that felt the size of a telegraph pole popped open the ring of muscle at her arse.

She hung, suspended between the four men, her body on fire. Every inch of skin from her toes to her scalp shivered.

A slow, slow lapping made itself felt at her outer labia. The muscular tip of a tongue dipped between her inner lips – and dug, twisting and writhing, licking at the sticky chocolate that coated her.

'Mmmmphr!'

It might have been audible: Fern couldn't tell. The gag stuffed her mouth, the head of Jonathan's cock stuffed her bottom, and Nadia's tongue stilled in her cunt. She was held for one second in bonds of flesh: no chains or cuffs, but the grip of strong male hands.

Slowly, Nadia's tongue began to thrust in and out, in and out; dipping to delve into her cunt, sliding out to lap flatly across the hood of her clit, flickering in butterfly licks around her clit itself, tantalisingly close—

Two hands closed on her breasts, fingers gripping hard; Fern realised they were not the hands of one man. A third set of fingers pinched hard at one nipple, sending a flash of ecstasy from her breast to her cunt.

Two hands cupped her butt-cheeks, easing them apart.

Slick with lube, Jonathan's cock slid up her arse. The burning sensation in her ring translated into some other sensation; the feeling of fullness as he stuffed his length up her made her whimper through the gag.

His hands closed on her bum. Slim female hands gripped her thighs. Nadia's tongue began to thrust in alternate rhythm, dipping deep. Jonathan's hips shifted, drawing his cock back, and she could feel it quivering with the need to come. *He's right on the edge*—

Fern groaned. She couldn't keep her eyes shut: they flew open. Gilbert had one hand down the front of her shirt, grabbing her whole breast; Jordan Axley rubbed his palm just in contact with her other nipple through the cloth, and the bud of flesh throbbed with the desire to be grabbed, crushed, nipped, bitten—

She couldn't move her legs and hips: she might have been held in a vice. Completely helpless, Fern could only take it – the thrust of Jonathan's cock, spreading her arse-cheeks, filling her bottom deliciously filthily; Nadia's bent head, as the elegant woman licked the full length of her labia, trailed her lips back over dripping, sticky skin, put her mouth over Fern's clit and sucked—

Jonathan Parnell's hands closed around her hips and bottom, so tight that Fern yelled through the ball-gag, 'More!'

Fern felt her arse clench, gripping him; felt her hips lift, tilting her crotch into Nadia's waiting mouth—

With a cry of complete despair, Jonathan thrust his hips forward – she felt his groin ram up against her buttocks, felt the shudder and quiver of his release through his flesh – and heard him yell out as he emptied his balls into her waiting arse.

In the same second, Nadia's hot, writhing, muscular tongue thrust home up her – and Fern felt Nadia's body move; felt the free-handed smack that made Jonathan grunt in surprise and drove his body forward, right up her arse to his root.

Fire flowered in her full bottom, clenched her in its grip, flowed into her groin and, as Nadia's hot mouth covered her clit and bit down, exploded into pleasure that thundered all through her body, out to her fingers and toes.

Distantly, though a haze of pleasure and exhaustion, she heard Dani's voice calling out:

'Cut! *Print!*'